TAPPED OUT

NATALIE M. ROBERTS

BERKLEY PRIME CRIME, NEW YORK

THE BERKLEY PUBLISHING GROUP
Published by the Penguin Group
Penguin Group (USA) Inc.
375 Hudson Street, New York, New York 10014, USA

Penguin Group (Canada), 90 Eglinton Avenue East, Suite 700, Toronto, Ontario M4P 2Y3, Canada
(a division of Pearson Penguin Canada Inc.)
Penguin Books Ltd., 80 Strand, London WC2R 0RL, England
Penguin Books Ireland, 25 St. Stephen's Green, Dublin 2, Ireland (a division of Penguin Books Ltd.)
Penguin Group (Australia), 250 Camberwell Road, Camberwell, Victoria 3124, Australia
(a division of Pearson Australia Group Pty. Ltd.)
Penguin Books India Pvt. Ltd., 11 Community Centre, Panchsheel Park, New Delhi—110 017, India
Penguin Group (NZ), 67 Apollo Drive, Rosedale, North Shore 0745, Auckland, New Zealand
(a division of Pearson New Zealand Ltd.)
Penguin Books (South Africa) (Pty.) Ltd., 24 Sturdee Avenue, Rosebank, Johannesburg 2196,
South Africa

Penguin Books Ltd., Registered Offices: 80 Strand, London WC2R 0RL, England

This is a work of fiction. Names, characters, places, and incidents either are the product of the author's imagination or are used fictitiously, and any resemblance to actual persons, living or dead, business establishments, events, or locales is entirely coincidental. The publisher does not have any control over and does not assume any responsibility for author or third-party websites or their content.

TAPPED OUT

A Berkley Prime Crime Book / published by arrangement with the author

PRINTING HISTORY
Berkley Prime Crime mass-market edition / October 2007

Copyright © 2007 by Natalie M. Roberts.
Cover art by Mary Lynn Blasutta.
Cover design by Rita Frangie.
Cover logo by axb group.
Interior text design by Kristin del Rosario.

ISBN: 978-0-425-21801-3

BERKLEY® PRIME CRIME
Berkley Prime Crime Books are published by The Berkley Publishing Group,
a division of Penguin Group (USA) Inc.,
375 Hudson Street, New York, New York 10014.
The name BERKLEY PRIME CRIME and the BERKLEY PRIME CRIME design
are trademarks of Penguin Group (USA) Inc.

PRINTED IN THE UNITED STATES OF AMERICA

10 9 8 7 6 5 4 3 2 1

Praise for

Tutu Deadly

"A fun mystery with an irreverent heroine and a steamy romance!"　　　　—Jessica Conant-Park and Susan Conant,
authors of the Gourmet Girl Mysteries

"A tour de force of silly fun with enough romance and murder to keep cozy readers on their toes!"
　　—Susan McBride, author of the Debutante Dropout Mysteries

"Blending the humor of Janet Evanovich with chick-lit quirkiness, Roberts adds sassy prose and a spunky heroine to create a new series to watch."　　　　—*Library Journal*

"Roberts's charming new series is a winner—a one-sitting read with laugh-out-loud moments, a wacky heroine, and enough red herrings to populate a fish market."
　　　　　　　　　　　　　　　　—*Romantic Times*

"[An] upbeat mystery . . . with many familiar details of life in the dance-studio world."　　　　—*Dance Teacher*

"A humor-filled romp . . . "　　　　　　—*Gumshoe Review*

"A fun and funny new series with a unique and wacky heroine. Jenny Partridge is fresh and endearing."
　　　　　　　　　　—*The Romance Readers Connection*

"Jenny is a great cozy heroine."　　　　—*Cozy Library*

"Roberts leaves you with that one thing every good author should generate—a desire for more."　　—*Fresh Fiction*

Berkley Prime Crime titles by Natalie M. Roberts

TUTU DEADLY
TAPPED OUT

This one's for all the dancers of Elite Dance Force, who have inspired this book in so many ways. In particular I must mention Savanna Kemp, my "weekend and dance competition daughter," because if I don't she'll never forgive me, and you know how dramatic teenagers can be. And since I am thanking her, I also have to give a shout-out to my best friend, Tracee, Savvy's mom. We've spent a lot of time together at dance events and competitions. And we're still friends. Go figure.

ACKNOWLEDGMENTS

So many different people contributed to this book, but first I want to mention the person who has contributed so much to the series: Calista "Cele" Cates-Stanturf. Cele has read both *Tutu Deadly* and *Tapped Out* countless times with a keen eye, open heart, and a genuine love for the character Jenny T. Partridge. She is an invaluable part of my writing process. Gary and Karin Tabke and Jennifer Apodaca have also been a big part of Jenny's creation and are among her biggest cheerleaders. Gary, aka Officer Friendly, answers all of my police questions and helps keep me on the straight and narrow regarding proper police procedure.

I, of course, am always indebted to the incredibly talented girls that dance with my daughter and on our team, under the direction of Misty Robbins, and to their psycho dance moms. They aren't *all* psycho, of course (come on, you *know* who you are!). But to those who are: Please, never change. It gives me lots of fodder for the books.

I must thank my agent Karen Solem, who is open and honest, and never hesitates to steer me straight, and also my wonderful editor, Sandra Harding, who is just "the bomb." She makes writing these books a dream and a joy. I feel incredibly lucky. I also want to thank Cati Dallas and Brenda Butcher, my Dancing Daughter's ballet teachers, for their dedication to the craft and for sharing their own stories with me, as well as answering any questions about dance I might have. I am also grateful to have Jenni Baxter to lean on, vent to, and share experiences with as we work at the studio. She makes what could be a difficult job a lot of fun! And last, but certainly not least, I need to say thanks to Carissa, my oldest daughter, who wants nothing to do with dance—except to watch. Thanks for the patience.

ONE

"Oh, Carmen? That hurts a bit. Carmen?"

The woman holding the hairbrush over my head—and what looked like a considerable chunk of my hair in her left hand—had a glazed, slightly off-kilter look on her face. I could see her in the mirror we both faced, and it wasn't a comforting sight.

"Carmen? Can you let go?" It seemed some of my hair was trapped in the brush, too, and it was in danger of joining the hair in her hand. Somehow, I just knew that bald would not be a good look for me. I should have known this would be a mistake.

Since I never have any money, I am always looking for ways to pinch pennies. One of the ways I do that is working in trade. I do something for the psycho dance moms whose little darlings learn at my studio, and they do something for me in return. Usually this works. Sometimes it backfires. The more psycho the mom, the more often it turns into a huge mess.

I'm Jenny T. Partridge, and as you might have guessed,

I'm a dance teacher. I live and work in Ogden, Utah, land of the Mormons, lake stink, and winter inversions that bring bitter cold temperatures and zero visibility. Everyone who goes through the public school system in Utah knows how the Mormons got here—it is a part of the fourth-grade curriculum. I heard once that the Great Salt Lake stinks because it has no outlet, but my father—a retired schoolteacher—told me that it is because of the dead plants and animals and the shallow water. *Eww.* And the inversion? My good friend James Marriott, who just happens to be a very flamboyant gay man—something everyone knows except his Mormon mother—claims it is God's curse on Utah for being so culturally backward. You can't take that too seriously, because of course, James claims a distant relationship with the very wealthy Marriott hotel chain owners, too. A family connection I highly doubt.

And I don't agree with James that Utah is culturally deprived. After all, we have Ballet West with its internationally known production of *The Nutcracker*; we have the Odyssey Dance Theatre with its annual production of *Thriller*; and here in Ogden, we have historic 25th Street, site of many movie shoots *and* of my studio—located just above Priceless Pearls, an antique and pawn shop. Oh, and the lead singer of the New Wave–inspired band The Killers is from Utah. Please do not ask me about the Osmonds. I am not going there.

Nonetheless, I don't love my home state much during the month of February. Despite the fact it is the shortest of all the calendar months, it can seem very, very long. During an inversion, you can go weeks without seeing the sun—and sometimes your hand in front of your face. Think of an inversion as the thickest of fogs. One that brings bone-chilling temperatures along for the ride. If Stephen King planned to write about a killer fog that came to stay one winter day, froze everything, ate the sun, and turned the residents of a town into raving lunatics, he could do his background research by hanging out along Utah's Wasatch Valley in February.

But this is where I live, and where my dance studio is located, and so I have to make the best of it.

Anyway, since I had the February blahs, I thought Carmen Jensen's offer of a free hairdo, in exchange for some private lessons for her daughter Melissa, sounded like a great deal.

Goes to show you what I get for thinking. I probably should have scheduled the appointment for a time before I rearranged the Petites dance and put thirteen-year-old Melissa in the back row. Melissa loved to dance, but her body wasn't listening to her brain, and the coordination was not there. I arranged my teams by age, size, and most important, skill—Tots, Minis, Smalls, Petites, and Seniors. Sometimes younger girls ended up on older teams, because they could dance better than others—usually because of natural talent. But I couldn't exactly make a thirteen-year-old a Tot. Melissa was a Petite only because of her age and size. She had the desire but no skill to back it up.

I completely applauded her love of dance. But when I saw her butchering one of my choreography routines, I lost all sympathy. Melissa was hopelessly uncoordinated. And all the tea in Japan was not going to get her going in the right direction.

So when I rearranged the dance—preparing the team to compete at the Hollywood StarMakers Convention and Competition, which was coming to town at the end of the week—I moved Melissa back to the third row, far right. I understood that this was the equivalent of putting a baseball player in right field, but I always hoped that the psycho dance moms wouldn't have that same understanding.

Unfortunately, they usually did. And Carmen obviously did. Based on the fact I that I was now missing large chunks of my hair, Carmen was totally clued in to what had happened.

"Uh, Carmen? My hair is attached to my head, and you're hurting me by pulling it. Ouch. Carmen, it hurts!"

The multicolored blonde standing over me narrowed her eyes, and I could almost swear evil flashed out from them. We were in the salon she ran out of her house, and I was suddenly fearful she was going to chop me into pieces and hide my body where it would never be found. You might laugh, but I promise, this dance teacher business can be very dangerous.

It hadn't been all that long since someone killed one of my psycho dance moms and tried to frame me for the murder. That wasn't the best time of my life, although I met a really hot detective because of it. Even with that factored in, I did not want to repeat the experience. I shuddered and looked up at Carmen. Another psycho dance mom, just like the one that tried to kill me. When I called them "psycho," I was not kidding.

Carmen yanked at the brush holding my hair and I winced and cried out.

"Carmen, maybe we should just do this another day, huh? Maybe, say, when you aren't quite so stressed out?" *Or maybe after you've been dosed with some heavy-duty antipsychotic drugs.*

"It hurts, huh?" she said, laughing without humor. "I'm really sorry. Sometimes these things do hurt. Yes, they do. They hurt really, really bad, and then someone tells you, 'Well, sorry. That's just the way it is.' That's life. Life in a nutshell. Sometimes things just *hurt.*"

"Oh, man, I just remembered, I have a solo lesson. Let's reschedule this," I said, anxious to get out of the chair and Carmen's house before I was completely bald. I tried to stand up, but she still had my hair caught in the brush—that was, the hair she hadn't already pulled out of my head.

"Nonsense. You said you really needed a change. Some highlights. A few layers would do wonders for this . . . er . . . your hair." She dropped the hair—my hair!—she'd been holding in her left hand, and it fell to the floor. Then she picked up a pair of sharp scissors, and my heart really started pounding.

"Yes, but you know how upset these mothers get when . . . I mean, I really have to . . ." I stumbled over the words, not wanting to provoke her any further.

"No, no, it'll be fine. Just sit tight and I'll make you a new woman."

Those just might be the most frightening words you will ever hear coming out of the mouth of a psycho dance mom garnishing a pair of scissors.

I was in big trouble.

Two

Two hours later I walked into my studio, my hair tucked up under a jaunty camouflage hat, which was adorned with a black skull—the latest style. Hats actually weren't a fashion accessory I usually adhered to, but necessity is the father of invention. Or something like that. Amber Francis, my assistant dance teacher, was already there, which was a shock, since she and James were almost always late.

She gave me a funny look as I sauntered in and unlocked the office, walking into it. She followed behind me. Both Amber and James had keys to the front door, but not the office.

"Nice hat. New?"

"Yes."

"You're not really a hat person, Jen."

"Thanks, Amber. Is that your way of telling me I look like crap?"

"Pretty much."

Since Amber never looked like crap—with her long, flowing blond hair that always fell perfectly down her back, unless it was pulled back in a neat ponytail for dance; her dark blue eyes; her small waist and large chest—I took offense. She just didn't get how hard it was to be a short, redheaded, thick-waisted thirtysomething like me.

"Gee, thanks, Amber. Love you, too."

"No offense meant, Jenny, but that hat makes you look like Britney Spears on one of her worst days. I almost expect to see you barefoot and walking into a public restroom."

With a flourish, I pulled off the hat and revealed my new do. Platinum blond hair, cut to my shoulders, choppy and layered, and flat-ironed to my head so I looked like a mutant seal.

"Good God. How did that happen?"

"Carmen Jensen."

"Oh, I see. Well, I suppose she's holding your real hair for ransom somewhere? And when you move Melissa back to the front row, somewhere close to the fifty, she will return it?"

"Something like that. So I guess you better get used to it."

I wasn't terribly fond of my new hairdo—and suspected no one short of an alien from another planet would be—but it was going to take more than that for me to move Melissa onto the front row and anywhere near the fifty, which is the prime dancing spot. Right in the middle, dead center. It's where the audience or judge's eyes automatically go. And having Melissa there would be a death knell to my career. I'd rather have the mutant-seal hair.

We heard the noise of children chattering and stepped out of the office and back into the studio. The Minis flowed in through the door, dropping their coats and dance bags on the outer edges of the dance floor. They plopped down to pull off snow boots and winter shoes and layers of clothing worn to keep out the chill. Soon they would be in dance clothes and shoes, and out on the floor—so long as my ancient furnace held out and the heat stayed on.

Frostbite and hypothermia were not conducive to good dancing.

"Who are you?"

I looked down to see Maribel Fulton tugging at my arm.

"It's me, Marble."

"Jenny? You don't look like you. How come you made your hair yellow?"

"Oh, because I was tired of red. Needed a change."

Maribel's mom, Marlys Fulton, came through the door, shivering even in her heavy down coat. She stopped short when she saw my hair, her eyes wide and a little aghast. "Dance mom?"

"Yep."

"Carmen?"

"Yep."

Marlys just shook her head and turned toward the office. "I'll get you an appointment with Ricardo."

"I cannot afford Ricardo."

"I cannot afford to look at you that way. It's my treat. Early birthday present." Since my birthday wasn't until July, it was really early. But I'd take it.

Marlys was that way. She was a dance mom, but a fairly grounded one. Her daughters Carly and Maribel both danced with me, and were reasonably talented, especially Carly, and Marlys didn't freak out if I moved them off the front row from time to time.

She also did office work and the studio books in exchange for tuition. I usually got the better end of this deal, since she was always having to rescue me from one scrape or another. Not my fault! Things just seemed to happen around me.

Marble, who had recently been moved up from the Tots to the Minis, and who was the youngest one on the team—a source of much contention for other Tot moms, who were crying favoritism and nepotism and a bunch of other isms I had never heard of—continued to gaze up at me with wonder in her big brown eyes, and I finally turned away and clapped my hands. "Let's dance." The girls slowly came to attention, except the stragglers who were late and still filing in. Maribel left my side and headed up to the front of the room obediently.

The line of late five- to seven-year-old girls ended, and behind them came Kayla Beckerson, mother of Kinley, arms tight by her sides, lips clenched, forehead wrinkled. She'd need Botox before the end of the day if she held that face for very long. She marched toward me with intent. Great. It was turning out to be a high-drama day at the old Jenny T. Partridge Dance Academy.

I really needed to make up a flyer. One that said, "If you live in Utah and are looking for a place for your daughter to dance, here are a few things to consider: Are you looking for a highly trained, passionate teacher? A program that is solid and building a good reputation? Are you mentally sound and stable, and if not, are you taking your medication faithfully? Have you been hospitalized for mental illness at any time in your past?"

I didn't really need any more psycho dance moms. I already had plenty.

I stared at Kinley Beckerson's mother and wondered if she was going to punch me. The little girl trailed behind her, peeking out from time to time, then ducking back behind her mother. For the record, I did not deserve the title of Dance Nazi! I did not. I couldn't help it if I wanted things done right. I had a higher standard.

And Kinley was a dime-a-dozen dancer. In other words, she danced exactly the same as millions of other five-year-olds. Not very well. I could put her on the back row of every dance, and that would suit her just fine, because she had no interest in turns, jetés, or extensions. She spent more time coming up with excuses *not* to dance than she ever did actually trying to do the steps. Her stomach hurt. Her head hurt. She needed water, or she was going to die.

Her latest—she had a poisonous spider bite that was

going to slowly spread and eat away her leg—had put me over the edge. February, besides being dismal, dreary, and darned cold—it had been ten days since I had seen the sun—was the cusp of competition season. In fact, I had already signed up some teams—the better, older girls—to compete at the Hollywood StarMakers Convention and Competition at the end of the week. Of course, Kinley was not on one of those teams, but I didn't really have time to waste forcing someone to dance who would rather be employed in the cast of a soap opera.

I threw her out of class last Wednesday. And she stomped off crying—boy that leg worked just fine then!— and now she had returned with her mother.

"What is the problem here?" Kayla Beckerson asked. She had a permanent scowl. In fact, I sometimes wondered if she'd had it tattooed on, because I'd never seen her smile. Not at Kinley. Never at me. Just never.

"She's not interested in dance," I said. "She says her leg hurts. Says she has a poisonous spider bite. Says she's sick. Last week she told me she had an erectile dysfunction. Too much TV? Bottom line, Kayla, she doesn't want to dance. And I'm tired of trying to make her."

Hmm, maybe the February doldrums were getting to me. I usually didn't tick off paying clients. Even paying clients with five-year-old hypochondriacs for children.

"It's a mosquito bite," Kayla said with disdain. "She's been whining about it since last week. Just do what I do. Tell her to buck up and get back to work."

"It's the middle of winter during an inversion. There are no mosquitoes out. In fact, I'm surprised there are still humans alive, it's so cold. She doesn't want to dance."

"Whose side are you on?"

Whose side? "Well, frankly, mine."

"Let me tell you something, Jenny T. Partridge. She's going to dance. You are the dance teacher. You make her dance. I am paying you to do that. You *work* for me."

This was one of those times I really wished I had a shotgun like they did in the old Westerns. With one of those handy, I bet I could make Kinley dance. Or maybe that was that *Goodfellas* movie. Anyway, since I didn't have a gun, it wasn't going to happen.

"Look, Kayla, maybe tennis would be her thing. Or maybe piano. Have you tried piano?"

"She takes piano lessons, thank you very much. She needs to dance."

"Why?"

Her eyebrows went up and the scowl went from angry to ludicrous. "Why? Why?" She practically spit the words out at me.

"Yes, why?"

Her scowl deepened. "Because, all well-rounded children dance, and if she's ever to get the acclaim, respect, and fame she deserves, she must be well-rounded."

"Acclaim? Respect? Fame? She's five. Maybe you have a few years to worry about that . . ."

"I wouldn't expect you to understand," she said, her voice dripping with disdain. Kayla Beckerson came from money. In fact, I thought money was her maiden name, because she never hesitated to throw it out in conversation. Money was also her best friend. I wanted money to be my best friend, but instead it treated me like a passing acquaintance. It wasn't terribly fair. She could afford to throw money at a lost cause like Kinley's fame, at least as far as dancing went. The child would never be a dancer. I had no problem with her paying the money, but sooner or later you had to be realistic. In my current mood, sooner was today.

"Of course you wouldn't, and that's neither here nor there, Kayla," I answered calmly. I was proud of myself for maintaining my cool. "Kinley does not want to dance. You can keep bringing her to class, and I'll keep trying to teach her, but it isn't going to have much impact. Her heart is somewhere else."

"Oh, *you* just worry about teaching her, and *I'll* worry about her heart," Kayla said, sounding as though she intended to throw her young daughter on the ground and rip the organ we spoke of right out of her body. She was more than a little scary. "And if you don't do it, I'll find somewhere else that will."

"I can give you some suggestions . . ." *Perhaps drive you there?*

"Are you being sarcastic?"

"Jenny? Never," Amber said as she came up and grabbed Kinley's arm, pulling her out from behind her mother. "Kinley will be just fine, won't you, Kinley?"

"Nooo, nooo, I fink I have a snakebite."

Amber just rolled her eyes and hauled Kinley to her place on the floor.

"You!" Kayla hissed, pointing at her daughter, who kept looking over her shoulder fearfully at her mother, "Dance."

Then she turned back to me, pointing the same finger. "You! *Make* her dance."

She turned and headed for the door, then stopped just before she got there and pivoted to face me. "Oh, and Jenny? You probably shouldn't try to do your own hair. I can recommend someone to fix that mess. Just give me a call." Ice and venom dripped from her words. I would never, for the life of me, understand why some people lived to torment others. If I were Kayla Beckerson's daughter, I'd probably fake cancer if it meant getting away from her.

The door reverberated a bit as it slammed behind her, and I winced and reached a hand up to touch this unfamiliar-feeling hair. So much for getting rid of psycho dance mom and her hypochondriac child. She was apparently still on my Minis team. Great.

"Jenny?" Marlys said, walking out of the office with the cordless phone in her hand. "There's a guy on the line, and he says he's from StarMakers. Bill, I think? Wants to talk to you."

Amber had the Minis warming up and the class reasonably under control, so I gave them one more warning glance and then headed into the office, taking the phone from Marlys, who sat back down at the desk and started tapping

out something on the computer. My dad had brought the
PC to the studio, after refurbishing it at home, and it worked
like a new one, even though I knew it had been previously
owned by the Weber School District. Dad got it at one of
those sales they have from time to time. He was pretty
much a whiz at everything, including guilting me into Sunday dinners with my mother and her heartfelt sighs over
my single, destitute state.

"Hello," I said into the phone. "This is Jenny."

"Jennifer, it has been waaay too long. How are you, dar-
ling?"

The familiar tones of Bill Flanagan rang out clearly
across the phone line. We had a history, Bill and I. We'd
danced together on the Camelot Dance Troupe ten years
before, and since he was one of the few men who didn't
have the same sexual preference as I did, we had dated for
a bit. But we were both flighty and creative, and therefore,
a very, very bad match.

Two artistic types rarely made it for the long haul. But
we'd managed to stay friends, and always went out to dinner when Bill came into town. And of course, he paid,
because he ran a successful dance competition and convention, and I . . . well, that was obvious.

"Bill, are you here already? I thought you wouldn't be
here until at least Thursday or Friday."

"No, Jen, we flew in early to get set up, and wouldn't
you know it, things are already getting messed up. Two of
my instructors just bolted. Bolted! I suspect that jerk Aiden
Bright lured them away, but you would think they would
have some sense of obligation to me and stick this out. Or
at least tell me they were leaving!" Bill's voice was distraught and tense, a condition in which I rarely saw him, so
I knew he was pretty unnerved by the situation.

"Who is Aiden Bright?"

"Oh, you know him, Jenny. He used to have a normal
name—Aaron Brown. But then, he became so full of
himself—and his money-hungry greed—that he decided
he needed a moniker that was a better fit. And Aiden

Bright, director of Tomorrow's Stars Dance Competitions, was born. He basically ripped me off right down to my formula for the dance competitions and conventions. And now he's trying to plunder my help."

I did know Aiden Bright—or at least Aaron Brown—and I suspected he slept with snakes for company. He was the lowest of the low, and I had no doubt that he would steal, plunder, and ravage to get his way at anything. But as far as I knew, he was nowhere near Utah.

"Well, didn't they fly in with you, Bill?" I asked.

"Of course. This is a stopover on our tour, so we've been together for about two months now. We take the same flights, stay at the same hotels. But no one has seen Twila Clark or Eldon Ramsay since we got to our hotel here in Ogden. They went to their rooms, and we were all supposed to meet up for dinner last night, and they weren't there. I've called and called, and they aren't answering."

"Uh, that sounds kind of weird, Bill. Maybe you should call the police."

"Why? I know it's that fink Aiden."

"How do you know that?"

"Bonnie found some correspondence that he sent to Twila, inviting her to be a part of his 'stellar' production."

Bonnie French was Bill's longtime girlfriend and business partner. She was, by trade, an accountant. Perfect match, I guess, for someone like Bill, who tended to live life by the seat of his jeans.

"How did Bonnie find it?"

"Twila just left it sitting on the table after we had drinks one night. Guess she had a few too many, because Bonnie picked it up to return it to her, and one thing led to another, and . . ."

"Too much information, Bill. Why are you telling me all this?"

"I need help. I have three hundred kids signed up to attend this convention and not enough teachers to go around. Can you and James fill in?"

As though on cue, I heard "Hello, dahlings," come from

the other room, and knew James had arrived at the studio. I looked at my watch. Fifteen minutes late! Why was I not surprised?

"Jenny? Are you still there? Can you help?"

"Well, Bill, I'd like to, of course, but I'm trying to get my teams ready to compete, and I have lessons to teach, and it's really close to solo season, and . . ."

"I'll pay you of course. It will be twenty-five hundred dollars for two days' work."

"When did you want me to start?" There were times when I had a serious lack of common sense, but this was not one of them. I could almost hear that hallelujah song you always heard around Christmas playing in my brain. Maybe that or *ching ching*. Fire logs in my fireplace. Socks without holes.

"Let's meet for lunch tomorrow, and I'll give you more details and a class schedule. Can you come up with a jazz routine that quickly? You'll need one for young girls, teens, and older teens. The older group starts at fourteen and on up. The middle group is eleven to thirteen, and all the girls under ten are in a group together. Usually the dancers that come to our conventions are from serious teams, like yours, because we aren't cheap, so the routines should be fairly challenging. Can you do it?"

"You know me and choreography."

"Yes, I do. You could choreograph your way out of the *Titanic*."

I chuckled. "I guess that's a compliment."

"Oh, and will you have James call me?"

We set up a time to meet for lunch in the coffee shop of the Marriott Hotel, where the convention was being held, and I hung up the phone.

"That call surely brightened your outlook. Although with hair that color, you could be a frigging beacon."

"Marlys, do you have to keep reminding me I look like Courtney Love?"

"Yes, yes I do. You have an appointment tomorrow at nine with Ricardo."

James sauntered into the office and stopped short, his eyes opening wide as he gaped at me. "What. Have. You. Done?"

"Carmen," Marlys said.

"Jennifer, I swear, you have got to stop cutting corners. If one of your dance moms was a tattoo artist, would you do that in trade, too?"

"Hmm, I'll have to think about that one—no!" Nobody was getting near me with needles. "And you are late. You were supposed to be here fifteen minutes ago and teach the Minis, so that Amber and I could work on the routine for the Petites and Seniors. You know we have to change the ending. And they are coming in early to do it. Amber and I need time to—"

"It was an emergency. I could not help being late."

"Emergency?"

"Half-price sale at Hollister. My friend, Nick? You know, that absolutely beautiful boy with an amazing face and no brains in his head? He called to tell me they got a huge shipment they didn't have room for, and so everything was going to be on—"

"Shopping. This is your emergency?"

"I wouldn't expect *you* to understand," James said, glancing over me in my Target dance attire.

"I wouldn't expect *you* to get a paycheck this week."

"Kids, kids," Marlys said, chuckling. "James, go teach. Jenny, you and Amber work on the routine. I need to do books, and the two of you are distracting me."

James just harrumphed and headed out the door, and I followed closely behind.

I decided not to tell him about Bill's dance offer just yet, because I was a little peeved with him. That was nothing new. Except I usually didn't have the upper hand, like I did today. I'd let him know about Bill's offer—eventually. James had gotten me into a bit of trouble in the past, first convincing his mother we were a couple, and then convincing her I was a lesbian, and last of all, trying to set the wife of his longtime paramour Cullin after me. I was his fall guy. And I did not like it. I was not yet over being angry at him. Although it was hard to stay mad. He was one of my best friends. So there was just an edge of tension between us. It would probably remain there at least until he came out of the closet to his mother.

THREE

AROUND 6 p.m. I decided the Petites routine was finally clean and ready to perform. Whenever we attended a competition, especially a national one, we couldn't afford to look sloppy or out of sync. The other teams competing at Hollywood StarMakers would be the best Utah had to offer. If I was going to make a name for myself, I had to stand up to them and at least win with a couple of routines.

For that reason, I'd had to hide a couple of girls in the back, which took some interesting dance camouflage, because although they could do the moves, they were in the awkward teenage phase that comes after childhood cuteness and before graceful young adult, and they were all knees and elbows.

As a dance teacher, I had the opportunity to observe the different stages kids went through as they grew. Not every young girl hit the awkward phase, but those who did were quite a sight.

"Okay, girls, I'll see you tomorrow, when we will do dress rehearsal. Make sure you wear your costumes. You don't have to do makeup, but please have your hair done, so I can make sure the look is right."

Marlys stood beside me and handed out notes to each girl as they left. I knew she'd covered all the bases for me, as she always did, giving the girls competition and arrival times, a checklist of things to bring, and other basic information. During the competition, the teams would go on one after the other, and it was always chaotic. Most competition directors tried to intersperse each studio's routines throughout the performance schedule so the dancers would have enough time to change, but at least one quick change per competition was inevitable—and usually it was a nightmare. Sometimes costume changes came so quick we were stripping girls down and throwing different costumes on them, a bevy of dance moms helping whoever needed it. And all the time, Marlys would watch the schedule to make sure each team got on the stage at the right time.

With Marlys by my side, we managed to make it work. I'd be lost without her. The convention the next day was always a relief, as it was a time for the girls to learn from excellent teachers they hadn't worked with before, and the only competition was for scholarships given out by the competition-convention directors. Of course, those psycho dance moms always pushed that to the next level, too. Girls came to conventions with the newest dance clothes, perfectly coiffed hair, and even light makeup. Truthfully, there wasn't much about dancing that was relaxed and stress free.

"Jennifer, I think we need to move spots in this routine," James called out from the other dance room. My studio had originally been used for storage, and when I moved in it was one big room, but my dad had helped me wall it off into two rooms, so I could run two different teams at a time.

I walked into the studio where James and Amber were running the Seniors dances, and stood at the front with them. Amber turned on the music, and the girls began the sequence of chene turns that turned into a difficult fouetté sequence. It was a hard way to start a jazz routine, but it made quite an impact. This time more than usual, as Sami McNeil crashed into Allison Woller.

Allison hit the ground hard, and Heather Marcuson tripped over her and ended up in a heap with Stacy White and Marysa Jenkins.

When the dust finally settled, only about four girls were still standing, one of whom was Sami, who was fourteen and a bit of a drama queen.

She surveyed the wreckage with wide eyes and covered her mouth with her right hand, tears streaming down her face.

"I am the worst dancer in the world. The worst. I am horrible. I can't dance. I can't! Look what I've done."

"Knock it off, Sami," I said. "I've seen a lot of dancers in my time, and believe me, you are not the worst. But if you would spot your turns, you wouldn't risk losing your balance and falling out of them. And then you could avoid hurting other people."

Allison glared at Sami as she and the other girls got back to their feet.

"No, seriously, Jenny, I am awful. You need to pull me out of this routine, because I am ruining it for everyone." Her words did not match the look in her eyes. In the big brown orbs I could see need and pleading. She needed positive reinforcement, and she needed it *now*. Drama queen or not, she was like most girls her age—very, very insecure. I looked at James, and he raised his eyebrows as though to say, "You're the teacher."

"James, will you please take Sami over to the other room and help her understand the importance of spotting these turns?" I asked.

"Why, of course, Jennifer. I would be happy to do that." His formal manner told me he would not be happy to do that and was, in fact, going to get me back but good as soon as possible.

I worked with the rest of the Seniors for the next hour. Amber had left as soon as I came into the room, because, as usual, she had a hot date. Sami rejoined us about halfway through, and her turns looked much, much better after the one-on-one with James. He drove me crazy, but he was a darned good teacher and dancer.

"Do I get private-lesson pay for that?" James asked as the girls filed out.

"No, but you do get a big thank-you, because you did a great job. She looks much better."

"Of course she does."

"Of course." I sighed. "You need to call Bill Flanagan, Mr. Big Stuff. He needs us to teach at the convention."

"He does? How delightful. And are we getting paid for this endeavor?"

"You can work that out with Bill. I'm just giving you the message."

"Jenny? What is wrong? I do love sparring with you and all, but you just don't seem like your normal self. Are you still mad about that stuff with my mom? I promise, I told her that you and I had decided just to be platonic friends, and that you were never a lesbian. Not even one time."

James was right. I was still angry at him for the messes he kept getting me into. But he was my friend. I had to get over it. The only problem was, I knew it wasn't true. He wasn't going to stop. I *knew* him. It would continue until the end of time. My only choices were to tell him to get the heck out of my life, or to accept it. I wasn't quite sure what I wanted to do. I decided to play nice for the time being. "It's February. I look like Courtney Love on crack, and it's freezing cold. And Tate hasn't called me for a week."

Whoa, where did that come from?

"Ah, man trouble. That I understand. He'll call, Jen. He's probably just busy on a case."

"Yeah, probably." Tate Wilson was the Ogden City police detective who had pretty much saved my life last Christmas, and he was also hot, hot, hot—something I could not put out of my mind. We had kept in touch, talking usually three to four times a week, and had gone on a few dates, too. But it seemed like something always got in the way of taking the relationship that one step further. Not the least of which was my own fear. It was hard to say what terrified me more: consummating my passion for him or never seeing him again. Did that make any sense? Probably not. I was pretty confused.

"Can I make a suggestion?" James asked.

"When have you ever waited for permission?"

"Right. Go back to red. Blond is a not a good color on you."

I sighed. "Call Bill. His number is written down on the blotter in the office."

I got home around 9:30 p.m. and hit the On button to my answering machine before I even shed my coat and gloves. The digital display showed fourteen messages. I didn't get excited. This wasn't my first rodeo. It was probably all psycho dance moms.

Beep. "Hi, Jenny, this is Tamara Williams, April's mom. I can't find the right color dance shoes in April's size, and I was wondering if it was okay if she just wore black . . ."

God no.

Beep. "Hi, Jenny, this is Tamara again, April's mom. Do you really require this brand of tights, because I found a sale on a different brand of them at . . ."

Beep. "Hi, Jenny, this is Tamara, April's mom. I just talked to Brenda Steed and we agreed that it really shouldn't matter what brand of tights they wear, as long as the color is the same, right?"

Sigh. It did matter.

Beep. "Hi, Jenny, this is Tamara . . ." I hit the Delete button. I would see the woman tomorrow morning for Pete's sake, at her daughter's solo lesson.

"Hi, Jenny, it's Mom. Are you coming for Sunday dinner? I'm making prime rib and funeral potatoes. Oh, and we have the nicest new neighbor, and he'll be here, and he's very anxious to meet you. Call me."

Sigh.

Beep. "Jenny Partridge? If you value your career, your

reputation, and your studio you will stay away from Star-Makers. This is not a joke. I suggest you take it seriously."

What the heck?

Chills ran up my spine as I tried to recognize the asexual voice. This was really strange. I had just told Bill Flanagan a few hours before that I would help him out. Now I was getting death threats?

Beep. "Jenny, this is Tamara, April's mom . . ."

I quickly fast-forwarded through the rest of the messages. Of all my messages, at least nine were from Tamara Williams. Four were hang-ups. And one was a death threat.

I didn't know whether to laugh or cry. So I didn't do either. I called Detective Tate Wilson.

FOUR

LATE took only about fifteen minutes to get to my door. I'd been wallowing in self-pity all week, because I hadn't heard from him once since we had almost fallen into bed together. That had been on our last date, where we drank a little wine at a great Italian restaurant and ended up almost in the same spot we'd been before—at my front door, kissing passionately, his hands and mouth exploring, my body melting. The last time we'd gotten this close, James had interrupted us with his shenanigans. This time, there was no interruption. He'd edged me toward the bedroom, his hands on my body, his mouth on mine, making it hard to breathe. Really, really hard to breathe. I started to gasp, and I did the whole hyperventilation thing and started to cry, and he'd gotten a bit of a panicky look himself, probably at my reaction.

After I calmed down, he'd acted all understanding. And then he left and didn't call me. I wasn't about to break down and call him, so I'd gone about my business like it wasn't bothering me. Except, apparently, I had been slightly cranky. So I screamed at the Smalls and made a few of them cry. Who could blame me?

Tate was six foot something, gorgeous, broad shouldered, and lean muscled. He had black hair and the most beautiful blue eyes I'd ever seen. And he had a scar over his left eye that made him slightly dangerous. I couldn't resist him.

Except I had, because I was fighting some emotions I didn't want to explore. I didn't handle rejection well, so I figured that if I didn't give him the chance, he wouldn't be able to walk away from me. Hmm. That was fuzzy logic. My favorite and only kind.

Now he stood at my front door with a quizzical look gracing his strong features. His eyes surveyed my body and then lit on my head and stopped. My hair! I'd forgotten about the mess that was my hair. His mouth quirked up on one side like it did a lot—at least when he was around me.

"Blond? I was a little bit attached to the red, really. And how did you get it straight? I've never seen it that way. Not even once."

"Psycho dance mom. Long story. Marlys made me an appointment to get it fixed tomorrow."

I motioned him inside since I was shivering and it was about four hundred degrees below zero outside. The fog had settled in, and I could barely make out the streetlight on the corner and the shape of my Pepto Mobile—my pink Volkswagen Bug.

After I shut the door he leaned down and gave me a gentle kiss that left me wanting more, but he pulled away and walked over to my answering machine.

He shed his down jacket, draped it over the kitchen chair, and sat down at the table. My apartment wasn't that big, so the kitchen table served as a desk, really. I never served meals, or even sat down to eat at it. After all, ice cream was best eaten in front of a television, out of the container. Who needed dishes? Less work. Plus, I never had any money so I got by eating a lot of Cup Noodles and Top Ramen.

It was the only reason my mother was able to lure me home and into her evil matchmaking soirees. I needed substantial food once in a while.

Tate hit the On button and listened to Tamara's messages, his grin growing with each one. It faded as soon as he heard the threat.

He played it back about five times, and then shook his head and turned to me. I walked over to the table and sat down in the chair next to his. He ran through my caller ID until he got to an entry that said, "Blocked call."

"They made sure you couldn't trace it. And the voice is altered. Probably one of those machines you can buy at any RadioShack. I'm assuming you don't recognize it?"

"No. But I'm curious how anyone at all could even know I'd agreed to work for Bill this weekend. He just called me today."

"And Bill is?" Was it my imagination or did I hear a hint of something akin to jealousy in his voice? Something was definitely bothering him.

"Bill Flanagan. He runs Hollywood StarMakers, a traveling dance competition and convention. We danced together years ago at Camelot, and we've stayed in touch. The dance world is a small one."

"Okay, so this Bill calls you and asks you to teach. Just today. And it starts this weekend? Poor planning?"

"No, apparently two of his teachers just cut and run. Bill thinks they were lured away by another guy who runs a similar competition and convention. He's not a very nice guy."

"And is it possible that this other guy is the one who called you?" Tate's voice had taken on a hard edge. It was his "cop voice." It made me squirm whenever it was directed at me—like now.

"You tell me. I couldn't tell squat from the voice. It sounded mechanical."

"What is this guy's name?"

"He goes by Aiden Bright now, but he used to be just plain Aaron Brown. I've run into him a time or two, and believe me, he is cutthroat. He will do whatever it takes to get what he wants. Back when he had a studio in Salt Lake City, there were rumors he was behind the attack of a certain star soloist—a girl who was competing against his top dancer. Somebody beat her up in the bathroom of a dance competition, right before she was supposed to go on. Very Tonya Harding-ish," I said, referring to the ice skater who had arranged to disable her main competitor, Nancy Kerrigan, at a skating match.

"Girls getting beat up in bathrooms at dance competitions? Are you kidding me?"

"Unfortunately, no. She was only twelve, too. Probably scared her off dance for life."

"This is one weird world you live in, Jenny T. Partridge."

"Hey, you hear about it on the news all the time. Little League baseball. Football. Soccer. Any competitive sport. It brings out the worst in some people. Dance is no different."

"Indeed."

I figured I didn't have to do much more explaining since Tate had been front and center during the poisoned cookie-dough fiasco that had recently enveloped me and me studio. One of my dance moms ended up dead because of arsenic-laced cookie dough being offered as my studio fundraiser—and since she and I were definitely not best friends—it had looked pretty bad for me. Thank goodness things had turned out okay. Well, mostly okay. There were still psycho dance moms, and Tate had seen exactly what psycho dance moms were capable of.

"So, what would this guy have to gain by frightening you off, if that is what happened?"

"No clue. I just know that two of the teachers who have been with Bill for the past two months have disappeared. And he offered to pay me a lot of money. It's going to take more than a voice from some neuter person to scare me off this gig."

"Neuter person?" His smile came back briefly, then disappeared again.

"Yeah, you know what I mean."

"So, why hasn't this Bill reported the missing teachers?"

"He said he knows they went to work for Aiden. So why bother?"

Tate shook his head. "Get your coat. We're going to pay Bill a visit."

I wasn't sure I liked having my own personal detective escort, since he was pretty proactive. I was of the opinion that many things would work themselves out if you just gave them time. Of course, this outlook rarely worked out for me, but a girl could dream. I'd planned an evening of a warm blanket, a fire, and some microwave mashed potatoes and gravy. I was famished, and as usual my stomach was letting everyone in the vicinity know about it.

I shivered and my stomach rumbled, and Tate pulled into the Burger King drive-through. This was becoming a habit with us.

I ate as he headed downtown toward the Marriott Hotel, where I'd told him Bill and his crew were staying.

I knew there was probably something intrinsically wrong with this sorta-relationship thing between us, especially since he was always feeding me. But since I was starving, I wasn't going to think about it too deeply at the moment.

We pulled into the parking lot of the Marriott and I finished up the last of my French fries, offering him a few. He declined. I'd never seen him scarf down junk food the way I did. I'd never really given it much thought, but now I had to wonder if he thought I was a huge pig.

"What?" Tate said, turning to me after he shut off the engine. "You have a funny look on your face."

"Do you ever eat anything or do anything that isn't good for you?"

"What kind of question is that?"

"Just curious. I've never seen you eat fast food. Even

when you are buying it for me. And your life seems pretty much in control, all the time."

"You don't really know me that well."

"I guess I don't." A little pit of something gnawed in my stomach. Was it sadness? Fear that I'd lost my only chance to connect with Tate?

"I swear, I can see the wheels turning in your head. Look, don't worry. We have plenty of time."

"Well, you kind of just disappeared after I . . . after I . . ."

"After you freaked out when we got close to making love?"

"Um, yeah, that."

"And now, because I didn't call you all week, you thought we were through."

"Well, I did wonder . . ."

Tate reached over and put his hand on my chin, pulling me toward him and leaning into me. "Jenny, I'm not a one-night-stand kind of guy. I'm not a take-home-to-mother kind of guy, either, but you and I are going to connect. And when we do, it's going to be good. But I don't force myself on anyone, ever. You have to want it, too."

He kissed me, hard, and I felt my heart stop—really, I swear it did. No wonder I freaked out. This man had both my head and my body in a dither.

"Now, let's go find your friend Bill and ask him more questions about these missing teachers—and find out who would leave you a message like that."

"Obviously, it had to be someone from inside his organization," I said. "Because no one else—except Marlys and James—knows about it."

"James. Maybe it's one of his tricks. He does stuff like this all of the time." Tate was right. James was constantly getting me into hot water, mostly because he used me as a front to hide his homosexuality.

"He really doesn't have anything to gain here, though. And James does a lot of crazy stuff, but usually it amounts to planning weddings for us that will never take place or spreading rumors about me to cover his own lifestyle. But he never does it maliciously, and it's not about scaring me."

"You really ought to rethink this friendship with him."

"I've known him a long time."

Tate just shook his head.

"Besides, what would he gain from scaring me into not working with Bill?"

"Maybe he wants to do it, instead of you."

"He gets to do it, too. Bill asked both of us. Are you trying to find ways to implicate James?"

"He makes me nervous."

"He thinks you're hot."

"I did not need to hear that."

I giggled and opened up my door. "Let's go find Bill."

The person working the hotel's front desk would not tell us Bill's room number, but obligingly rang his room. There was no answer.

"I know where to find him," I said. I pointed to the hotel lounge.

Sure enough, when we pushed through the door we spotted Bill sitting at a table with about four other people, including his girlfriend, Bonnie. I'd met her about three times, and she was always more than a little cold to me. I figured she must know that once upon a time Bill and I had been more than just friends.

"Hey, Bill," I said as we walked up to their table. He turned to me and a puzzled expression crossed his face. Then he looked closer.

"Jenny?"

"Yes, it's me."

"What have you done to your hair?"

"Uh, just a temporary change." I could smell his boozy breath from where I stood, and I knew that wasn't good. Always a partier, Bill drank even more heavily when he was stressed. Even drunk, he knew this hair thing just wasn't right. I couldn't wait to get it fixed. He jumped to his feet and embraced me in a big, sloppy hug. He was already five sheets to the wind.

Bonnie glared in my direction.

"Why'd you come down here?" Bill asked after indicating we should pull up chairs and join his group. "Couldn't wait to see me?" Both Bonnie and Tate's faces hardened at that comment. Great.

"This is Tate Wilson, Bill and Bonnie. He's a, uh, friend of mine."

"Pleased to meet you," Bill said, enthusiastically pumping the hand Tate offered. Bonnie just nodded, although the look she gave Tate was a lot nicer than any look she ever gave me.

"This is Enrique Perez and Jason Kutcher," Bill said, pointing at the other two people sitting at their table. "Enrique teaches tap, and Jason does pop and hip-hop."

"Hello," said Enrique without a trace of an accent, even though he looked as if he could start spouting eloquent Spanish at a moment's notice. I was betting he grew up being called "Ricky," possibly in the suburbs of California. You had to have a shtick in the dance world, or you didn't get far. But his shtick didn't matter, because he was truly one of the most beautiful human beings I had ever seen. Thick, glossy, sleekly styled hair. Dark complexion. Deep, dark brown eyes. Gorgeous. Alas, just from looking—and from experience in the dance world—I was almost certain he was playing for the other team. Sad day for the ladies. Bonus for the guys like James. *James.* Oh Lord, I saw trouble coming. Oh well, couldn't worry about it now.

"Yo," said Jason. He had that Justin Timberlake look going on, and I recognized his name. He'd done choreography for some of the big names like Mariah Carey, Janet Jackson, and Madonna, although I'd also heard he was somewhat of a thug. A successful thug. Bill must be doing really well to afford his fees.

"Jason is just doing this city and Las Vegas with us," Bill explained. "He has a busy schedule, so I was lucky to get him."

Jason didn't comment.

"So, what brings you down here tonight, Jenny?" Bill asked again.

"Well, I got a really strange phone call on my answering machine tonight. It warned me not to participate in your convention. I just wondered who would know you asked me to teach."

Bill's face hardened. "You're kidding. I didn't tell anyone except Bonnie and some of the other teachers. We were shorthanded. They all knew that."

"Nobody has seen or heard from Eldon and Twila, which is very irresponsible of them," Bonnie said in her nasal voice. "Not to mention they signed contracts with us, so they could be in some legal trouble, too."

"Did they check into the hotel with you?" Tate asked.

"Yes, of course. We all took the shuttle here from the airport and then went to our rooms. Then they never showed up for dinner. We always eat dinner together, like one big happy family."

Enrique frowned at that comment, causing me to wonder why. "Excuse me, I'm really tired. I think I'll go to my room." He stood up and reached a hand out to me. "Pleased to meet you, Jenny. I look forward to working with you. Nice meeting you, also, Tate."

He was very polite, and formal, but not terribly effusive or friendly. After he left, Bonnie made a little moue of disgust, and also stood up. "I need to get my beauty sleep. Bill, you really need to get to bed, too. We have a lot to do tomorrow."

"I'll be up soon, Bon."

She said a general good night and then wafted off. She was rail thin, with long, sleek, dark hair that probably required no straightening at all, and she was always perfectly manicured and coiffed. I could still smell her perfume—something expensive, I was sure, but not a scent I could identify since Bath & Body Works sprays were as expensive as I got.

I felt like Cousin It next to Bonnie. I was glad she was gone.

"So tell me 'bout the phone call," Bill said.

"Nobody else seems really worried about it," Tate commented, looking after the rapidly departing Bonnie. Enrique was long gone from our sight. It *was* kind of weird, I thought, that nobody said anything about the strange call. Maybe they were all angry at me for coming to work for Bill. But why?

"Did you give anyone else Jenny's phone number or leave it laying around?"

"Course not. It's saved in my phone, so I just hit speed dial."

"You're on his speed dial?" Tate asked me, lines hardening his face.

"We're friends," I said defensively. "And it's my work phone."

"But you got the threatening phone call at home."

"Well, I am listed in the phone book. I've always wanted Madonna and Britney to be able to reach me when they needed me to work on their next tour."

"I didn't have her home phone number," Bill said, nodding. "And I didn't look it up. I don't have her cell phone number, either. How come I don't have your cell phone number, Jenny?" He was starting to slur his words.

Tate gave him a stern look, and I ignored the question.

Jason still sat at the table with us, but he was staring at some sports roundup program on the television above the bar.

"This just doesn't make a lot of sense," Tate said. "And I have to wonder if the two people who just left don't have something to do with the threatening phone call. After all, neither one of them was very friendly."

"Well, Enrique is tired of just teaching tap classes—he says it's too confining and has put a straight jacket on his career—but it's the only thing he does well enough to teach. His jazz technique just ain't all that great. So he wasn't thrilled I wouldn't give the classes to him, and I called Jenny instead. And Bonnie . . . well, Bonnie just doesn't really like . . . I mean . . ."

"Bonnie hates me. Which is pretty stupid because she doesn't even know me."

"Yeah, I agree. But she's a woman. You know how you guys are."

"Uh, what do you mean by that?"

Tate started laughing.

"Just that you are all the time jealous and demanding, and when someone doesn't do every little thing you want, you just throw temper tantrums and go off in a huff, and . . ."

"Uh, Bill? Is everything going okay with Bonnie?"

He sighed and hunched over. "No, not really. She's getting really demanding. Trying to get us to branch out, do more cities, and how the hell am I supposed to pull that off? Do you know how many of these traveling convention-competitions there are?"

"A lot, but yours is different. I get flyers for at least fifty, and this is the only one I attend," I told him reassuringly, patting him on his shoulder.

"Back to the point, it's obvious that whoever called Jenny is very aware of the moves you are making, and so we have to consider it might have been Enrique or Bonnie," Tate said, irritation lacing his voice.

"No, no, they wouldn't do that," Bill said. "I know them better than that."

"Enrique would, my man," Jason offered, the first words he'd uttered since "Yo."

"Why do you say that?" Tate asked him. The other man never moved his eyes from the television screen, but he answered the question.

"Because he thinks he's the bomb, dig? But he wants to be more than he is. And it's all about the Benjamins. He's a dance climber. Wants to be on the top level, when all he does is *tap*." He said the last word with great derision. And I picked up only about half of what he meant.

"Is tap a bad thing?" Tate asked.

Jason just snorted.

"Tap is an important part of every dance education," Bill intoned, again slurring his words. "The movement and rhythm involved is an important part of America's dance heritage, and—"

"Tap sucks," Jason said.

"I feel like I landed on Mars," Tate said. "So you don't like tap dancing. Still, tell me why Enrique would make a threatening call."

"Told you, dude. He wants to move up. Thinks he has the jazz and hip-hop moves." Jason sniggered a little bit. "He hip-hops like a bunny rabbit."

Bill's eyes were starting to take on a decidedly unfocused look. "Hey, Bill, maybe we can talk more about this tomorrow," I said. "You should get up to your room. We'll talk more at lunch tomorrow."

"Yeah, I think you're right. Glad you came down, Jenny. Why did you come down again?"

Tate rolled his eyes.

"I'll help you to your room, Bill," Jason said, standing up. "Look, I'm not saying it was Enrique. Just saying it's possible. There's been some weird shit going on here, even just since I came into town. He's worried. Bill got me started, way back, so I figure I owe him. If you're looking for someone, I'd look first at Enrique. Then check out Aiden Bright."

Bill mumbled something I didn't quite catch, and we watched as Jason led him toward the elevator.

"That didn't get us very far," Tate commented.

"Well, at least we have some possible suspects?"

"We?"

"Yeah, we. This isn't exactly a case now, is it? You are not on official business. In fact, you're on Jenny T. Partridge business. So, yeah, it's 'we.'"

"Great."

As we pulled up to my apartment building, Tate offered to come in and sleep on the sofa. "After all, you did just get a death threat. Although that appears to be a fairly regular occurrence with you."

"As much as my sofa loves you, I think I'll be okay. The next time you stay over, Tate, I think it should be in my bed. But I'm not sure I'm ready for that yet. I hope you understand."

"Do you promise to lock up tight, and that includes the chain lock?"

"Yes, Tate."

"And call me if anything happens. Anything at all, no matter how small?"

"Yes, Tate."

He sighed and then ran his right hand through his dark, thick hair. "I shouldn't leave you alone, but I have to be up really early tomorrow. The department has me on a case that's requiring a lot of overtime, and yet I still feel like I'm getting nowhere."

Overtime? That made me feel slightly better about his noticeable absence from my life in the last week.

"What kind of case?"

"The really ugly kind you don't want to hear about."

"But I'm interested in you. I'm interested in what you do." I was, really. But he was right. I didn't want to hear ugly details. I was kind of weak-stomached that way.

He leaned in and kissed me gently. "Thanks for trying, but I think I'll spare you on this one."

He opened up his door and walked around to my side, opening my door before I could jump out on my own. He walked me to my front door, arm around me. I felt him tense, and then he pushed me behind him and drew his gun.

"Police. Freeze!"

I froze, so the command worked.

"Don't shoot. Don't shoot," came a frantic voice from the gloomy fog on the side of my apartment. Wow, Tate was good. I hadn't even seen anyone there.

"Come out, hands up. Slowly," Tate ordered.

"Don't shoot," said the voice again, and I noticed it was heavily accented with a Polynesian slant.

"Elder Tuatuola?" I asked, not knowing anyone else

who had that particular accent. Except . . . something was different.

"Yes, it's me. Don't shoot. I need a place to hide." He came out slowly, hands up, wearing his standard missionary white shirt, but he had on dark blue sweatpants, and no tie. He also had on a big white down jacket, but it wasn't done up. And it made him look like a slightly deranged Eskimo. Noticeably missing was his name tag identifying him as a missionary for the Church of Jesus Christ of Latter-day Saints.

"What do you mean you need a hiding place?" I asked him. "And something is different about you. What is it?"

"Why are you sneaking around Jenny's apartment at this time of night?" Tate asked, but I noticed he'd lowered his gun.

This wasn't good. Elder Tuatuola—I did not know his first name—was one of the Mormon missionaries who almost got poisoned at my house—it was an accident!—and he seemed to have become addicted to the adrenaline that came with trying to convert me. Since I'd been raised by a Catholic mother and a Jack Mormon father, I'd pretty much just never made a religious choice and stuck to praying when I really, really needed something. The fact that I didn't have a specific religious affiliation made me a bit of a target.

Elder Tuatuola and Elder Martin, his companion, had been visiting me regularly despite the fact their mission leader thought I was the Antichrist. But Elder Martin had recently been transferred to the Evanston, Wyoming, mission—possibly because of the bus incident. Don't ask.

I knew this because he had come by before he left, and asked if he could write to me. It was kind of cute. Kind of.

Elder T. hailed from Samoa and spoke in broken English. That was it! "Hey, you aren't talking like you normally do. What's up with that?"

He shrugged his shoulders. "People expect me to not speak English clearly and have an accent, so I give it to them. It got us in more doors, and it made a lot of members happy to feed us. I know, I know, it's not very honest, but this mission is for the birds. I want out. And the truth is, I want to dance. I want to dance with you. I can teach at your studio."

"Uh . . ." It didn't happen too often, but I found myself speechless.

A light flipped on over my neighbor's porch, and I quickly said, "Maybe we better take this inside."

"Yes, inside. It's too cold out here. Darn cold," Elder T. said. He still had a slight accent, but his English was a whole lot better. He rubbed his gloveless hands together and frosty breath filled the air in front of him.

Tate gave me a look, his eyebrows raised.

After we got inside, Elder T. shed his down jacket and plopped into my man-eating sofa. It was old, and the springs were mostly gone, and it swallowed people regularly. Elder T. was so big he didn't even make a dent in it.

"Well, this is an interesting situation," Tate said, and I saw that gleam of humor in his eye, even though he was trying to hide it. "Although I'm going to tell you right now, I really would advise against trying to hide away this particular runaway missionary. He's not exactly, well, inconspicuous. Actually, I'd probably advise against trying to hide *any* runaway missionary. But this one in particular would be hard to miss."

I looked over at the big Samoan sitting dejectedly on my couch. He caught my eye and said, "So will you help me? Can I dance at your studio?"

"Uh, well . . ."

"Hey, he wants to dance," Tate said. This time I heard the laughter in his voice. Heard it! "You can't fight the rhythm. If the feet want to dance, they want to dance."

"I'm good. I was applying to the university dance program when my parents convinced me to do the mission thing."

"You aren't really from Samoa, are you?" I said accusingly.

"Yeah, I am, really. But I've been here in the United States for a while. I was about twelve when my parents moved us here to Utah." Hence the accent, minus, of course, the broken English he used before.

"Isn't Samoa warm?" I asked. "Why would anyone move here from a warm place? That's just nuts."

"They wanted to be closer to Mormon headquarters. So we came. And I tried to be a good son. But I don't want to be a missionary. I want to dance. To teach dance. You should see my choreography. Darn good."

I had to think fast. "Well, see, here's the thing, Elder T. I don't think you can just bail on your mission. I mean, I'm sure there are regulations and . . . well, what I mean is, don't you think there might be trouble if you just disappear? When people disappear, all kinds of bells and alarms and whistles go off, and the police are called. The police! Like him." I turned and pointed to Tate. "Tell him, Detective Wilson. What do they do to missionaries who run?"

"Uh, well, frankly, I have no idea. I would guess they would report him missing."

"Yes, missing."

Elder T. was beginning to look alarmed.

"And they would notify his parents that he had gone missing, of course."

"Oh, wow, you can't do that to your parents, Elder T. They would be frantic. Even when you are older, parents get frantic when their children go missing. And I think your church kinda frowns on missionaries bolting on the program, you know?"

"You know how many people I've baptized?"

"No."

"Not one. Zero. Zippo. None. I'm not a good missionary. Even the accent didn't work when it came to convincing people to get dunked. But it did get us lots of free meals." *Hmmm, maybe I should consider an accent . . .*

"Well, I wouldn't take that too hard, pal," Tate said. "I mean, you're in Utah for hell's . . . er, heck's sake. There aren't a lot of people left here to convert."

"And perhaps your heart is not really in it," I said. "But that's neither here nor there. See, the thing is, Elder T., I didn't even know you could dance."

"Oh yes, I am very good at dance. Very good."

"Well, then I think we need to start at the beginning," I said. "You need to call your warden, er, that guy that always gives me dirty looks, and tell him that you are planning on leaving your mission. Then maybe you can call your parents and arrange for them to come get you. Then when things get straightened out, you can come back out and show me your, uh, dance skills, and we'll go from there."

It sounded reasonable to me. Even Tate nodded his head.

But Elder T. was shaking his. "No, they won't let me leave. I know them. I could tell you stories of how far they go to keep missionaries on their missions. I have to think of another way. If I could just stay here for a few days . . ."

"I don't think they can make you stay on your mission, Elder T.," I said gently. "If I remember right, you have to choose to go on a mission. And it's a little odd that you are here in Ogden, too, because usually they send you at least a little farther from home, don't they? Just in case you want to, well, do what *you* want to do."

"Please don't call me 'Elder.' I'm not a missionary anymore. And the truth is, originally, they sent me out to the Washington, D.C., mission, but I got very sick, so they sent me home and then reassigned me here."

I started to get a little suspicious. "You got sick?"

"Yeah, I think it was a tapeworm, man. Or something like that."

"From Washington, D.C.?" Tate said. "I know there's a lot of weasels and rats there, oh, and snakes, but I don't think tapeworms are a big problem."

"Maybe a parasite. Something."

Apparently, Elder Tuatuola had something in common with the little soap opera queen on my Minis team, Kinley Beckerson. "You made it up, didn't you?" I said. "You weren't sick. You were trying to get home, and you made up the sick story."

His lips tightened up for a moment, then his face fell and his shoulders sagged with dejection. "Yeah. I just wanted to come home. Then they sent me here, instead, where I could be close to 'medical care' and parent pressure. This time, I am not going back. And I'm going to dance."

Boy, when he made his mind up, he was darn stubborn.

"What's your first name, anyway, since you don't want us calling you 'Elder'?"

"Salesi. But I go by Sal."

"Well, Sal, it seems to me that you just need to call your parents and tell them the truth."

"You don't understand," he said, shaking his head gently. "If I leave, I'll bring shame on my family. They were so proud. But I hate it. I'm miserable. I want to dance."

He was really stuck on this dance thing. And it didn't appear he was moving off my couch. I was generally pretty creative, mostly because my life forced me to be, but I wasn't seeing an answer to this situation.

I knew I could make one phone call, though, and find the answers. Problem was, I'd rather walk through a pit of vipers than do it.

FIVE

TATE was insistent that Sal return to his apartment, where his constant companion—someone named Elder Perkins who Sal called a "greenie"—had to be wondering where the heck he was. But Sal wouldn't budge.

Since Tate and I had no clue how the Mormon Church handled runaway missionaries, we decided we needed help. And the one person who knew everything there was to know about everything was my Auntie Vi. She was the gossip maven of Ogden, a devout Mormon, and the "mother" of two ugly, fat dogs. She had plenty of money, too much time on her hands, and a very interesting sense of Mormon style. And she knew everybody, everything, and who to call to get things done.

I swallowed my pride and picked up the phone. This wasn't going to be pretty.

"Hello?" Auntie Vi chirped, despite the late hour. I knew she was a night owl, always watching Jay Leno and other late-night talk shows.

"Hello, Auntie, it's Jenny."

"Jenny? My long-lost niece? I haven't heard from you in months. Why, at least since Christmastime."

Long lost? It was freaking February. *Sheesh.*

"I know. I'm just really busy getting ready for competition season."

"So, to what do I owe the honor of this call?"

"Well, I sorta had a question."

"Oh?"

I could visualize the look on her face as she heard those words. She loved helping people. Mostly because it gave her something to hold over the person's head.

"Yeah, I was just wondering, say . . . well, what would happen if a missionary decided he didn't want to finish his mission, and wanted to go home. How would he go about that?"

"Jennifer," she gasped. I could hear the scandal in her voice. This was going to be all over town tomorrow. "Please, tell me you have not gotten involved with an innocent missionary and caused him to want to desert the Lord's work."

What was I, the Jezebel of Ogden? "Auntie, this is just hypothetical. It's a question for a . . ." I looked at Sal sitting on my couch, watching me closely, his big brown eyes pleading. "It's a question for a friend, one of my dance moms, who has a son. Yeah, and he's not happy out in the mission field. She doesn't know what to do. He wants to come home. How do they handle it?"

"Well, he'd have to go to his mission president, of course, and they'd sit down and discuss it." She still sounded skeptical—probably thought I was hiding an innocent missionary in my closet, possibly tied up with rope and duct tape—but at least she was answering the question. "They would probably do some prayer sessions, and some more interviews, and they would give him a mission companion that would help him spiritually."

I was beginning to see Sal's problem. "But what if he didn't want that? What if he just wanted to come home?"

"Well, Jennifer, all missionaries get homesick. It's

normal, and so the leaders would do their best to help him realize the importance of his work and get him feeling better so he could finish his duty to the Lord."

"Auntie Vi," I said, getting a bit impatient. Sal just shook his head and Tate watched both of us with bemusement plastered across his face. He clearly enjoyed all the weirdness that was my life. "You aren't listening. He wants to come home. He doesn't want to be a missionary anymore."

"Jennifer, it's just not that simple."

"Okay. Well, thanks, Auntie Vi. Let's do lunch sometime."

"Wait! Wait, Jennifer, please . . . Please promise me . . . You haven't done something wrong, have you? You haven't lured away a young, innocent missionary to . . ."

"Good-bye, Auntie Vi."

I hung up the phone. Tomorrow, my name would be on the lookout list for missionaries across Utah: "If you see this woman, run!"

"Okay, so I get your point. It's not very easy to get out of this mission thing," I said to Sal.

"Nope," Sal said. "Told you."

"But the truth is, you are really close to your parents. I mean, technically, if someone would just drive you to Salt Lake City, you could really just do it, right? It's not like you're a political prisoner or anything like that. Or in jail."

"I know I have to tell them," Sal said. "But I need to build up the courage. I'll do it tomorrow. Please just let me stay here tonight, on the couch."

"Even *I* know that is breaking some cardinal missionary rule," I said.

"I'm not a missionary."

"He isn't staying here," Tate said. "Not alone with you."

"He's a missionary."

"I'm not a missionary."

"Fine, you take him home. Because obviously he can't resolve this tonight."

"You want me to take him home?" Tate raised his eyebrows.

"Do you have a better suggestion?"

"We could all stay here."

"I only have one couch."

"I know." He smiled that wicked smile, and my face got all hot and flushed, and my palms sweaty. Sal's eyes got big, and I swear his brown complexion went a shade of auburn.

"I don't think that will work," I said, gulping.

Tate laughed. "Fine, let's go, Sal. I have a spare bedroom in my condo. But in the morning, you are going to have to come clean with your church leaders and your parents."

"I know," Sal said, sighing. He hefted his big body off the couch. I couldn't see how this man could dance. Did he mean some sort of Polynesian-type dancing? Hulas? I had no idea.

"After I get this worked out, Jenny, can I show you my stuff? My choreography?"

"Yes. After you get your situation worked out."

"Okay. Thanks."

After Tate and Sal left, my apartment felt much larger, and colder, and I shivered a bit. Tuition wasn't due for about fifteen days, I was out of fire logs, but there was a bright spot on the horizon. I was going to earn some serious money this weekend, and for once, maybe I could put a little away for a snowy day. Uh, well, for all my snowy days. Or was it rain? This was Utah. It definitely had to be snow.

I went into the bathroom and washed my face, ran a brush through my foreign-looking hair—who was that blond seal in the mirror?—and then decided to go to bed. Tomorrow I would meet with Ricardo, get my natural red back, and then have lunch with Bill and find out more about the job—and of course dig a little deeper into Bill's problem, and figure out who had made the mysterious phone call warning me away from teaching for Hollywood StarMakers.

For now, I was going to sleep, and dream about a certain hot detective. That was pretty much guaranteed.

A loud boom woke me from a sound sleep. I sat straight up in bed and listened but heard nothing else. The noise had not sounded good. Much, much louder than a backfiring car, and certainly not a gunshot—although those had been heard here, before, on my little street in Ogden. Monroe was below Harrison, and unfortunately, the farther west of Harrison you traveled, the worse the neighborhoods got.

I got out of bed and left my room, padding to the front of my apartment, where I could see a bright orange glow reflecting through the window. I pulled aside the drapes and my mouth fell open. Something was burning, flames leaping and bursting from it. People were starting to gather, coming out of the apartments around me and also the nearby houses.

They all had on coats and jackets over pajamas, and they were watching like it was the Fourth of July fireworks. The flames penetrated and almost dispelled the thick fog, and I could clearly see all the people standing back from the bonfire. Nobody was running for a hose, but since it was the dead of winter, of course, there were no hoses out. Then it hit me.

It was a car burning. A car that was very familiar. A car that was parked where my . . . *My car!* I headed out the door, irritated that I had to unlock both the dead bolt and the chain, having been guilted by Tate into using them faithfully. By the time I reached the watching crowd, dressed only in flannel pajama pants and an old T-shirt that said "Shut up and dance," there wasn't much left of the Pepto Mobile.

I shivered as I stared at the raging inferno. I could feel the heat radiating off the car, even standing twenty-five feet away, and I guessed it was a good thing since I had no shoes or coat on. But it was my car. My independence. My way to get around Ogden.

And it was gone. This was one dead Bug.

I heard the sirens in the distance, and my heart thumped painfully. First the warning phone call. Then the burning car, shortly after I *ignored* the threatening message and went to see Bill at his hotel.

This was either one father of a coincidence, or someone was deadly serious about me not teaching for Hollywood StarMakers.

SIX

THE policeman who had taken the report had looked at me strangely when I told him my name.

Twenty minutes later I understood why. Tate pulled up in front of my house, minus the runaway missionary. The officer who had been first on the scene had probably recognized my name, and been close, because Tate had assigned him to watch my house. That was the kind of thing he did.

He quickly came up to me and put his arm around me. "You okay? You know, I ask you that a lot, Jenny. You might want to think about working in an office or something."

"One would think that teaching dance to small children would not be a terribly dangerous job," I said. "Of course *we* know better. But maybe it was an accident."

"Well, the fire department is pretty much saying it wasn't. Someone smashed the window, doused the inside and out with an accelerant, and lit a match. That usually doesn't happen by accident."

"Where's Sal?"

"I left him back at my place. He took a bath, singing at

the top of his lungs—I think it was a Christina Aguilera song—and then he disappeared into my guest bedroom and I heard some pretty loud snoring. I have to say, he's a little odd."

"Ya think? I guess that's why he's attracted to me."

Tate chuckled, and then he took off his coat and made me put it on. Only then did I realize I was shivering. Outside. In February, during an inversion. In my pajamas. Without shoes.

"Let's get you inside. Hey, Stevens, you done with her?" he yelled to the policeman who had taken my report.

"Yep. Just tell her not to leave town."

"Funny," I said, without even cracking a smile. This was not an amusing situation.

Tate led me back into my apartment and shut the door, then locked both locks. "I'm not leaving, so you might as well accept it. I know you aren't ready for this relationship to move any further, so I promise to wait. But it's not going to be easy. And I am not looking forward to sleeping on that couch. It's a little too fond of me."

"Do you think you could just lay with me, in my bed?"

"Do I think?"

I blushed. "I'm cold, I'm scared, and all I'm asking is for you to hold me. I know, I know, it's a cliché. But I am really kind of freaked out right about now."

He took my hand and led me into the bedroom. "Get back into bed. I'm going to the bathroom, and I'm going to take off my clothes. Don't freak. I have boxers on, and I won't remove them. But I can't sleep in my clothes."

"No, you can't." The stark terror that had filled me every time I thought about making love with Tate was gone. It had been replaced by stark terror, period. Wondering who the heck wanted me hurt or dead now.

"Get into bed, Jenny," he said.

I climbed in obediently and pulled the covers up to my chin. He put his gun and holster on my dresser, emptying his pocket of his keys and wallet. I listened as he entered my bathroom and shut the door with a soft snick. I heard bathroom noises and running water, and then he came out, his clothes folded neatly in his hand, wearing nothing but his boxers.

My heart stuttered.

His chest was broad and taut, his abs firm. He made my heart flutter.

Tate set his clothes on the top of the dresser and then flipped off the light, making his way to the bed.

He climbed in and then reached over and pulled me close. "Try to sleep, okay. I'm here. Nothing is going to happen to you."

I felt warm and safe in his arms—and terribly aroused. Probably the fear talking. Who would maim an innocent pink Volkswagen Bug? What kind of monster?

The kind that wouldn't think twice about hurting a thirty-something, eccentric, redheaded dance teacher. Or at least most days I was redheaded.

Once again, I was in deep trouble.

$\mathcal{S}$EVEN

I woke up to the smell of smoke. Panic filled me, and I sat straight up, afraid something else was being firebombed, but then realized the smell was coming from me. Left over from last night.

I heard my shower running and knew Tate was already up and getting ready for the day. I looked at the alarm clock on my bedside table and saw it was only 6 a.m. Since the firebombing happened around 1 a.m., by the time all was said and reported, I hadn't gotten a whole lot of sleep. And my eyes were complaining about it.

I flopped back down in my bed and closed them. No car. No money to buy a new car. The only good thing was my father was a stickler for the important things, and he and my mother always paid the insurance on my vehicle on time. It was their way of showing support. Of course, an old Volkswagen Bug wasn't terribly expensive to insure. And I'd had it quite a while. And I would not get much to replace it.

I saw a Pinto in my future, and it was not something

I wanted to contemplate. I opened my eyes, wide, mostly to dispel the thought of driving one of the world's ugliest and most hated cars.

Tate came out of the shower fully dressed, wearing the same clothes as the night before. He smiled when he saw me watching him.

"I need you to get up and get dressed, okay, so I can drop you off."

"Uh, drop me off where? There is no dance this early."

"Do you ever think of anything but dance?"

I considered his question for a minute. "Yes, food. Funeral potatoes. French fries. Potatoes in general. Chinese food is good. Food and dance. That's about it." Except sex. Sex with him. But I wasn't going to own up to that.

Tate just shook his head and laughed. "I think you need to stay with your parents for a while. Until we figure out what's going on."

"Oh no, I am not doing that." I sat up again. "Are you insane? Have you met my mother? Are you aware she is so worried about marrying me off that she invites a different man to our house at least once a month? Can you imagine what she would do if I was actually staying under her roof?"

"No, actually, I haven't met your mother. And I'm sorry, Jenny, but you aren't safe. I'm totally serious here. I also think you need to tell Bill Flanagan you can't do the convention. I'm pretty sure that's what is causing all of your trouble."

"Tate? I have to do the convention. It's a lot of money for a few days work, and you are pretty much aware I need money, right?"

"You won't have much need for it if you're dead."

"Well, that's an intelligent comment." I knew that wasn't a terribly snappy comeback, but it was six in the morning. What did he want?

He sighed. "Jenny, someone is not messing around. You need a safe place to stay. And no amount of money is worth your life."

"Yeah, and without money, I have no life. I'm not going to my mom's. Or my Auntie Vi's, so don't even suggest it."

"Marlys?"

"No room. She has too many kids."

"Amber?"

"Studio apartment. But James has—"

"Never mind, you are coming to my house."

"Uh, you already have a houseguest."

"Who is leaving today."

"Fine. Your house. At least for now. Until I figure something out. You don't happen to have a bicycle, do you? Or a skateboard?"

He chuckled and pulled me up out of the bed and into his arms. He kissed me, hard, and I could feel his arousal through his jeans. I had to tiptoe to reach his mouth, and he moved one hand down my back and rested it on my behind.

Anticipation skittered up my spine, and into a couple other unmentionable places, and he pulled back and stared at me, a half smile on his face, his left cheek dimpled, his eyes wicked and sparkling. Could I really stay at this man's house and resist him? And further, did I want to even try?

My heart skipped so loudly I could hear nothing but a roar in my ears, and that incessant ringing of . . . ringing? Were my ears ringing?

Tate shook his head. "Saved by the bell," he said wryly, then picked up the handset of the cordless phone off my dresser and handed it to me.

"Uh, hello," I said, my voice shaky.

"Jennifer T. Partridge, what in tarnation is going on?"

Even through the roaring in my ears, I recognized my dad's voice. Oh boy. I didn't know how she knew, but I was fully aware that Auntie Vi had placed an early morning call to my parents, and I was in deep trouble again. Dad only used my full name and the "tarnation" curse when he was pretty steamed about something my meddling aunt had told him.

"Hi, Dad, just had a small incident with a fire. Uh, well, not really small. The Bug's pretty much toast. How much insurance did you have on it?"

"Someone burned your car?" Despite his harsh tones, I heard the concern in his voice. My dad was not an emotional man, and he didn't show love easily, but I always knew he cared, even if he showed it by building me a personalized jewelry box or making umpteen trips to my studio to work on the furnace. Some people told you they loved you, over and over again, but never acted on it, so those were just words. My dad never said it, but he always showed it.

"Yeah, pretty much. It had to be loaded on a flatbed truck, because the tires burned, too."

"Jenny . . . your mother isn't going to like this."

"No, I don't imagine she will. But do you think she'll let me borrow her car?"

There was a pause, and then he said, "Come by. You can drive the truck."

"Okay, Dad. I'll be there in about half an hour."

"Jennifer?"

"Yes?"

"There isn't any truth to this rumor I hear about you leading a Mormon missionary astray, is there?"

I sighed. "No, Dad, no truth at all."

Button down the hatches. It was going to be a bumpy ride.

Tate promised to stop and buy me a blueberry muffin and a mocha latte at Grounds for Coffee, but not until we had made sure that things were proceeding well for the runaway missionary.

It was still terribly dismal outside, pea-soup fog. Eleven days since I had seen the sun.

Elder T. sat on Tate's living room couch, dressed in the same clothes he had been wearing when he showed up at my house: white dress shirt, blue sweatpants. Not a good look. Next to him sat a twelve-year-old wearing a suit and tie, and a name tag identifying him as Elder Perkins. Okay, so he probably wasn't really twelve. I think you had to be out of high school to serve a Mormon mission, but he sure looked young. And very, very, nervous, especially every time he glanced over at me.

In a chair across the room sat the Church Leader Man (I didn't know his official title, although I was sure he had one) who always glared at me as though I had Beelzebub tattooed somewhere on my body. I was starting to really not like this guy, although we had never actually spoken. Surely his time was about up in this position. Didn't they reappoint Mormon leaders all the time, being as the positions were all on a volunteer basis? If I was going to keep running into Mormon missionaries, I really hoped they'd find someone new for the job soon. Someone who didn't know about the poisoned cookie dough and the crazy bus ride. That was back when I was having all my trouble with the arsenic cookie dough and not knowing which psycho dance mom wanted me dead. Truth was, I was never sure just who was chasing me, Marlys, and the two missionaries. All I knew was it was just some lunatic in a silver Humvee. Maybe it was this guy, because he really had a nice glare worked up this early morning, and I swear if his eyes could shoot lasers at me, and through me, they would.

Never mind that I was totally innocent in all of this. Elder T. had come to me! Next to Elder Perkins was another older man, also in a suit and tie, with gray hair and a kindly—although slightly nervous—smile.

"Jenny," Sal said, jumping up when Tate and I walked in. "Help me explain to them. Please."

"Oh no you don't. You aren't pulling me into this. I had nothing to do with this," I told the three males staring at me with horror on their faces, as though Sal had just announced I was pregnant and he needed to be released now so we could plan the wedding. Sal's face fell at my words.

"Then perhaps you could explain why Elder Tuatuola

said you helped him in his escape, providing this place for him to stay." Church Leader Man did not believe a word I said. I could tell.

"Escape?" Tate said, amusement tingeing his voice. "This is my place. I am Detective Tate Wilson, of the Ogden City Police Department, and Sal here showed up late last night at Jenny's saying he wanted to go home. He really doesn't want to be on this mission anymore. Jenny had nothing to do with it. He refused to return to his apartment, so I let him stay here. He promised to call you first thing this morning."

"And I did," Sal said, nodding happily, smiling at everyone. No one smiled back, including me.

"Elder Tuatuola has made a serious commitment to the Lord," said Church Leader Man, his lips pressed together in a very unattractive way. "I am not sure why anyone would want to encourage him to abandon that commitment. I think the best thing here is for us to return to the mission home and discuss this further." I could interpret that statement. He meant he intended to get Sal as far away from me as possible.

Sal shook his head furiously, alarm rapidly spreading across his face, replacing the happy smile of moments before. I remembered Auntie Vi's recitation of what would probably happen to Sal, and sighed.

"Look, he's done. He does not want to be on this mission anymore. He's really sorry about it, he is. But he wants to go home. And really, you can't stop him, right?"

Church Leader Man's lips pressed even tighter together, and I feared in a moment his head just might explode.

"It's not that simple." The other man spoke up. "There are papers to be drawn up and people to notify, and of course, we are ultimately concerned for Elder Tuatuola's well-being." What was this? The religious variation of good cop–bad cop? Good elder–bad elder?

"Yes, papers," intoned Church Leader Man.

"Maybe we should pray together," suggested Elder Perkins, his voice squeaky and high, adding to the illusion he was just passing puberty. I swear I could see a few zits on his chin.

"Yes, it would be useful to pray," said Good Elder.

"Lord have mercy," I dutifully answered. "Look, I have a truck to pick up, so I really don't have time for this, but I'm telling you right now, praying isn't going to help. He is set on going home. He does not want to be out here. Surely you aren't going to try to make him stay on his mission, doing something he doesn't want to do?"

"Oh no, we would never do that," said Good Elder.

"Then let him go home," I said. "See? Simple."

"Not so simple. But I would not expect you to understand," said Church Leader Man, who I was now beginning to realize must be inherently evil himself. What other explanation could there be for this man getting between me and the blueberry muffin and mocha latte that Tate had promised me? The devil was at work here. My stomach rumbled in agreement. And what was with all these people implying I didn't understand anything?

"What the heck is that supposed to mean?" I was getting a bit fired up at this guy's attitude.

"I'm not leaving," Sal said, his voice firm. "I mean I am leaving, my mission. But not leaving here. I'm not going back to that stupid little apartment with the lumpy mattress and the cockroaches that come out at night. I'm not putting on another suit or another tie as long as I live. I'm not tracting door-to-door, and I'm not going to any more Sunday church meetings, either. I'm done. D. O. N. E. Done."

"Didn't you used to have an accent?" Elder Perkins asked, his voice perplexed, as though he had just noticed something amiss. "And you talked different. Real different."

"This just won't do," Church Leader Man said. He was starting to sound a little frantic, and a lot less angry, which earned him a few sympathy votes from me.

"Look, I understand your dilemma here, Elder, uh . . ."

"President Goff. I am the president of this church mission, and it's my responsibility to see that all the missionaries are cared for, kept spiritually fed as well as physically. He's been entrusted to my care. I can't just let him go."

"I'm twenty-one," Sal said. "I'll be fine."

"President Goff, I don't really see what you can do, short of keeping him prisoner, and that's not legal. Even in these circumstances, the police department frowns on that," Tate said, his voice calm and reasonable. "I can't make him go with you, and you can't take him forcefully, so I'm afraid there is nothing else that can be done."

"But . . . But . . ." President Goff sputtered. "I can't just *leave* him here." He shot a nasty glance in my direction, losing all the sympathy points I had just given him.

"You don't really have a choice. Now, I need to get to work. So, while I understand your problem, I need you to leave. Now."

The three men stood and Sal rose, too.

"I'm going to have to call your parents and your bishop, and tell them what has happened," Goff said to Sal, the consequences of that action relayed in his somber tone.

"I already called them," Sal said. "They are on their way to get me now. I thought they'd be mad, but they were just sad. But they understood."

Wow, he must have some really cool parents.

The three Mormons left, leaving Sal behind, and as soon as the door was shut he collapsed on the sofa and put his right arm over his eyes, sighing heavily.

"So, when will your parents be here?" I asked, since Tate was giving him nervous glances and frowning at me, as though to say, "Get him out of here."

"I didn't really call them. I was just buying time," Sal admitted. Tate groaned. "I called my cousin Sampson, though. He's on his way up from Murray. Should be here in about forty-five minutes."

"Okay, well, I guess we can wait until he gets here," Tate said. He obviously had no intention of leaving until the runaway missionary was long gone—nothing but a funny memory. Kind of.

I took a moment to look around Tate's condo. It was on the east side of Harrison, in a very nice neighborhood, and I had to wonder how he could afford such plush surroundings, especially on a cop's salary, because plush it was. Expensive wood and leather furniture—I was the queen of pressboard, and I knew just about everything there was to know about cheap furniture, and where to buy it. I felt like I had landed in the ritzy section at R.C. Willey, a local furniture store. I didn't dare touch anything.

"This is a very nice place," I said cautiously. "What did you do, hijack an R.C. Willey's delivery truck?"

Tate chuckled. "No. Family money."

I waited for him to go on, but he didn't. And it bugged me. I didn't know a lot about Tate Wilson. I knew he was raised in Brigham City, and that he had a half sister, product of an affair his father had, who was somewhat of a wild child.

But I didn't even know her name. Now he had family money?

"I don't like that look you are giving me," he said.

"I just realized I know absolutely nothing about you, and that you really aren't doing much sharing," I said honestly. "Makes a girl wonder why."

"I'm one of the good guys," he said with a mysterious smile. "Trust me."

"He good guy," intoned Sal from the sofa.

"Hey, you're doing it again," I said accusingly, turning to Sal. "We both know you speak English better than most people in Utah, so knock it off."

"Sorry," Sal mumbled, looking miserable. "Force of habit."

I suspected Sal had a long road ahead of him.

After Sal's cousin Sampson picked him up—Sampson was a goliath of a man, taller and rounder and just bigger in general than Sal—they drove off in a tiny white Nissan Sentra. I swear I could see the car settle and drop close to the ground as the two big men got inside.

I found Sampson's size, his appearance, and the situation Sal was in all appropriate, considering the whole Sampson and Goliath thing from the Bible. I mentioned this to Tate as we drove to Grounds for Coffee. It was probably a mistake.

"Sampson and Goliath?"

"Yeah, you know, the giant story, and the kid who shot him with a bow and arrow?"

"I don't think I've ever heard that version."

"What? Didn't you ever go to church?"

"Never mind." He said "never mind" to me a lot. It was starting to bug me. That, along with the fact he was Mr. Mystery, and I just didn't know all that much about him.

"No, tell me."

"It's Samson and Delilah, without the 'p,' and David and Goliath. You got those two stories a little mixed up. And it was a slingshot, not a bow and arrow."

I could feel my face turn red and hot, and I turned to stare out the window. Why didn't I just shut up when it came to these things? Ask me about piqués or arabesques, and I could answer knowledgeably. The rest of the time I sounded like a blathering idiot. And why did he know so much about the Bible, anyway?

We went through the drive-through of the coffee place, and soon I was sipping a mocha latte and eyeing a blueberry muffin, wondering if I could eat it in the car without getting crumbs everywhere. I decided against it. I already felt stupid enough.

When Tate pulled up in front of my parents' old red-brick home on the east side of Ogden, I grabbed my purse, jumped out, leaned in and thanked him for the coffee and muffin and for playing interference with Sal, and then waved good-bye.

As usual, he completely ignored my subtle hints and got out of his side of the car and walked toward the house with me.

"I really don't need an escort here," I said. "I'll be safe

from most things except attempts to marry me off. And possibly overeating."

"I don't mind. I want to meet your mother. I've heard so much about her. And I really never met your father, either, except in passing."

"Yeah, when you were holding a gun pointed at Auntie Vi."

"Hey, I thought someone broke into your apartment again. I'm a cop. I don't walk into situations unprepared."

"Yeah, well, you're walking into one now," I muttered under my breath.

"What did you say?"

"Jennifer, hello. What on earth have you done to your hair? And what brings you home?" My mother's voice interrupted our conversation.

"Uh, Dad said I could borrow the truck."

"And why would you need the truck? And who is this with you?"

So far she had asked four questions. I knew more would follow. My mother rarely said anything that wasn't a question, either implied or real. She was at her coy best, the Miss Manners personality she put on whenever she saw someone as a possible suitor for her daughter. Usually her sights were set wrong. Today, they were dead-on. I kinda saw Detective Tate Wilson as a suitor, too.

She wore her hair up in a nice twist chignon and had on dark blue velour casual sweatpants, white shirt, and matching jacket. Her lined face was friendly and inquisitive, but I was worried.

I'd known my mother all my life. She was really good at setting traps, and catching things in them—usually me.

"Aren't you going to introduce me, Jennifer?"

"Uh, yeah. Mom, this is Detective Tate Wilson of the Ogden City Police Department. He gave me a ride over here because . . ." *Ulp*, a trap, and I'd set it myself! I could hardly tell her that he had spent the night at my house, even if it was mostly innocent.

"Hello, Mrs. Partridge," Tate said, intervening. "I dropped by this morning to give Jenny a ride over here, since there was an unfortunate incident regarding her car."

My mother's face blanched a bit, and then she decided to ignore it. My mother's greatest dream in life is for me to be married off, safe and sound, with a few kids and a nice, boring husband. So far, I'd been a huge disappointment. She didn't like knowing that I was living my life on the edge, although how she got around it was a mystery to me.

"Will you come in and have some coffee?" she asked Tate. "I mean, if you drink coffee, of course. I know a lot of people around here don't, and I certainly wasn't trying to offend you, but if you would like a cup . . ."

"I'd love one," Tate said.

"Jenny?"

"Already have one," I said, nodding my head toward the hand that held my latte.

"That is not coffee, Jennifer. That is espresso, and they are two very different things. It has to do with the way the beans are brewed, and—"

"Thanks, Mom. What would I do without you to correct me?" I figured she was probably wrong, since I suspected she had never had a cup of espresso in her life. She was Catholic. Coffee was a required part of the religion. Espresso was not. But I would let it go. I gave her a look, and she ignored it.

"My pleasure, dear."

TATE and my mother hit it off famously, and they chatted for quite a while about Brigham City, where my mother had an aunt. She'd spent some time up there, and they even knew some of the same people, which meant she already knew more about Tate than I did. That really irritated me.

Finally, I broke up the little tea—er, coffee—party and said I needed to get going. I had an appointment with Ricardo to try and get my hair color back to its natural red.

I'd awakened with a big, blond, frizzy mane. Straight ironing only worked for a few hours, apparently, especially when you had hair like mine.

"I can drive you," Tate offered.

"No thanks. Dad said I could use the truck."

"Yes, he said something about that before he went down to the diner to have coffee with the boys. He left the keys over there. Incidentally, what happened to your car, exactly?"

Why was she asking? She didn't really want to know. If she had the details, she might have to take to bed for a week. My mother would have been better off with Marcia Brady, of television's *The Brady Bunch*, for a daughter. Noses horribly swollen by footballs and jealous sisters were things that were easy to deal with. Blown-up cars and psycho dance moms were not.

"Um, it sorta blew up. Okay, thanks, Mom. We'll be going now." I stood up to escape while my mother was still in shock and slack jawed, but Tate apparently didn't understand that this was modus operandi at our house—shock and awe, or shock 'em and run—and he stayed seated.

My mother opened and closed her mouth a few times, and then finally regained her composure.

"It 'sorta' blew up?" she asked.

"Yeah, real freak thing. Maybe some gang member thought it belonged to a rival gang and firebombed it."

"A gang member thought a pink Volkswagen Bug belonged to another gang? What gang? The Pink Ladies?"

My mother found her sense of humor—or was it irony?—at the most inappropriate times.

"The police are still investigating, Mom. We don't know yet. But I have to run. I have a hair appointment, and I don't want to be late. Do you want your daughter looking like this for even another hour?"

My mother sighed deeply. "What have you gotten yourself into now, Jennifer?"

"Nothing, Mom. Tate, let's go!"

My mother gave up the questioning, mostly because she

really didn't want to know the answer, and said, "Tate, would you like to join us for Sunday dinner? I'm making fried chicken."

"I'd be honored," Tate said.

Great. Great? Was this great? I didn't know how I felt about it. Usually, whenever my mother invited someone over to dinner, I was nervous about it. I guess I was nervous about this, too. But for totally different reasons. He knew all about me, and would soon know more.

And I knew very little about him.

Tate followed me out, my mother standing at the door, watching us and beaming, as I headed around the side of the house and to the back. There, parked on the side of the garage, on an old cement strip, sat Bessie. She was older than me, more stubborn, in much worse shape, with a constant oil leak, and my father loved her. He'd been driving the 1963 Dodge truck when he'd met my mother, and he still had her. He still drove her, actually, once a week. Just to make sure the truck still ran. It ran.

"You're going to drive this?" Tate asked, eyeing the truck.

"My dad is a spectacular mechanic. It runs better than it looks."

"I sure hope so."

I got into the truck and started her up. It took about four tries before the engine kicked in and gave a throaty rumble as it warmed up, smoke coming out the tailpipe, mixing with the fog inversion.

It was just as dreary now, at 8:30 a.m., as it had been when I woke up a few hours earlier. Gotta love that inversion.

"Are you sure this thing is legal?"

"Yes, my father is a by-the-book kind of guy."

"Are you sure it's safe?"

"Yes, enough already. It's safe. And right now, it's all I have."

"Okay. I have to get to work. But I want to know you are safe, so keep in touch."

He slid a key off his key chain and handed it to me. "Here's the key to the front door of my condo. When you're done, go back there. I'll meet you, and we'll go to lunch with Bill together."

"I don't think the lunch invitation included you," I said, not unkindly, but honestly.

"I don't care. I'm coming. See you at noon."

EIGHT

RICARDO was a miracle man. Okay, maybe miracle was too much. My hair was no longer platinum blond, and he had trimmed off a lot of the damage and made it as close to my natural color as he could get it, but he couldn't do much about the choppy shag style that Carmen had given me.

"I suggest lots of hair gel and a blow dryer," he said, handing me some of what he called "product." I told him I couldn't afford it. He said it was "on him." I must have been a worse mess than I'd realized.

It was nearing noon when he finally finished, so I decided to just head over to the Marriott—since Ricardo's salon was on 25th Street, not far from my studio—and meet up with Bill.

Tate would not be thrilled, I knew, but he'd already told me in one phone call that he'd got hit with some sticky paperwork regarding the case he was working on—the one he couldn't tell me about—and would be cutting it close to get home by noon. I lucked out when I called him the second time and got his voice mail. I left a message, like the big orange coward I was, and told him I would be just fine on my own.

The truth was, I wasn't entirely comfortable with the fact I knew so little about him and he knew so much about me. In fact, it was starting to make me downright antsy.

And to have him tell me how busy he was, when I checked in—like he asked me to do!—well . . . This, after he acted like it was a major deal that we stick together so he could protect me. *Hmmph.*

I entered the lobby of the Marriott and caught sight of Bill, head in his hands, sitting in a chair. Next to him was James, chattering incessantly. Bill was obviously feeling the effects of his little bender the night before. James, as usual, did not care or notice. The world revolved around James, most of the time. You couldn't tell him otherwise.

"So, I thought I would do this little combination—"

"Hey, James. Hey, Bill," I said, interrupting.

Bill looked up, and I almost jumped, his eyes were so red and bleary and scary looking.

"Yikes," I said, involuntarily. "You don't look so good."

"I don't feel so good," he said, his voice a low mumble. "Although *you* look better than you did yesterday."

I decided to let that comment pass. "You need something in your stomach. Let's go eat." Okay, I was protecting myself here, too. I needed food. The blueberry muffin had definitely worn off.

"*Urk.* Food." Even though he complained, he stood and lurched toward the hotel restaurant, James following, still talking about his planned choreography, pretty much ignoring me. He hadn't even said hello. And he definitely hadn't commented on my hair.

The hostess seated us, and James continued to talk, while Bill just sat there, looking straight ahead, not speaking.

"James, chill," I finally said. "Can't you see Bill isn't doing too well?"

"What? Oh, well, I guess he does look a little rough."

Geez, talk about self-involved. And to think people accused *me* of that.

"Hi, my name is Traci, and I'll be your waitress. Can I start you out with an appetizer or something to drink?"

Bill blanched and turned green, then jumped up and ran out of the restaurant, and, I guessed, straight for the nearest restroom.

"What in the world is that all about?" James asked. Our waitress looked a little stunned.

"I'll take a Diet Coke with lime, and bring him a Sprite and some saltine crackers," I said, pointing to Bill's empty seat.

"I would like a Perrier with just a splash of lemon, please," James said. "In a glass, of course."

The waitress gave him a funny look and then walked away, shaking her head. Bet she was wishing we hadn't been seated in her section.

"I repeat, what on earth is going on with him?" James asked again, his voice slightly petulant, with a why-is-the-world-not-revolving-around-me tone to it. Nothing unusual about that.

Bill came back to our table and sat down. He looked slightly better, although he was still very pale and his eyes rimmed with red.

"Sorry about that. Not feeling too well this morning."

"Bill, I'm worried about you," I said as the waitress came back with our drinks and four packages of saltine crackers she set in front of Bill.

"It's just the stress of my teachers disappearing, and being on the road, and everything else combined, you know?"

"You need to slow down. Have you considered not doing so many cities next year?"

"Are you kidding me? Bonnie is trying to add more. She's working on growing our venture."

"Then maybe you need to slow down on the, uh, booze."

"Jenny, it's not that. Last night was an aberration, but it was the stress. The truth is, I'm worried about pulling off this convention. Do you think you and James are up to it?"

"Oh, don't you worry about Jennifer and me. We are pros at the last-minute substitution game," James said. "We will make this your best convention and competition yet. You just wait."

Bill didn't look entirely convinced, and I wasn't sure whether to be offended or understanding. After all, he had been working with the missing Twila and Eldon for quite a few cities now, and I'm sure it had to be a little bit worrisome to add someone new at this date. But I was a professional. He'd known me a long time. I screwed up a lot of things, but dance was not one of them. Usually.

The waitress returned and I ordered a club sandwich, James asked for a salad, and Bill got a bowl of chicken noodle soup.

As she turned to walk away, she bumped into a tall, blond, handsome man in a suit. "Oh, excuse me," she said, simpering slightly as she batted her eyelashes up at him. I followed her gaze and couldn't blame her. He had the kind of sky blue eyes that mesmerize and hypnotize, and probably a few other "ize" words I couldn't come up with at the moment. He was hot. Chiseled face. Immaculately coiffed hair. I already mentioned the eyes. Broad shoulders, tan face—tan? It was winter here—and those eyes. Did I mention those? And then there was the suit, and the hard stance, and the alert gaze under the good-old-boy demeanor.

All put together, it spelled c-o-p. I'd been around a few in the past few months, and had actually worked with some during a short stint with the sheriff's office as a dispatcher, and I could pretty much recognize them now on sight.

He walked to our table and looked at the three of us, his gaze stopping on me for a minute—be still my heart—and then moving to James and Bill. His eyes wavered back and forth between them, weighing both men.

"Bill Flanagan?" he finally said, choosing James.

"No, but I can be anything you want me to be," James said with a breathy sigh. He wasn't as good at recognizing cops as I was—or maybe he just didn't care because the guy eyeing him was very, very handsome.

"I'm Bill. Can I help you with something?" The cop turned away from James, a look of relief on his face.

"I'm Agent Carson Keller with the Federal Bureau of Investigation. I need to speak to you about a missing persons report we've received."

"Jenny!" Bill said, turning to me, his eyebrows knitted together, consternation on his face.

"Hey, don't look at me. I didn't call them."

"Well, then your detective friend did. I told you guys they just took off to work with Aiden Bright. I don't need anything else, like cops sniffing around, to make this convention a disaster."

"Actually, Twila Clark's mother reported her missing, Mr. Flanagan. She hasn't been able to contact her daughter for two days, and she got no answers when she contacted you, so she called us." Keller spoke with the dulcet tones that only came from a born-and-bred Southern boy. I'd known one of those, back in my Camelot Troupe dancing days, and he could have talked me into jumping off the Mormon Church Office Building, naked, just because he "med it ahll sand so nahss." The man could have had me committing mass murder, and all I'd remember was how pretty his eyes were and how hypnotizing the sound of his voice was. That accent sorta made me melt. Keller's was having the same effect on me right now. "I checked in with the Ogden PD, and that's when I found out that you knew they were missing but hadn't reported it."

"See?" Bill said to me, his red eyes nearly blazing, giving him a sort of demonic look. He was starting to scare me.

"Hey, they called Tate. What was he supposed to do, lie? He's a cop. And he said you should have reported them missing from the very beginning." I was feeling a little bit irritated at Bill Flanagan. Okay, a lot irritated.

"FBI, what a fascinating job. I would love to sit down and chat with you about it," James said to the agent, his head cocked slightly, displaying what he considered his better side. Evidently, the accent plus the extreme good looks had the same effect on him.

"Uh, well, uh," Agent Keller said, extreme discomfort crossing his face. James was nothing if not obvious. "Look, Mr. Flanagan, we need to sit down and discuss the disappearance of these two people, and also you need to answer some questions as to why you didn't report them missing. I need to know everything that happened up to the time they disappeared."

"But I can't," Bill said, despair slipping into his voice. "I have to meet the hotel events planner at one to set up the rooms for the competition and convention tomorrow, and at two I have a photo shoot with the local newspaper and an interview with a reporter. I have too much to do. That's why I didn't report it. Besides, if you just checked with Aiden Bright you'd find out they jumped ship to work for him, and left me hanging, so I had to hire the only people I could find."

"Hey," I said, more than slightly offended now. I was downright pissed. "I'll have you know that I am a really good choreographer and dancer. And you know it, Bill!" I pointed my finger at him.

Keller just shook his head at Bill's suggestion that the conversation couldn't happen right now. "Sorry, but we have to talk now. Time is of the essence when we have missing people, and not only that, but I would think if you're innocent, you'd be more than willing to sit down and tell us where you were when they went missing and why you didn't report it."

"Aiden Bright, I'm telling you. Aiden Bright!"

"We've contacted Mr. Bright. He's not heard from them or seen them in months, Mr. Flanagan. We've already verified his story."

"They're not with Aiden?" Suddenly, all the air seemed to go out of Bill and he deflated like a popped balloon. "You mean they're really missing? They might be in danger?"

"Yes, they are missing, and it's highly likely they are in danger. Or dead."

"Oh God, no." Bill put his head back in his hands. He

looked almost as bad as he had when I first saw him today.

"Look, go talk to the agent, Bill. Clear it up. Give him the information he needs. It always works better that way. Be completely honest. I'll meet with the hotel director and help get the rooms and the stage set up. You should be finished with Agent Keller by then, and can make your photo shoot. Okay?" I didn't know why I was taking pity on him, especially since he had intimated that I was little more than a last-minute substitute, but he just looked so desolate.

"Okay," he said. "Let's go talk in my room. Bonnie is there, and you probably should talk to her, too. I didn't want to think they were really missing. I wanted them to be with Aiden, because that was the easy answer. And the safe one. Now I have to worry about this, too."

"Can I help?" James asked Agent Keller, brightly.

"Do you know the missing subjects? Are you a regular with this tour?"

"No, I'm just helping out like Jennifer, but I do know a lot of people in Ogden, and I'm certainly willing to volunteer my services to aid and assist the FBI."

"Uh, no, that's okay."

Bill rose and shuffled after Agent Keller, and I remained stubbornly in my seat. I was on a budget, and went without a lot, so I was *going* to get this meal. And make sure it got charged to Bill's room, too. Then I would meet with the hotel people and see what I could do to help Bill save his convention-competition.

I would also have to call Amber and remind her to be there to work with the Petites, who were coming into the studio for the dress rehearsal, so they could be ready for the competition. In fact, Amber was going to have to do a lot of covering for me, as I helped Bill get ready for the convention. Good thing I had Marlys. Amber was not exactly reliable.

And there was something else nagging at me. What was it? Was I forgetting something?

After our waitress delivered the food, including Bill's soup, which sat there untouched, James and I ate and chatted idly about dance, the convention, and what we planned to teach. And of course, the newest hot cop in our lives.

I took a bite of my sandwich then heard a loud beep, and looked around the restaurant.

"What was that?"

James just looked at me and said, "Sounds like you have voice mail."

I hadn't even heard my cell phone ring, although since I had driven here in Bessie and she rumbled pretty loudly, there could have been a nuclear explosion and I wouldn't have heard it.

It had probably sounded off a few times before, telling me that I had a message—or messages—but I mostly ignored it as someone else's phone. Wishful thinking.

I reached down to the floor and grabbed my purse, pulling it up and fishing through it for my cell phone. I finally found it, and when I looked at the display I groaned aloud. Seven missed calls? I clicked the little button to tell me who had been trying to find me—pyscho dance moms, I'm telling you—and saw that every one of the calls, save one from my mother, was from Tamara Williams. Probably another pressing question about tights. Or maybe . . . *Ack!* Between the runaway missionary and the Pepto Mobile explosion, I'd forgotten April's solo lesson this morning. That was what had been nagging at me. Oh, this was bad. Really bad. Most other moms would be understanding. While Tamara might pretend to be so, the truth was she would get little digs in as to how rude I was, and how I didn't like her daughter as much, and how other kids got better opportunities. And she'd spread little hints among the other moms, too. Discontent was like cancer. Given oxygen or air, it spread. And Tamara Williams was definitely dance cancer.

I sighed, hit the button to dial my voice mail, and put the phone up to my ear. James was eating, totally unaware of my angst, or probably ignoring it.

"Jenny, this is Tamara Williams, April's mom, and we're waiting here at the studio for April's solo lesson. Maybe you're running late. Call me. 555-6773."

Next message. "Jenny, this is Tamara William's, April's mom, and it's now twenty after, and you still aren't here. Call me. I don't know if we should leave or wait for you."

Next message. "Jenny, this is Tamara, April's mom . . ."

"Oh for hell's sake, does she really think I don't know who she is by now?" I groused aloud. "She calls me six or seven times a day. Sometimes more. I know she's April's mom, and I also know she's a gigantic pain in my—"

"Jennifer, what are you talking about?" James asked.

"I missed April's solo lesson."

"Oh Lord." He chuckled. "You are so going to pay."

The call waiting beeped in as I listened to the rest of the messages, and guess who it was? Yup, Tamara Williams. Did you know she's April's mom?

"Hello?" I said, deciding I better take this call before she filled up my entire voice-mail system with her messages.

"Jenny, it's Tamara, April's mom? We waited for you for an hour this morning for April's solo lesson, and then we finally left. You know, if you aren't going to make it, the least you could do is call. I guess it's okay, since April is off track right now, and not in school, but what if I had kept her home for her lesson?"

"Look, Tamara, I'm really sorry, but someone blew up my car last night, so I had to spend the morning . . . at the police station. Filling out paperwork. Answering questions. You know, that stuff. And I didn't get a chance to call you. I'm really sorry. Um, and since solo season doesn't start for April until late next month, I promise to get at least two more practices in with her, okay?"

"She needs the time, Jenny. She is having trouble with the arabesque, and no matter how much she practices at home, she just can't quite get the timing on the kick-arounds."

"Tamara, I understand. Will you just let me get through

the Hollywood StarMakers Convention and Competition, and then next week I promise we'll do her two practices."

"Well, I didn't hear about you canceling Addison Westley's practices, did I? Of course, since Addison is a favorite . . ."

Lord, I groaned silently. Addison's mom Sandi and Tamara were best friends on odd days of the month and bitter enemies on even days, mostly because their daughters were the same age, the same level, and competed against each other all season long. *Stupid psycho dance moms.*

"Thanks for reminding me. I'll call Sandi right now and reschedule for Addison. Good-bye, Tamara. I'll set up April's lessons for next week."

I clicked the Disconnect button before she could get another word in.

I quickly finished my club, and when the waitress came back around I told her it needed to be charged to Bill's room. "Um, somebody is going to have to sign for that."

"I'll sign for it, but it has to be charged to Bill Flanagan's room."

"And are you staying in that room?"

"No, but you can call him and ask. I'm one of his staff members, and this was a business lunch. He just got called away by the FBI."

"Do you even *know* what the room number is?"

I didn't. Great.

"No, he forgot to tell me, but when the FBI comes looking for you, you usually move quickly. I'm sure that was on his mind, instead of telling you what his room number was. But I know you can look it up."

"Well, I'm sorry, but—"

"Charge the freaking lunch to his room," I practically yelled, and then sat back a little bit alarmed by my behavior. Perhaps things were starting to get to me, but I did not have enough money in any account in any bank anywhere in the world to even begin to cover this tiny lunch, and Bill had to pay. Or I'd be washing dishes.

"Uh, I'll ask my manager," she said, and scooted off.

James watched me closely, an unidentifiable look on his face, and I snapped, "What?"

"Jennifer, I am very worried about you."

"It's just stress. I'll be fine."

He shook his head and started to say something, and then stopped, his gaze moving from leaving me to something behind me, his eyes opening wide, his mouth dropping slackly.

I turned and saw the beautiful Enrique walking toward us, and I knew trouble was already on its way. Like I needed any more.

"Hello, Jenny, it is an extreme pleasure to see you again," Enrique said, grabbing my hand and kissing it. Definitely more friendly than he had been when I met him the night before. "Who is your friend?"

"This is James Marriott. He'll be teaching for the convention, too. James, this is Enrique Perez. He teaches tap."

"James, it's nice to meet you."

"Oh, and it is nice to meet *you*," James said, finally gathering his senses together enough to speak. "I'm James Marriott. And I am a huge fan of tap."

Liar.

"And what do you teach, James?" Enrique asked, trapping James with his dark, chocolate stare.

"If you two will excuse me, I have to go meet with the hotel events planner to make sure the main ballroom is set up for the competition," I said. Both men ignored me.

As I walked away, I dialed Sandi Westley's number and sighed with relief when it went to voice mail. There were certain numbers, of certain dance moms, that I had memorized. Not because I called them all the time, but for the opposite reason. I needed to be able to screen calls, and knowing the numbers of those I didn't want to talk to really helped.

I left a message telling Sandi I would reschedule Addison's solo practices for the following week, and then disconnected, quickly trying to find the main ballroom of the hotel.

I knew that sooner or later the fact I was only taking Michelle Nunez, Trinity Hansen, and Marlys's daughter Carly to solo at the Hollywood StarMakers Competition would come into play, so I was going to avoid that until after the competition—if I possibly could. People thought I gave Marlys favors because she worked for me. Frankly, given all the crap she had to deal with, I probably should do her favors, but that wasn't my way. I was taking Carly because she was a good dancer, and her solo looked awesome. And that was the bottom line.

I'm sure that was part of the reason Tamara was so upset I hadn't worked with April. Since *she* was convinced her daughter was the best dancer on my team, she was sure I would change my mind and take April, too, once I saw how good she was.

Like I hadn't just watched her daughter two days before that. The truth was, April was a competent dancer for her age. But StarMakers was a national competition and convention, and while April won at local venues, she just wasn't ready to compete with the best of the best.

But try telling her mother that.

I found the sign that pointed to the main ballroom, and followed the arrow, opening up a door to see a large room with a stage on short risers set in the middle. A host of workers were setting up chairs in rows, following the directions of a petite, auburn-headed woman. She looked competent, and everything appeared to be going as it should. To the left side of the stage a group of workers were connecting wires and speakers for the sound table, and another man was putting up a large projection screen that would be used to show video flashes of the winners when the competition was over.

Bill ran a classy production, and this one promised to be no different—other than the fact two teachers were missing and the FBI was here questioning Bill, that is.

I introduced myself to the events planner, who said her name was Sarah York, and told her I was helping Bill out. "I thought his assistant was Bonnie French," she said.

"Um, I think she just does financial stuff."

"Oh, okay. Well, Jenny, can I get your cell phone number, in case we need to make contact?"

We exchanged numbers, I told her the room looked great, and then I left the ballroom, my cell phone ringing as I did. The caller ID said it was Sandi Westley. Wasn't answering that one. Sometimes I loved technology, even though I had a hard time mastering it.

I headed for the elevators, dialing Amber's number as I walked. I knew she took classes at Weber State University in the mornings—late mornings, of course, as Amber didn't do early—and so I left her a message reminding her I needed her to cover the Petites extra practice, and be at the studio at 1 p.m. She got out of class at 12:30 p.m., so I knew she'd get the message, and since we'd already talked about it, she knew the plan. Sometimes she just needed to be reminded. She lived with her phone by her side, mostly since she always had one hot guy or another calling her, begging her to go out with them. Me, I got psycho moms.

I hit the Up button and then realized I still had absolutely no idea what room Bill was in. Lucky for me—or was it?—the elevator doors opened and there stood Bonnie. She gave me a nasty glare, then walked out of the elevator and headed toward the front of the hotel without even acknowledging me. "Hey, Bonnie, wait," I said, following her.

She stopped and turned, giving me an evil look. "What?" she snapped.

"I need to talk to Bill. Do you know what room he's in?"

"If he didn't tell you what *our* room number is, then obviously he didn't want you to have it," she said, disgust dripping from every word. She gave special emphasis to the fact they were sharing a room. Man, this woman had serious issues with me. What the heck had Bill told her that got her so fired up and hateful toward me? Or was that just her nature? I suspected a little of both.

"He's been a little preoccupied, but I need to talk to

him. I checked on some things he asked me to do for him, and I need to update him on—"

"He asked you to check on something? Please. Bill says you can't even walk and chew gum at the same time. I can hardly believe he would put our business in your less than capable hands."

Now that was just not nice. I clenched my fists together at my sides, mostly to keep from hauling off and decking Bonnie French. "Tell me, did you have to take lessons to become such a raving bitch, or does it just come naturally?"

She blanched at my use of the "b" word—and frankly, so did I, since I rarely used profanity—and then turned on her heel and walked away.

Great. I had just had a fight with a woman I barely knew, and I still didn't know what room Bill was in. I walked back toward the elevator doors just as they opened and Bill and Agent Carson Keller came out.

Thank goodness.

"Jenny," Bill said, his face still white. "Thanks for covering for me. Does everything look okay? Are they getting it all set up?"

I had a tooth to pick with Bill, considering the nasty thing that Bonnie had said, but that would have to wait. "Yes, everything looks fine. The competition stage and sound system are almost completely set up, they're finishing up with the chairs, and the events planner seems like she really knows what she's doing."

"Oh, thank goodness."

"I'll be in touch," Agent Keller said to Bill. Then he turned to me. "Can I ask you some questions?"

"Uh, me?" My heart fluttered a little, and dismay filled me. Why did I feel like I was cheating on Tate just because my stomach tickled like a million butterflies had taken flight inside it?

"Yes, just a few questions. I realize you didn't know the missing dancers, but I thought you might have some insight."

Insight? Me? I hoped I wasn't glowing. After Bonnie's nasty comments, however, I needed to hear some nice things. *Yeah, you tell yourself that, Jenny.*

"Sure, I could take a minute. But then I need to put together a routine to teach tomorrow. We start classes as soon as the competition ends, right, Bill?"

"Yes," he said, but he was glancing around the lobby as though looking for something, and not paying a lot of attention to me. Maybe a five-foot-four witch-on-wheels named Bonnie was on his mind. I suddenly felt very, very sorry for him. What had he gotten himself into?

"Is there a schedule, Bill?"

"What?" His attention snapped back to me. "Oh, yes, the schedule. Let me go get you one. Where will you be?"

"We'll be in the lobby for a few minutes," Agent Keller answered.

"After that I'll probably head to my studio. It's practically in the parking lot of the hotel," I told Bill. I pointed to the south, in the direction of my studio, and gave him the address. "You can find me there, if you don't come back down with the schedule before I'm done talking to Agent Keller."

"Okay," Bill said, scanning the lobby again. "Have you seen Bonnie?"

"She probably jumped on her broomstick and took off," I said, my teeth clenching together at the sound of her name.

"Huh?" Bill said. I could see Agent Keller fighting back a smile. I guessed he'd already interviewed Bonnie.

"Nothing. She went that way." I pointed to the front of the lobby, and he scurried off in that direction.

After Agent Keller and I settled into chairs in the lobby, he asked me my full name, and then if I'd ever met Twila or Eldon. I told him no.

"How long have you known Bill Flanagan?"

"Oh, about ten years. We danced together in the Camelot Troupe in Salt Lake years ago. And we touch base when he comes to town. And since I don't want any misunderstandings, yes, we, uh, dated for a while, but it didn't work out. We're both creative types and just didn't mesh."

"I wasn't going to ask that, but thanks for sharing." He smiled, revealing perfect dimples on both sides of his cheeks. His blue eyes reminded me of something we had not seen for several weeks—the sky!—and I found him mesmerizing. He might have been asking me to eat spiders, and I wouldn't have noticed, so beautiful were his eyes. And then I realized I was staring.

I blushed.

He looked amused, and I had to turn around, staring at the leaves of an artificial plant that decorated the lobby. I reached out and fingered them idly, trying to keep my hands busy.

"Anyway, he's a good guy. Flighty and flaky, and sometimes emotional, but a good guy."

"Has he ever had any financial trouble? Problems paying bills?"

"Uh, he's a dancer. He does it for a living. Of course he has had some lean times, but not now. His convention and competition are very successful." Me, on the other hand, that was a different story.

"Did he have a beef with either of the missing dancers?"

"Not that I know of, but I haven't really been around him much. I only see him about once a year."

"Anything else you can tell me?"

"Not really."

"Not even going to mention the threatening call you received, or the fact your car was firebombed?" *What? No more Mr. Niceguy there! I was so not eating spiders for this guy. That was not fair. And darn Tate anyway.*

And what *was* I thinking, anyway? He'd made me totally forget it all. I needed to pull myself together and stop acting like a teenage girl.

"Oh yeah, there was that. Someone doesn't want me here teaching, although I don't know why. I *do* have my suspicions."

Bonnie French did not look like someone who would firebomb a car, but she sure acted like one.

"And they are?"

"Well, Bonnie French is not a nice person. She seems to have a serious problem with me, too, which gives her reason to try to drive me away. Maybe she sees me as a rival. I don't know. But I'd definitely look into her whereabouts when the poor Pepto Mobile went up in smoke."

"Pepto Mobile?"

"Long story. Pink Volkswagen Bug. But seriously, she is probably the one behind it. At least behind the threatening phone call and death of my car. She has an investment in the success of the convention, so I can't see why she would do something to harm it, though."

"Okay, well, if you think of something else, here's my card." He pulled it out of his suit jacket pocket and handed it to me, smiling again. I melted a little.

"Sorry I couldn't be more help."

"It was just a pleasure to talk to you," he said.

Warmth again, in all sorts of regions of my body. What was it about this guy?

"Hey, Jenny. It is Jenny, right?" I turned to see who was calling my name, and noticed Jason Kutcher standing by the back exit to the hotel. He wore a big basketball jersey over a black T-shirt, expensive-looking shoes, and big, baggy jeans. Gangsta style, though this guy was as white as they came.

"Hi, Jason," I said.

"Where can a guy go in this town to get a decent drink and some good tunes?" he asked me. What, like I'd know? Did I look like the Tara Reid or Paris Hilton of Ogden or something?

"Um, well, there's Brewski's back there, although I don't know if they have music. I don't go to bars much."

"Ah, come on, Jenny, you look like a girl who knows how to have a good time," he said, moving in close to me—so close I could smell the alcohol on his breath. This guy had been at it for a while, and it was just barely past lunchtime!

"Well, no, not really. I'm pretty boring. There's some pretty good spots on 25th Street though."

"You gonna show me?" he said, leaning in even closer. "Intro-duce me to yo town. Fo shizzle?" He hadn't talked like this the first night I met him. What was up with this?

"Has anyone told you that you are not black?" I blurted out, then slapped a hand to my mouth. That probably wasn't the smartest thing to say. Sometimes my mouth just opened and words came out, and I had to eat them later. I preferred my food to have substance, and not taste of crow, so I was trying to curb that impulse. But Jason Kutcher wasn't bringing out the best in me.

"Yo, why you dissin' me?"

"Yo, bro, where I come from, bother someone and you can get your butt kicked."

"No harm, no harm," he said, backing off, palms up. He walked off down the corridor, and I sighed with relief.

I realized then that Bill had never returned with the schedule. I walked over to the front desk and asked them to ring his room. No answer. I'd have to get the schedule later. Maybe I could come back and see if Agent Keller was still around . . .

I walked to the back entrance of the hotel, still feeling all loose and quivery—and more than a little guilty.

"Snap out of it, Jenny," I said to myself as I pushed open the door and stepped out into the arctic air. I shivered and shrugged into the jacket I had taken off inside the hotel. The subzero temperatures cooled me off quickly and brought everything back into focus. Except I couldn't see two feet in front of my face, so there wasn't much to focus on. Stupid inversion.

I headed in the direction I hoped would take me to my studio, and felt the cold begin to seep into my pores, my joints aching. I'd danced for a long time, and done a lot of harm and put a lot of stress on my body, so that was another reason February inversions were so miserable for me.

Even though it was early afternoon, I felt totally isolated as I trudged toward 25th Street, walking through the parking lot of the Marriott, and chills that weren't brought on by the temperature began to sneak up my spine.

I turned around, but could see nothing behind me. Or ahead of me. Or even to the side. This was ridiculous. I walked faster, listening to the sound of my boot heels as they snapped on the tar. The unmistakable discordant sound of another human being, other steps, came from behind me, and I turned to see a shadowy figure running toward me.

Fear exploded in my stomach, and I turned and ran, not knowing how far I had to go to reach the metal stairs that would lead up to my studio, and praying that Amber was already there and the door was unlocked.

My pursuer got closer and I ran as fast as my boots would allow, my lungs threatening to explode in my chest as I realized I was holding my breath.

"Jenny, wait! Why are you running?"

James! I stopped cold and turned, relief and anger flooding my body.

"James, you scared the cement out of me!"

"Why? I just had some news to share, and I saw you headed this way. Well, I thought it was you, based on the drab coat and unfashionable boots, but I wasn't sure, so I was trying to catch up to you before I yelled your name. Didn't want to embarrass myself."

"Drab coat? Unfashionable boots?" I started to cry, but it wasn't James's insults. I was used to him. It was the pent-up fear that had gripped me as I ran from an unknown assailant. These were relief tears.

"I'm sorry, Jennifer, your coat isn't that bad. But the boots are kind of dismal. Target?"

"Wal-Mart. And I'm not crying because of that. You scared me."

"I'm sorry," he said again. "Let's get into the studio. I have something to tell you that will make everything better."

"Are you giving me a million dollars?"

"No."

"Have I been invited to go on tour with Christina Aguilera?"

"Uh, no."

"Then I doubt it is going to make everything better."

"But you will love it. I promise."

Nine

Once inside the studio, I could hear the music of the Petites dance, which would stop every once in a while, and I could hear Amber's voice as she corrected and "cleaned" the routine.

I poked my head in the door of the other room, waved at her, then went into the office, James following closely. We both took off our coats, hanging them on the antique hall tree. I put my purse down on the desk, then sat down in the swivel chair behind it. The phone answering machine blinked with about a million messages—probably all from Tamara Williams and Sandi Westley—and I just ignored it.

I had a pounding headache right in the center of my forehead, probably brought on by the recent scare and the pollution-filled inversion combined. James was sashaying around the office, too excited about something to sit still. I suspected that something was a some*one*. Namely Enrique Perez.

"So, what's your news?" I asked, wanting to get it over.

"Well, Enrique and I are having drinks tonight—isn't he just lovely?—and he promised to share the scoop with me about Bill and Bonnie. Apparently, they are not getting along at all. That's good news for you, right?"

"Good news for me? Why would that be good news for me?"

"Well, because of course Bill has carried a torch for you all these years, and I know you aren't too happy with the way Tate has been treating you, so I thought that perhaps this was an omen that you and Bill are due to get back together and—"

"Whoa, whoa, whoa . . . Slow down. What do you mean Bill has carried a torch for me?"

"Are you daft?"

"Are you an idiot?"

"No, I am not."

"Me, either, so what the hell are you talking about?"

James stopped and stared at me, a gleam in his eye. "You mean you really didn't know?"

"Didn't know what?"

"Bill was heartbroken when the two of you broke up. He spent months in a deep depression, only putting on a brave face when you were around. Apparently, you were clueless. When he finally hooked up with someone again, he picked the total opposite of you. Hence, Bonnie the Witch."

"Okay, I am very glad that she is exactly the opposite of me, because that woman is pure evil, but I really had no idea. I mean . . . are you sure?"

I was pretty floored by this news.

"Yes, dear, I had to listen to the man cry in his beer more than once, and it was not pretty. And he swore me to secrecy. So you can't let on you know!"

No problem there. Bill, carrying a torch for me? Did I feel anything for him? I searched my brain. Nope. Nothing. Except for a fondness, of course, that came from some good memories.

"Uh, no problem, James. But I won't be getting together with Bill anytime soon, so don't get your hopes up. And frankly, I think you are using your great skill of exaggeration."

"Maybe, maybe not. And as for hope? For you, I gave up years ago. But a boy can dream."

With that, James turned away with a flourish and walked into the other room to see how the Petites practice was going. I didn't think he was really interested in the practice. He just liked to leave every room and every occasion with a big bang. I muttered a bit as I exited the office and went into the first dance room. I sat down on the hardwood floor by the stereo, pulling out my big CD case to see what music I could find that would really stand out for my convention routines.

I couldn't decide if I wanted to do a traditional jazz routine or something funkier, so I pulled out some Ciara and some new Justin Timberlake music, as well as a couple of old Broadway classics.

I put on the Ciara and stood up in front of the mirror, stretching a bit as I let the music's rhythms and beats flow through my head.

After my muscles warmed up, I started to dance, moving with the music. The Ciara wasn't speaking to me, so I switched it out with the new Justin Timberlake jam, which was fun, fast, and had a great beat, but was kind of hip-hoppy—definitely not my specialty.

I could pull it off, and follow it, but I was more known for my stylized jazz routines. I pulled another CD from my case, and soon Christina Aguilera was singing "Ain't No Other Man," and I knew I had hit on at least one of my songs.

The song was fast-paced and exhilarating, and I lost myself in the music as I practiced some moves. I was so deep in the groove that I only barely registered someone was next to me, dancing, too. A big someone. A big, dark-haired someone.

I stopped, alarmed, and turned, only to see Sal Tuatuola, formerly known as Elder Tuatuola, busting a move beside me. And he *could* move, like no big man I had ever seen before.

He hadn't noticed that I had stopped, so I watched as he gyrated and turned and bounced to the music—all done with precision and skill, and a flair I had to admit I envied. How could this big Samoan man move so gracefully? And quickly. And . . . what was the word? The dude had the moves.

I sensed someone else standing next to me, and turned to see James and Amber, and the Petites, all standing behind me watching Sal give new emotion and depth to Christina Aguilera's song. His choreography was fresh and new, and his style was unique, but I could fully see my girls doing the moves—despite the fact they were being demonstrated by a large Samoan man who was a former runaway missionary.

When the last notes of the song faded away, he closed his eyes and did some deep breathing, then seemed to come back to consciousness, turning to see he had quite an audience.

He was dressed in white sweatpants and a white T-shirt with a "Dance Utah" logo on it.

"Hi, Jenny," he said, slightly sheepish, doing that auburn blush I had seen before. He ducked his head and then smiled shyly at James, Amber, and the Petites.

"Can we do that dance, Jenny?" Carly, Marlys's daughter, asked. "I mean, can we learn it? That was so cool. It looked like so much fun. Mister, you can really dance."

"Thanks," Sal said. "I'd love to teach it to them, Jenny."

"Uh . . ." I was speechless, not quite sure what to say.

"Jenny, we do have a competition coming up. It's hardly the time to be learning new dances," James pointed out, rather shrewishly. I didn't blame him. I was feeling somewhat shrewish myself. But that had a lot to do with James scaring the bejeebers out of me in the parking lot, and not a lot to do with Sal.

Sal Tuatuola was a natural talent, and very, very good.

"Maybe I could start after the competition?" Sal said brightly, not daunted by James's obvious lack of enthusiasm and my failure to jump right on the music wagon.

"I *am* going on vacation next week," Amber pointed out. "Maybe he could fill in while I'm gone, and you can see how things go. Who *is* he, by the way?"

One of Amber's many beaus had promised her a tropical vacation—that sounded sooo nice. I was jealous.

"This is Sal Tuatuola. Sal, this is James Marriott, Amber Francis, and those are my Petites."

"Hi, Sal," said a chorus of voices. James just nodded. Amber gave him a little coquettish wave.

"Hey, everyone. Oh please, Jenny. Just give me a chance," he said, his big puppy-dog eyes pleading with me. James's lips were tight.

"Oh, all right." I had been at a loss as to what I was going to do while Amber was gone, anyway. Not enough of me to go around. I'd considered cloning myself, but the idea of more than one Jenny T. Partridge was frightening even to me. "But I can't pay you much."

"No pay necessary. I will prove myself to you," he said, putting his fist to his heart, like an ancient warrior. He was making me a little bit nervous.

James rolled his eyes and stomped back into the other room as the Petites gathered around Sal and peppered questions at him in the rapid-fire way only teenage girls can do. He looked a little shell-shocked, as he backed up a bit, but I figured if he was going to teach them, he better get used to it.

I turned back to the CD player, flipped Christina back on, and Amber called the Petites back into the other room to work on their routine. James huffily put on his coat and gloves, and muttered something about finding somewhere quiet to work. He stomped out the door. Hello? We were dancers. Music was a must. He was sulking. He'd get over it.

I tried to get back into the groove, but Sal's moves were sticking with me. In the mirrors that lined the wall, I could see him standing behind me, watching.

"Show me that one thing you did," I said, motioning him next to me. He stepped up and said, "This step?" He effortlessly pounded out sixteen counts, with arms in perfect sync with his light steps.

"Yup, that one."

We worked together for a while, me suggesting some things and Sal suggesting others, until I had a good routine together for the teenage dance group.

"You should know I'm planning to use this for the Hollywood StarMakers Convention," I told him. "And I'm getting paid for it. I can't pay you a lot, but I will try to make it fair. But if that's a problem, speak up now, and I'll do something else."

"I would be honored. No money necessary," he said, his eyes sparkling at me, an adoring look on his face. *Yikes.* He was willing to work without pay *and* lend me his moves. What was next?

"Uh, okay, thanks, but we'll work it out. Now I need to figure out two more routines."

"You need my help?"

"Don't you have somewhere to be?" I asked, not unkindly, but he was making me more than a little nervous and antsy.

"No, my cousin Sampson won't be back until six or so. I had him drive me out here, and he had a friend he wanted to visit with."

"How did all that go with your parents?" I asked.

His face fell. "Not so well. I have brought shame to my family. My mother wailed for hours."

"Wailed like cried?"

"No, she was pretty much wailing. And beating her chest."

"Yikes."

"Yeah, yikes. I figure I'll stay with Sampson until things cool off. Unless Detective Wilson needs a roommate. That would definitely be easier, since Sam isn't going to want to drive me out here every day next week, when I'm working for you."

"Detective Wilson does not need a roommate," Tate said. He had come in through the front door in time to hear Sal's suggestion, and I could see it wasn't an idea he thought a lot of.

I eyed Tate, who look harried and tired, his hair a little rumpled, a five-o'clock shadow visible on his strong chin.

"It would just be for a week or two. Amber is going on vacation next week, and I need a teacher to help me out. Sal has volunteered."

"I keep strange hours, and I'm used to my own space. I'm not a good roommate."

I gave him a sharp look—pretty gutsy of me, really—and he said, "Oh fine. Two weeks. No more."

"Oh wonderful," Sal said, clapping his hands together and jumping up and down, and Tate's eyes grew wide. "I'm going to go see what the Petites are doing. Thanks again for the chance, Jenny. And, Detective, I will cook and clean—whatever you want. I'll be the best roommate you ever had. You will never want me to leave."

"Uh . . ." Tate had a slightly dazed look on his face.

"Thanks again, Jenny," Sal said, and then dashed into the other room.

"What the hell just happened?" Tate demanded, rubbing his jaw. "Is he, uh . . ."

"No clue," I said. "But he does seem to be a study in contradictions, doesn't he? I'm having a hard time putting a finger on just exactly *what* he is. Besides a very talented dancer and choreographer, that is."

"This is not turning out to be a good day."

"Hey, look at it this way. You get his services for a couple of weeks, while I get some help in my studio. You heard him. He can cook and clean."

"I do not *wish* to have his services, thank you very much," Tate muttered.

I couldn't keep back the giggle that bubbled up from my chest.

"Are you *laughing* at me?" he asked, his eyes narrowed.

"Um, no." But the laughter kept coming, and I couldn't contain it.

He tried to look mad for a minute but then finally conceded with a quirk of his lips.

"I'm sorry I didn't get back to escort you to lunch.

Things are getting really crazy on this case, and I just couldn't get away. I feel terrible."

"I'm a big girl, Tate," I said. "I've told you before, I can take care of myself. Well, mostly, anyway. I'll be fine."

"What about the threatening messages and the Pepto Mobile fire?"

"I'll watch my step, okay?"

"Okay. But you better be careful. Call me at the first sign of trouble, and I'll have cops there so fast your head will spin. You do have your cell phone, don't you?"

I was kinda notorious for losing and destroying cell phones, so I understood the question, even if I found it slightly irritating.

"Yes, I have my cell phone."

"Show me."

"Hello, Tate, I am not twelve."

"Show me."

I sighed in exasperation. "Fine." I walked over to the office and grabbed my purse and picked it up, fishing around inside until I came up triumphant, cell phone in hand. He'd followed behind me, and I waved it at him. "See? Here's my phone."

As if to prove a point, it rang shrilly, and I looked at the caller ID. Tamara Williams again.

"How do those stalker laws work? Do they work for cell phone calls?" I asked him.

"Stalkers? Is it another anonymous call?" He moved forward a bit, as though to grab the phone.

I sighed. "No, it's just a psycho dance mom. But it sure feels like I'm being stalked by her. She calls me more than my own mother. Ten times more. Maybe twenty."

"Okay, well, I'm glad it's not another threatening message." A look of sheer exhaustion crossed his face, and I was filled with the desire to take away those dark shadows.

"What's going on, Mystery Man? Why won't you tell me what you are working on? Why won't you open up to me?" I swallowed my fear of rejection and walked up to him, running my hand down his face and neck. He reached up and grabbed it, and then pulled it to his lips and kissed my palm.

"Some of the things I work on are way too ugly to darken your mind. I don't even want you to know. This is one of those things."

"I'm not fragile, Tate. Flighty maybe, but not fragile. This is your life, and I want to be a part of it. The way you don't tell me anything, well . . . I wonder what you're hiding."

"Hiding? I'm not hiding anything. Why would you think that?"

"I know very little about you and your life. I haven't met any of your family. Well, I mean . . ." I could feel the red rise, creeping from my neck upward, to engulf my entire face. Maybe the truth is all he wanted was a sexual relationship—not that we'd even managed that—and I'd assumed maybe it meant more. Maybe that was why he intended to stay the Man of Mystery. And if that was bothering me, did it mean that I really did *want* more from him?

"Why are you looking at me like that?" Tate asked.

"Like what?" I asked, turning away to hide my flaming face. He pulled me back to face him, and into him, tight up against his chest, lifting my chin with his hand.

"Like I just told you someone outlawed dancing and ice cream and anything containing potatoes."

"Hah, funny." I tried to turn my head away again, but he wouldn't let me.

"I'm not hiding anything, Jenny. But I'm not an open book. I never have been. It takes time to get to know me. Are you willing to put in that time?"

"You're a lot of work," I mumbled.

"So are you," he retorted, then he bent his head and touched my lips with his, gently at first, then harder and more insistent.

"Oh, oops, excuse me." We both turned to see Sal watching us, his mouth a sad frown, his bushy eyebrows low.

"Did you need something, Sal?"

"Well, actually, I was just going to make a suggestion

for the Petites routine, but I didn't know how you would feel about it."

"Go fix the routine," Tate said softly. "I have to get back to work."

"And I have two more dances to come up with." I looked up at Sal. "I'll be right in there, okay?"

He nodded his head and backed out of the office.

"He's making me nervous. He didn't look happy to find us together like that," Tate said. "Maybe he has a huge crush on you."

"Or maybe he has a huge crush on *you*," I suggested.

"That type of comment is not conducive to my allowing him to stay with me in my condo next week," Tate pointed out, concern and apprehension on his face.

"I'm kidding."

At least I thought I was. I had to admit, I wasn't totally sure.

I spent the rest of the afternoon with Sal, first working with the Petites and then choreographing two more routines for the other classes I needed to teach at the convention. He gave me some new and fresh moves, and I was enjoying the exchange of ideas and feeling really motivated and upbeat. Pretty good for a February blah month.

I had a feeling that he would really help give our routines the extra oomph they needed to make our competition season the best ever.

At 6 p.m. Sal's cousin Sam picked him up. The Petites had been dismissed the hour before, and Amber had packed it in at the same time, so I was alone in the studio. And since it was winter, in February, during an inversion, the outside world no longer existed, at least as far as I could see.

Between the fog and the dark, my studio might have been located on a deserted island with no electricity. Except inside, of course. I could see nothing when I looked out the window.

I hated February. I hated inversions. The good feeling that

came from seeing Sal's talent and optimism for our competition season dissipated fast. I needed to get home, start a fire, and eat some ice cream. In that order. Or close to it.

I straightened up, picking up the clothes and shoes left behind by the Petites, depositing them in the lost and found, and then turned off the lights in the studio, all except the one in the office. I gathered up my coat and purse, tucking my sports bottle filled with water inside, since I would need it the next day. I also made sure I had my cell phone—*See, Tate? I'm listening*—and just as I flipped off the light I heard the sound of footsteps, clanging on the metal staircase. I realized right then that I needed to use the bathroom, in a pretty bad way, but as usual, I had ignored it while I was dancing. My heart immediately set to thumping, even while reason and logic told me it was probably just James or Amber or one of the Petites coming back for something they forgot.

The steps stopped. I waited, not breathing, for them to resume. Nothing. It was a standoff. Mysterious footsteps, 1, Jenny T. Partridge, 0. Because I was frozen. I didn't dare move. I knew, even though I tried to tell myself differently, that something was wrong. Whoever had made those noises was there, waiting for me, to do . . . what? My eyes started to fog over, and I realized I better start breathing, and fast, or I would pass out. The ragged breaths I took, in and out, reverberated in my brain, louder than an atomic bomb—at least in my mind.

I stood for another five minutes or so—but it felt like an hour—and could hear nothing else. My bladder informed me I urgently needed to relieve myself, but I didn't dare move. I forced myself to breathe, and the fear dissipated slightly. It could have been a transient, just looking for a place to hole up. We got a lot of those here on 25th Street in Ogden, because we were so close to the railroad tracks and also to the missions that fed and sheltered the homeless.

Finally, I forced myself to move. I opened the door and peeked outside. Nothing. Well, not that there was nothing there, I just couldn't see anything, thanks to the dark and the thick fog. I considered calling for help, but since I'd heard no noise for a very long time, I decided that was probably foolish. I hated looking foolish. Grandma Gilly, my mother's mother, used to say, "Better to be thought a fool than be dead." Or something like that. I'm sure it was more eloquent, and proverb-y, but right now the exact words wouldn't come to me. Of course, she also used to tell me the story of the girl who cried wolf, so she sorta contradicted herself there.

Just about anything Grandma Gilly said I disagreed with. I much preferred Nana Marian, even with her endless supply of Books of Mormon and admonishments to find my salvation in the Mormon Church. Grandma Gilly just gave me the death stare—I swore she learned it from the nuns at that private Catholic school she went to as a young girl—and condemned me to hell with every sentence.

I realized my thoughts had strayed, and today I was grateful for my lack of focus, because I discovered I wasn't nearly as frightened. Plus I could hear nothing out there, and since I didn't want to look stupid, yet again, I decided it was time to go. Every bump in the night did not mean danger. I mean, I was a dance teacher in Ogden, Utah, for Pete's sake. I shut the door and quickly locked it behind me, and then ran down the stairs as fast as I could without slipping and falling. I should have stopped to go to the bathroom, but I just wanted to get home.

I couldn't see far in the thick fog, and I hoped I was headed directly toward Bessie, or I was going to be hopelessly lost. A loud, thrumming roar filled my ears, and I looked to my left to see the dim outline of two headlights, low set, headed straight for me.

I froze for a moment, doing my best deer-in-the-headlights impression as blood roared in my head and fear coursed through my veins, and then I took off in the general direction of where I had parked the old truck. The motor sounds grew closer; I glanced back and saw what appeared to be a four-wheeler. I was being chased by a four-wheeler, in my parking lot, on a February evening?

I kept running, staring back all the while, watching it gain on me. The closer it got, the better I could see it was a multipurpose four-wheeler, with a blade attached to the front for plowing snow. In fact, it looked just like the four-wheeler Jack and Marco—my landlords for the studio—used to plow our parking lot.

I reached Bessie just as the four-wheeler caught up to me; using all my agility, I dropped to the ground and rolled underneath the truck just as the snowplow blade slammed into the side.

Unfortunately, I rolled over my purse and heard a crunching noise, and then moisture began to spread across my clothes. Great, the water bottle had broken under my weight. I irrationally thought of all the things the water would ruin. *Get a grip, Jenny! Call for help!* My heart pounding, I opened my purse and frantically searched for my cell phone as I heard the four-wheeler back up a bit, maybe preparing for another ram at the truck.

I dialed 911 and reported I was being attacked by a snowplow.

"I'm sorry, ma'am, can you repeat that?"

"I'm under my truck, and a snowplow is ramming into it. You better send someone quick."

"A snowplow is ramming your truck?"

"*Help. Me!*" I screamed into the phone.

"Um, what's your address ma'am?"

"I'm in the parking lot of Priceless Pearls, 252 and 25th Street. My name is Jenny T. Partridge. And someone is trying to kill me with a snowplow!"

"Jenny?" A familiar voice came across the line. Alissa Miller was my close friend and confidante, and she worked as a 911 operator for Weber County.

"Alissa, help. Someone has me trapped here, under the truck, and I'm scared. I'm . . . I'm really scared." Hearing her familiar voice had forced me to face how terrified I really was. I didn't want to get chopped up by a snowplow. I wanted to have legs, so I could continue to dance. Legless dancing was not really the rage.

"Now be calm, Jenny. Help is on the way. Can you hear anything? Do you know who is driving the snowplow?"

"No, it's a damned inversion. You can't see anything out here. I heard the noise, and then . . . Wait."

The thick, stewy night air suddenly stilled, and I could hear nothing. The four-wheeler was silent, shut off. I heard the thump, thump, thump of footsteps coming near me, very near.

"You want to die, little girl, keep coming around Star-Makers," hissed an androgynous voice. "You seem to be failing to get the message. I am not messing around here. I *will* kill you, and it will be fun. Then I'll go after your cute blond friend. That'll be fun, too. Stay away or die."

If there ever were a time to pee your pants, even as an adult, this would be that time. I was proud that I did not. Not that I would ever share that story.

I heard the footsteps move away, then nothing, and in the distance I heard the roar of sirens.

"Jenny? Jenny, are you there? Are you okay, Jenny?"

"I think he's gone, but I'm not sure," I whispered into my phone.

"Stay right where you are. Don't move, okay?"

She didn't have to ask that twice. I was frozen to the spot. Maybe literally, as the temperature was well below zero and I had broken a bottle of water on the ground. This was not going to look good. My pride disappeared. How was I going to convince anyone that I had not peed my pants? *Sheesh*. Considering how badly I had to go, it was a wonder I hadn't. When my teeth began to chatter, I realized how cold I really was.

I saw red and blue lights reflect off the icy pavement and knew the cop car must be close. I heard the crunch of the tires and then the slam of a car door.

"Okay, Jenny, the police are at the scene. Tell them where you are." Alissa's voice was reassuring and firm.

"I'm here," I yelled. "I'm under the truck."

I heard the crunch, crunch of footsteps on the icy pavement, and then a firm voice said, "Come out, ma'am. Come out slowly, please, and show us your hands."

I tried to move, but I couldn't. I *was* frozen to the spot.

"I can't."

"Uh, ma'am? Please come out now."

"Alissa?" I said into the phone.

"Jenny, they are asking you to come out, hands up, just to show them it's you. What's wrong? Why aren't you coming out from under the truck?"

"Because when I was getting under the truck, I rolled over my water bottle and broke it. Now I'm stuck. I'm frozen to the pavement."

"You're frozen?"

"Pretty much, yeah."

"You're sure it was your water bottle?"

"Alissa! Could you please broadcast that across all the channels so all of the sheriff's office, Ogden Police Department, and surrounding areas can hear you?" I said, rather crossly. "Yes, it was my water bottle. I don't see the point in lying right now."

I heard her fight back a giggle.

"Do we need extrication equipment?" I heard one of the police officers say. Of course, I could only see his feet, since I was frozen to the pavement underneath Bessie.

This really sucked.

I knew it was only a matter of time before this story made its way around town. And I'm sure my water bottle would not be considered the source of my current predicament, even though it was true. *Sheesh.*

A plop on my head just added to my misery. A dark, thick substance ran down my face onto my lips, and I stupidly stuck my tongue out.

Ack! I had never eaten motor oil, but I had no doubt that was what I tasted. Several more thick, globby plops followed, coating my hair and face. It was cold enough to freeze water in just minutes, but the oil still managed to leak from Bessie.

It took both officers tugging at my arms to free me from underneath Bessie. They weren't too crazy about the rescue efforts, either, which made me feel like the kindergarten pariah. "It was a water bottle!" I said indignantly, when one of them wrinkled his nose after they had me standing up. "See?" I opened up my purse to show them the shattered hard plastic and all the frozen contents of my purse. They just didn't make those sports bottles very strong. My cell phone would probably be the only thing to survive, since I had pulled it out before it could get too wet.

"Uh-huh," said the officer with the wrinkling nose. I was too cold and tired and relieved to be alive to argue with him anymore. Let the rumors fly. *I* knew it was water!

When Alissa showed up on the scene, I was very relieved.

She took charge, heading us all back into the studio, where I had a change of clothing, since I practically lived there. I hadn't seen her much in the last few months, as she had applied to and been accepted into the police academy at Weber State University, and between classes and her job as a 911 dispatcher, she had little spare time.

I knew it was her dream, though, to be a detective, and I knew from experience she'd be a good one. The fact that she'd left work to come to my rescue meant a lot to me.

"Are you okay, Jenny?" she asked.

"Yes."

"What have you gotten yourself into now?"

"I'm not exactly sure. But as soon as I know, I'll give you a call and let you know."

She sighed, asked me again about my welfare, then told me she had to get back to work. "Do you want me to come stay over tonight?"

"No, I'll be fine."

"Okay, just call me." She was a tall, willowy brunette, and very, very beautiful. Men always went slack jawed around her. Tonight was no different. All the cops seemed to have forgotten about the killer snowplow incident, which had involved me, not her. Not her fault, of course.

When she exited my studio, attention finally returned to me.

I was frozen to the core, and afraid I would never warm up again. Now I sat facing a uniformed officer who asked me again for details of the crime. Which, by the way, was attack by snowplow. Believe it or not. I was a walking advertisement for Ripley.

When Tate walked in, I wasn't terribly surprised. But I *was* terribly embarrassed.

"Are you okay?" he asked. "There I go again. Every time I see you I am asking you, 'Are you okay?' There's something seriously wrong with that. You understand that, don't you? That I have to ask you, every time I see you, if you're okay? It's just wrong."

He turned away from me.

"Where did the four-wheeler with the plow come from?" he asked the officer who was questioning me.

"It's Marco's," I answered. "He keeps it in that little shed to the side of the building and uses it to keep the parking lot clean."

"And how did the assailant start it?" the officer asked. "I mean, I have two of them, and they require a key to start."

"The key would have been in it," I answered. "Marco and Jack like things convenient."

"Marco wants his stuff stolen?" Tate asked harshly.

"No, but he doesn't want to worry about where the key is, either. And the four-wheeler was in the shed, which is normally locked, so it usually isn't a problem."

Tate sent the two officers out to check the state of the shed, and he asked for Marco's number, so he could be called in to the scene of the . . . um, snowplow attack?

After that, he came up to me, but sort of kept his distance. "I heard this rumor . . ."

"It was water!" I said crossly, opening up my purse to show him the shattered plastic. In the warmth of the studio, my purse items were no longer frozen, but getting soggy and mostly ruined. Nice.

"Yeah, well, there are globs of black in your hair, too. In short, you are a huge mess."

"It's oil, from Bessie. I need a shower. And I'm freezing." I'd cleaned off my face as best I could, but I knew I was still a mess. And very, very cold.

"As soon as we're done here, I'm taking you home with me. I'll put you in the shower and warm you up."

"Oh man, a hot shower sounds really, really nice."

"That's not the part that's going to warm you up."

Be still my heart.

"And be prepared," he added. "There's a possibility I might not ever let you go. I might keep you prisoner, because my heart can't take much more of this anxiety about you and your state of safety. Every time I turn around, something is going wrong. Locking you up would solve all that."

I wasn't sure how to take that. Was that a declaration of love? Lust? Psychotic tendencies?

I decided to focus on the "not let you go" part. That would keep me going for a while.

TEN

MARCO showed up at the studio, Jack in tow, and was appropriately flustered by the break-in and snowplow attack. "I promise never to leave the key in the four-wheeler again," he told Tate.

"Jenny, I'm so, so sorry about this," Jack said to me. "Are you okay?"

Jack was really Jaclyn, a name she had never been too fond of, and she stood about four foot eight and probably weighed eighty-five pounds, soaking wet. Marco was six foot four and weighed at least three hundred pounds. They were the ultimate odd couple.

She fussed over me for a minute, while Tate told Marco the particulars of the crime. Someone had sawed through the padlock on the outside, which Tate assured me was relatively easy to do. How they knew the snowplow was in there was another story. Maybe they had just been looking for a weapon, anything, to try to get me.

"This makes no sense. None of it," I said. "I'm tired of

my life not making sense. How about some sense, huh? Can someone give me some sense here? Just a little bit. That's all I'm asking." Hmm. Perhaps shock was starting to set in. Either that, or I was freaking nuts. I preferred the shock theory.

"Time for you to go home, honey," Jack said gently, smiling. Her big blue eyes showed compassion. I'd known both her and Marco for the past six years, since I started renting my studio space from them. They were . . . unique. Utah is a pretty diverse place to live, despite what people might think. You have your active Mormons, your ex- or Jack Mormons, and then you have your non-Mormons, who come here mostly for the skiing or because of job transfers, and end up staying.

That was Jack. She had flown into Salt Lake City in 1971, on assignment for a newspaper back east. She discovered the resorts east of Salt Lake and spent about ten years there, taking a job with the local newspaper, until one day she made a fateful trip to try a ski resort just north of the big city. A resort called Snow Basin, located just above Ogden.

There she met Marco. Back then, Marco had been a healthy 230. A crazy big man who just loved to slash up the slopes. But shortly after he met Jack, he had a pretty major crash and spent a few months in the hospital. She'd tended to him during that time, and they'd been together ever since. Jack still skied, but Marco's knees couldn't handle it.

They compromised with trips to Mexico for deep-sea fishing. I'd heard tales of sharks and jellyfish and other things I didn't even want to consider. My daydreams of beach vacations did not involve things that bit and stung.

"We'll drive you home, honey," Jack said. "Are you done with her?" She directed the question at Tate.

"Actually, I'll take her home," Tate said, and I remembered the small bag I'd packed, one that was now at his house. I was staying with him, at least through the end of the week and the end of the convention that someone was determined to keep me from attending.

I'd be with Tate until we knew I was safe. The truth was, I knew I was in danger of losing my heart. Staying with him wouldn't keep me safe at all.

ELEVEN

I wasn't nervous at all about the night ahead of me. Probably because my nerves were all frozen solid. But as soon as I showered, and warmed up, I got a serious case of butterfly stomach. I washed my hair four times to get the oil out and then one more time just to stall.

I dried off with one of Tate's fluffy towels and then put on a clean pair of underwear, my warm flannel pajama pants, and a white cami. I topped that with a big sweatshirt that said "University of Utah." Hey, I was cold!

I towel-dried my hair and tried to avoid the mirror, knowing my tresses were now curling up tight to my head, and I had no way to smooth them. I wasn't about to paw through Tate's personal belongings looking for a hair dryer, and I was pretty sure he didn't have a curling brush.

At least I hoped he didn't, because if he did, that would mean another woman besides me had resided here, and I . . .

"Jenny? Did you drown? Are you coming out?"

Tate's voice was low and throaty, and it sent electric

shocks down my back. Wow, if his voice could do that, just imagine . . .

"Uh, yeah, I'm just trying to do something with this mop of hair I have. I'll be out in a minute."

"Okay, I'm in the kitchen. I made hot cocoa. I figured coffee might keep us up. I have other plans for that."

Ulp.

I stared at my hair in the mirror. Scary. Sort of like a mutant Chucky doll. Or Raggedy Ann gone bad. Oh well, there was nothing I could do to fix that.

I searched through my bag for some lip gloss, and didn't find any. I hadn't planned the packing really well.

I fluffed at my hair one more time, then headed for the door, the butterflies in my stomach having some kind of party. Maybe a parade.

Tate sat at the kitchen table, shirtless, arms behind his head, eyes closed. He opened them and turned his head to watch me come into the kitchen.

"Hungry?"

"Um, no, not really," I said, trying to look sultry and confident, and figuring that at best I looked like an escapee from a bad horror movie.

"I am," he said, rising from his chair and heading toward me. I backed up a few steps, and he stopped. "You're backing away."

"You scare me."

"Good scared or bad scared?"

I considered the butterfly swarm in my stomach and electrical arcs running up and down my spine. "Good, but still scary."

"Good scary, like thrilling?"

"Yes, yes, thrilling."

He moved toward me, and I swallowed hard. He pulled me into his chest, and I almost gasped. I always knew that electricity could exist between two people. I just didn't know it would be so real, and so, well, electric! He reached up a hand and tugged on my curls. "Very sexy. I like your hair like this."

"It's a little curly," I said.

"Curly sexy. Natural. I like it."

He liked the hair that gave me so many fits? I was falling seriously in love with this man. Oh no, more butterflies!

His cell phone, sitting on the kitchen counter, rang loudly. Of course.

I didn't know whether to cry or be relieved. On one hand, he was seriously hot, and I dreamed about him all the time. And he seemed to really like me. On the other hand, I didn't really know much about him. He kept himself distant from me, in so many ways. I wasn't sure I wanted to tie myself up with an emotionally distant man. If he was, in fact, emotionally distant. Plus, I suspected he got a lot of amusement out of watching my life.

"Wilson," he said into the phone, then stopped to listen. In the silence, I could hear ringing again, and recognized the tones of my phone. We'd spread out the contents of my purse on his coffee table, so they would dry, and my cell phone was not there. I remembered tucking it into the pocket of my winter jacket, and I moaned. We'd put the jacket in the laundry room, and as I walked toward it, I could hear the swooshing sounds of a washing machine. But, logically, the phone wouldn't be ringing if it were in the water, right?

Tate, Man of Mystery, to the rescue. He had searched my pockets and pulled out my phone, about four million bobby pins, a hairnet that had to have given him pause—I was not a lunch lady in my spare time; we used them to keep buns tight and hair from straying during competitions—and one toe topper, which looked a lot like a baby sock. All things I had picked up from the floor of my studio at one time or another. I wasn't really good at cleaning out my pockets. They were all sitting on the countertop on the side of the washer and dryer, next to my phone.

The call had switched into voice mail by this time, of course, and I grabbed it and checked the caller ID. Tamara Williams again! Would she never give up? I'd call her back when I had time. Would I never have a normal life? Would my phone ever be filled with messages from admiring males? Or at least one admiring male? One who just happened to be in the other room right now?

"You need to make some changes, Jenny," I told myself. First off, I figured, was to take a chance, be brave, and dive in, at least where Tate Wilson was concerned. I didn't know where this relationship was going, but I was sure as heck never going to find out if I never even allowed it to get out of the starting gate.

I walked back into the kitchen, only to find Tate missing. Had he gone back to the bedroom, and was he waiting for me there? Candles burning? Scented massage oils on the dresser? Clothes on the . . .

Nope. He came out of the door fully dressed, just as I reached it. "Sorry, Jenny, I've been called out. It's this case we are working on. I'm not really happy about leaving. Seems like we keep getting interrupted."

Yeah, it did seem that way. I tried not to let my disappointment show. Every time I got up my courage, and decided to move ahead, and behave like an adult, something like this happened. Signs from God? Nah, that would probably be lightning. Or a flood.

He leaned over to give me a quick kiss, told me to get into bed, and promised to get back as soon as he could.

"I'll be waiting," I said. Of course, the minute my head hit the pillow I fell asleep, but Tate was always pretty amazing in my dreams. For now, that would have to do.

TWELVE

I spent the morning luxuriating in Tate's king-sized bed, which was the most comfortable place I'd ever slept in my entire life. He'd come in sometime in the very early morning hours and collapsed next to me, snoring lightly. I woke up when I heard him, but pretended sleep, because the fear was back. My bravery sure hadn't lasted very long.

And it didn't matter, because he was obviously putting in some long, hard hours in whatever this mysterious case was. I woke up a few hours later to find him gone, a note on his pillow—his pillow! Isn't that kind of like those romantic movies?—that said, "Had to get back to work. Make yourself at home. Looking forward to tonight!"

Butterflies again. I told them to quiet down, and I dozed on and off until around noon, when I finally forced myself to get out of the comfortable bed and dragged myself into Tate's shower. It was large and roomy, and beautifully tiled, and was just a shower, unlike mine, which was in my bathtub. The water stayed hot for a really, really long time—unlike at my place, where you were lucky to get a quick five-minute shower before it turned lukewarm, then cold.

After I washed my hair and washed the soap off my body, I reluctantly turned off the water and dried myself with a big, fluffy towel.

I could get used to sleeping and showering here. *Ulp.* I probably ought not to go there.

After making myself a grilled cheese sandwich and some tomato soup—hey, Tate said to make myself at home!—I drove Bessie back down to the Marriott Hotel, where I was due to help with the competition, which started that afternoon. The fog was still thick, and even though it had been twelve days since I had seen the sun, I felt like singing. I liked Tate's bed. Even more, I liked Tate's shower. Best of all, I liked Tate. Even though he made me nervous, and I was always dreaming of him in rather, uh, naughty ways.

I felt myself blushing, despite the fact that I was all alone.

I parked close to the entrance, because after last night I was still pretty nervous, even in the daytime. Since it was still a nasty inversion, it wouldn't be hard to sneak up on anyone. I wasn't going to take any chances.

Down by the double doors that led into the main ballroom I could see a large white truck, with the Hollywood StarMakers logo on the side. Though the teachers and staff flew into each city, they had a lot of sound equipment, trophies, plaques, and other paraphernalia necessary to run a dance competition, so they had a truck that drove from location to location. That's a job I would not want. I watched as two burly men unloaded the truck, took out what looked like some very big speakers, and wheeled them on a dolly into the hotel.

I walked into the hotel and went straight to the main ballroom—and into sheer chaos. Bonnie, dressed in black leggings, a denim miniskirt, and an embossed, very tight T-shirt—emphasizing what I was sure was a very expensive boob job—was yelling at Enrique, who looked ready to haul off and hit her.

James, early for once in his life, stood back and watched

the altercation, while dancers of all sizes and ages—from eight to eighteen—milled around in their travel suits, hair done up, makeup on. They were ready to compete. They were also watching the spectacle, eyes wide. Not good for business.

So why was Bonnie yelling at Enrique? And where was Bill?

"What's going on?" I asked James, as I sidled up beside him.

"And you had better do what I tell you to do, because I am in charge here. This is my company, too," Bonnie the Beast yelled at the tap dancer. He stood with his arms crossed, wearing a tank top that emphasized his biceps. I suspected he knew that, too, based on the smoldering look he wore on his face. Although right now, the smoldering look was suffering, undercut as it was by anger.

"Bill has taken off. No one has seen him since late last night. Bonnie said they got in a fight, and he left the room, and no one's seen him since."

"Hello? He's missing? Has anyone called the police?" I yelled. The whole room went silent, and there were about a million or so pairs of eyes trained on me. Okay, maybe not that many, but you get the idea.

"Uh, Jenny, he probably just got another room and is sleeping off his, well, you know. He's sort of been . . ." James put his hand up like he was holding a cup and made glug-glug sounds, while tipping back his head and opening his mouth.

I supposed it made more sense to think he was in another room in the hotel than to think something bad had happened, but since I'd been chased just the night before by a crazed snowplow driver, I was inclined to lean toward the foul-play theory. If *that* could happen, anything could happen.

"Look, just since I agreed to help Bill out, someone has left me threatening messages, firebombed my car, and chased me with a snowplow! Given that—plus the two others who are missing—I think we should suspect the worst and call the police."

Slowly, a buzz started up in the room again, since I had

lowered my voice. People began talking and turned away from what was no longer a spectacle.

I reached into my purse to grab my cell phone and came up empty. Drat! I'd turned it off—after I'd received about two hundred phone calls from Tamara Williams—and left it on Tate's dresser last night. This morning, I'd forgotten to grab it and put it back in my purse.

"Somebody needs to call the police. Or at least Tate. Of course, Tate is the police."

"We can't afford to alarm people when Bill has just wandered off in a drunken stupor," Bonnie said with a nasty edge to her voice. What did Bill see in her? "He'll be back around when he comes to. For now, this competition needs to get started, and I am in charge."

"People aren't numbers, Bonnie," Enrique said scathingly. "You have no clue how to run this competition. All you do is keep the books and tally up the competition scores."

"What, like dance is that hard?" Bonnie said, scorn in her voice. "Like telling people 'You're on' is that difficult? Please. A monkey could do it."

I did not much like Bonnie, and she had just fallen a few more notches in my esteem with her derisive comments about dance.

"Let me borrow your cell phone, James," I said. He reached into his pocket, then a look of alarm crossed his face.

"Damn, where did I leave it?" He was just as bad as I was at keeping track of a cell phone.

"Oh wait, I remember," he said, a coquettish smile on his face as he eyed Enrique. Great. Just great.

Enrique smiled back. Bonnie gave a huge sigh of disgust and tromped off.

"She has no clue how to do this," Enrique said. "And we are scheduled to start the competition in ten minutes. Jenny, if I do the announcing, will you make sure each team is lined up and ready to go? We have to keep this thing on schedule or we'll be running routines past midnight, and these kids are too young for that."

"Why is no one worried about Bill?" I asked, exasperation filling my voice. "Two other dancers have disappeared. I've been threatened and attacked. And now he is missing, and no one is worried. Why is no one worried?"

Enrique walked closer to me and leaned down so he could semi-whisper in my ear. "He's been doing this kind of thing for the past three cities, Jenny. I'm really worried about him. That beast Bonnie is driving him to drink, and he's so unhappy with her. He needs a good woman. Someone who has something in common with him. Someone he relates to."

I stepped back a bit. "Uh, well, maybe you can line him up with someone."

I turned to glare at James, who was watching Enrique closely.

"Oh, I think the perfect woman for Bill is closer than we realize."

James giggled. He *giggled*. I was so going to kill him. He was always getting me into this kind of trouble, whether by telling his Mormon relatives we were a couple, or by pointing out my behavior to draw attention away from his own.

"Well, good luck with that. Now, give me the lineup. And call the police! I don't care if they find him in a room. There's been enough going on that we need to report him missing."

"Bonnie probably tied him up and hid him in her broom closet," Enrique said.

At that moment, twelve girls ran up and surrounded me. My Petites had arrived for the competition, as they were in the first division. The Seniors would compete a few hours later.

Carly and the two other girls I had picked to do solos were standing together, nervously rubbing their arms. They wore costumes that were a little plainer than we were used to, since our regular costume designer was more than a little cuckoo, and, it turned out, had some warrants out for her arrest. Since she was currently a fugitive from the law, whereabouts unknown, I had to resort to ordering costumes from a catalog and putting crystals on them to make them snazzier. It worked pretty well, but I really missed Monica. A part of me really hoped she would get those pesky warrants straightened out and come back to Utah and work on costumes for me. Selfish, I know. What can I say? I was no Madame Teresa.

"Hi, Jenny," Carly said. "We're all ready. We're excited. Should we go warm up?"

"Definitely. You guys all look great! Remember, run your routines to counts a few times before you have to perform."

Marlys sauntered up behind the girls, Marble clinging to her hand. She looked really calm, but I knew her better. She was pretty nervous for Carly, who would be performing her solo routine for the first time, and this was a major competition. It could be very nerve-racking, especially for the mothers. Since only the older teams were competing here, Marble was in her street clothes.

Carly and the other Petites ran off to find the dressing room. I saw Tamara Williams milling around near the back of the room, and I gave her a little finger waggle.

"I need to talk to you," she mouthed at me.

I nodded, then turned to Marlys, trying to look really, really busy. Which didn't take much trying because I actually *was* pretty frantically busy.

"Marlys, Bill is missing," I said to her. "No one can find him. Will you please call Tate and tell him? No one else seems to think it's strange, because I guess he's been drinking a lot, but after all that's happened to me, I suspect foul play."

"All that's happened?"

"Oh yeah, you don't know. It's been an eventful few days. First someone called me and left a warning message about working for StarMakers, then someone firebombed the Pepto Mobile, and last night, after practice, somebody chased me with a snowplow!"

"What the . . . ?" Marlys asked. "Are you okay? You tick off another psycho dance mom? I mean, I know Carmen messed with your hair, but this seems a little extreme."

"Yeah, I'm okay. I don't think it has anything to do with the psycho dance moms, although if Tamara Williams calls me one more time I'm going to have to change my phone number."

"Still bugging you about April's solo?"

"Yeah, and when she finds out that Carly is doing her solo here, she's going to be even less pleased."

Marlys just shook her head and tightened her lips. She turned to look at Tamara and her eyes hardened. "Too late. She's spotted her, and she has to know that Carly is dancing her solo, because she isn't in the team costume yet. Why is she talking to her? What is she saying? Is she trying to psych her out? Carly's worked hard. She's so excited you picked her, because that means her hard work and dedication paid off. The only person who wants April to dance is Tamara. April would rather text boys on her phone, or go to movies with her friends. Dancing is only social for her. She's not bad, but it's not enough to push her beyond local competitions."

"Yeah, I know. Look, Carly earned this. I just wanted you to be prepared for the fallout."

Marlys frowned. She shook her head, turned away from Tamara, who had walked away from Carly, and then pulled her phone out and hit a speed-dial button. Don't ask why Marlys had Tate on her speed dial. In a roundabout way, it had a lot to do with me and some trouble I'd gotten into a few months ago, where this *really* crazy dance mom wanted me dead.

It still irked me that people acted like I needed taking care of. I didn't. Most of the time, anyway.

Since I knew Marlys would handle reporting Bill's disappearance, I hurried over to where Enrique stood with the lineup. The solo competition would go on first, followed by teams. It would probably be a late night, with routines scheduled to compete until 10 p.m., and awards to follow shortly after that.

"Okay, let's go over this," Enrique said. "You up to the challenge? We have to keep the girls moving on and off the stage fast. We can't afford to fall behind. So remember, if someone isn't there, like if they have a quick costume change or something, you find the next group, fast, and we announce a change in the schedule. We have to know who is up, so the judges can follow each routine, though. So it's kind of a balancing act."

"Right," I said, feeling butterflies in my stomach. I'd never run a big competition before. I'd be cutting my teeth on one of the biggest, at least as far as importance.

"We start with solos, and those begin right at three o'clock. From there we move to team, youngest teams first, then up to older teams. There are four categories: jazz, hip-hop, lyrical, and character. There are also five group sizes: extra small, small, medium, large, and company."

"So, basically, I'm doing what?" I asked, my head spinning with all the information.

"You are making sure the next routine in the lineup is here, and if they aren't, you need to track them down. You will be letting me know if we have to make a quick lineup change, or if someone isn't there, if I need to make a call over the microphone. You also watch the sound table for music trouble. If they signal you, you need to let me know that we need to call the director and have them come up, with either a new tape or a new CD. Okay?"

My head began to swim. "Do you always do this with Bill, Enrique? I mean, I thought that Bonnie was his partner."

"Bonnie doesn't do much but her nails. She is in charge of tabulating, and that's about it, at least as far as the competition goes. I've backed Bill up since I joined him. And despite all that, he hires people like Jason Kutcher who are extremely arrogant and full of themselves, and meanwhile Bill won't let me teach anything but tap. And before you say anything, yes I'm bitter. But that's the way it goes."

"You didn't have anything to do with . . . Never mind." I was no detective. Why was I asking these questions? In fact, I was a big fat coward, and I was starting to regret I'd even begun to say the words. Enrique, to my misfortune, caught the meaning.

His eyes hardened and his lips tightened. "No, I had nothing to do with Twila or Eldon going missing, and I'm not a street thug, despite the fact that my last name is Perez."

I flushed. "I didn't even think of that, Enrique, I promise. I'm sorry I made you mad. I promise that never occurred to me. I mean, look at me. My last name is Partridge. I get a lot of crap about that, let me tell you."

His lip twitched at that comment, and I could tell by the way his face relaxed that he had at least partially forgiven me. "Okay, let's get into place and get this show on the road."

The next few hours went by in a blur. I did a reasonably decent job of keeping the teams on time and in line to get onstage, especially after I recruited Marlys to do some of the running and finding of missing teams for me. My soloists did a great job, and Carly really stood out on the stage, her turnout excellent and her technique in top-notch form. The other two did well, but their showmanship was lacking. When it came time to shine, Carly really knew how to turn it on.

I saw tears running down Marlys's face after her oldest daughter finished, and felt a lump in my own throat. Carly had started her dancing career with me. If things kept going the way they were headed, she had a long career ahead of her.

My teams did well, too, and I felt that they looked better than any of the other competition teams. Pride swelled my chest.

And as they say, pride goeth before you fall on your behind. Or something like that.

I turned away from the last team on the stage to find myself face-to-face with Bonnie, followed closely by Tate Wilson.

"Did you find Bill?" I asked, the question directed at Tate, since I would rather kiss an asp than talk to Bonnie again.

"No, there's no sign of him."

"I'm telling you, he just checked into another room and is sleeping off a killer hangover somewhere," Bonnie said, her voice a plaintive whine. "We fought last night, mostly because I told him I was tired of his drinking and that he either needed to get help or I was leaving him. He was totally distraught and drank even more. Then he disappeared."

Enrique was up onstage, getting ready to announce the awards, and he looked over at Bonnie and me and gestured. She had a handful of papers in her hand, apparently the tabulated scores, and she walked away from Tate and me without another word, handing the papers up to Enrique, then stomping off.

"She's a real piece of work," Tate said. "I spent the last twenty minutes questioning her. And her story doesn't waver, and yet I don't really feel like she's telling me everything."

"I think you should lock her up until she gives you the answers you want," I said spitefully.

"You do, do you?" Tate asked, amusement underscoring the rhetorical question. "That's not generally how the police department does things, although I will certainly take it under consideration."

"She's a witch."

"Me-oow."

"Don't get funny with me. She has been nothing but nasty to me since she saw me on Wednesday. I don't feel like I have to be nice back, thank you very much."

Tate chuckled, then his face grew grave. "There really is no sign of Bill Flanagan. He didn't check into another room, and I've checked hospitals and clinics, and he's not there, either. Not even any John Does who might be him. It's like he just walked out of the hotel room into the night and disappeared."

"That's not that hard in this inversion. It surprises me that more people don't disappear every year when it comes to town. But he has to be somewhere."

Enrique began announcing the awards, and I tried to listen for the names of my dancers and teams, without totally blowing off Tate and my concerns about Bill.

"Go listen to the awards. I'm going to ask a few more questions of the staff, and then I'm going to put out an ATL—attempt to locate—on Flanagan. With the other two missing dancers, I just don't think we can take any chances."

"Do you need my help?"

"No, I need you to stay in the crowd and don't disappear. Don't make yourself a target. Something bad is happening here, although it's hard to believe a dance competition could be the arena for crime."

"Hey, you've seen how crazy these moms can be."

"Yeah. Now go and listen to the awards. I'll come find you in a few minutes." Then he pulled me close to him and kissed me lightly on the lips. "Just a little hint of what's to come," he said in a low voice.

"And the third place winner in the soloist teen division is . . ."

"Oh, this is Carly's division. I have to go listen."

"I'll be back soon," was all he said.

I ran up close to the stage and felt my nails biting into my hand as Enrique announced the second-place winner, Karen Something-or-other. I started jumping up and down, as I realized Carly had won. I saw Marlys doing a similar move and knew she had realized it, too. The only one who didn't seem to understand was Carly, who sat with the other soloists on the stage, her fists tightly clenched, her face tense.

When Enrique announced her as the winner, she opened her eyes wide and then jumped to her feet, the other team

members dancing around her. She took her plaque and trophy, and beaming widely, she searched the crowd for me.
As soon as she saw me she smiled even bigger and held up
the trophy.

"I won," she mouthed.

"You did good," I mouthed back.

$\mathcal{B}$OTH of my teams won first place, and I congratulated
the girls, who were on a high after starting off the season,
at such a prestigious competition, by winning. Carly even
won high-point soloist, and a huge trophy. Marlys was
beaming ear to ear.

"What did Tamara Williams say to you, earlier, before
you went on?" I asked Carly, after she had calmed down a
little bit.

"Oh, it was weird. She told me to make sure I didn't fall
off the stage. That's weird, isn't it, Jenny? I mean, why
would I fall off the stage?"

Yikes. Sounded a little bit like a threat to me.

"Oh, she was just being silly, Carly. Way to go." I knew
it was time to confront Tamara Williams and tell her to
chill out, and it was not a conversation I was looking forward to having. But, of course, it was not the first time I
had had to do it.

I knew all competitive sports were the same way, and
sometimes people forgot dance was a sport. But I'd had
parents get in fights, sometimes physical, threaten each
other, threaten someone's child . . . You name it, it had
happened.

Usually, if I sat a parent down and told them they were
"over the top," they would get it. At least for a while, until
I had to remind them again. But not always. Tamara
Williams was a little scary. But I had to do my job as a
teacher, and sometimes that meant controlling the parents.
And if that didn't work, asking them to leave and find another place to dance.

After the girls cleared out, we were left with a mountain

of abandoned dance shoes, clothes, pieces of costumes, and even some stray underwear—all par for the course at a children's dance competition.

The hotel staff member I asked handed me a large garbage bag, and I went around gathering up the left-behind items, putting them in what would become the lost and found, at least for the next day or so. I even found a small gold locket that looked expensive, so I tucked it inside a shoe it was sitting next to and put them carefully in the bag. Someone was going to come looking for that.

When the room was relatively clean, I turned my attention to the hotel events planner, who was directing her workers to stack up the chairs and prepare the room for dance classes the following day.

There were about four rooms, including the big ballroom, which would be partitioned off tomorrow to make classrooms in which each of us teachers would run our routines with different age groups of girls.

Jason Kutcher and Enrique were having some sort of heated argument in the entryway of the ballroom, and I moved closer to try and hear what they were fighting about.

"No, you can't take off just because Bill is gone. This convention is going on as planned, and you need to stick to your contract, or Bill will have to sue you."

"Bill ain't nowhere to be found, dude, and this ship is sinking fast. I don't hitch myself to any sinking ship. I'm a star. I have too much to lose. I was doing this as a favor for my main man, but being as he has bailed, I'm bailing, too. It ain't my bag, anyway, teaching little untalented pains in the—"

"Whoa, whoa, who are you calling untalented?" I said, barging into the conversation. "Some of those pains in the . . . I mean girls, are my students. Who the heck do you think you are, anyway? They are just little girls, you moron. They have to learn somehow." Nobody called my girls untalented. Well, nobody but me, anyway.

Both men stared at me. "Well, sorry, but you're not very nice. I bet you weren't even hired by Bill. I bet Bonnie hired you, because you act just like her. You wanna talk about a pain, then you should look in *her* direction!"

Jason flushed when I said that, and turned and stomped away.

Enrique stared at me, eyes wide, and I said, "She's standing right behind me, isn't she?"

He nodded, fighting back a smile.

I turned to see Tate Wilson and Bonnie, standing together. Bonnie's nose was scrunched up, as though she smelled something really bad, and her eyes were narrowed and angry. Her perfectly arched eyebrows were knitted together, and her lips were pursed.

"Just exactly who do you think you are?" she said to me. I decided to take that as a rhetorical question. "I see you're trying to take over my life, and my job, but it isn't going to work. Bill loves me, and he said you were so irresponsible that you couldn't even put your shoes on without getting confused. Walking down a hallway, you would get lost, Bill always said. And he also said you eat like there's no tomorrow. Which probably explains this." She pointed at my middle, which wasn't terribly trim but not terribly fat, either, and I decided she had gone too far.

I pulled back my arm to swing and felt it catch. I turned to see Enrique holding me back, keeping me from decking Bonnie the Beast. I pulled my arm out of his grasp and put both down to my sides. Assaulting Bonnie probably wouldn't be the wisest idea. Tate nodded his approval.

"Look, this has gone far enough. I think everybody needs some sleep. We'll start a full-scale search for Bill tomorrow," Tate said.

"Hmmph," Bonnie said, then stomped off.

"Hey, Enrique, where should I put these?" I asked, motioning to the large garbage bag full of dancer's paraphernalia. "It's all things the girls left behind."

"Just set it over there. I'll ask the hotel staff where a good place for lost and found is."

"Let's go, Jenny," Tate said. "You have to be back here

pretty early. I'll drive you and drop you off in the morning. You can leave Bessie here."

"Bessie?" Enrique said.

"Bessie's a truck. She's old. She's tired. And her heater doesn't work too well."

"My heater works fine," Tate said in a low growl.

"Good night, you two," Enrique said, giving us a little wave, before he leaned into me. "Never mind Bill. I see you have something else going, and it appears to be working for you just fine."

THIRTEEN

OF course, in Jennyworld, things rarely worked out like that. First of all, I didn't dare leave Bessie in the Marriott parking lot. My father would kill me. So Tate followed me to his condo. I was hot for Tate, and apparently, he was hot for me, and I was determined not to panic, but once again, duty called. His cell phone rang and put an end to our interlude. He had to go, and I spent the night in his bed, in a deep, dreamless sleep. At least as far as I knew. The alarm went off at 6 a.m. and I groaned as Tate pushed at me, urging me to get out of the bed and into the shower. Since it was Saturday, he didn't have to get up right away.

I was jealous.

"When did you get in? I didn't even hear you," I said sleepily, rubbing at my eyes.

"It was late. Around 4 a.m. And I know you didn't hear me. Good thing you are at my house, and I'm not trying to assault or hurt you, because you weren't moving. I tried to wake you, but I had to take your pulse just to make sure you weren't dead."

"Um, I'm sorry," I said. "I guess I didn't realize how much all this has worn on me. And worn me out."

"Don't apologize. It was late, anyway. The right time will come."

Ulp. I showered, ate some cereal, and went back into the bedroom to kiss Tate good-bye. He mumbled something sleepily and then caught me off guard when he pulled me down onto the bed beside him.

"Faker," I said, laughing, as he wrapped me in his arms.

"No, no faking. There will be no faking in this house," he said, his voice a low, sleepy rumble.

"I promise no faking. Ever. But right now, I have a convention to go to, and dancers to teach. And money to earn. So I have to go."

He groaned and then released me.

"I'll stop by and see how things are going. We're going to meet with the FBI this morning to talk about the three missing persons cases tied up with this convention. Jenny?"

"Yes?"

"Please be careful."

"I promise."

EVERY morning I walked outside hoping that the inversion—and mucky fog and chilling temperatures—would be gone. No luck. Thirteen days since I had seen the sun, and the fog was thick as tomato soup.

I got to the Marriott at around six forty-five, and since warm-ups were slated for seven thirty, I had a few minutes to myself to run over the routines in my head.

I walked into the main ballroom to see if Enrique—and hopefully Bill—were there, but didn't see either one. Instead, I ran headlong into Bonnie and a crying girl and her tearful mother.

"Jenny, where on earth did you put the lost-and-found items you gathered up? Enrique said you had the whole thing under control, but no one can find the bag, and this little girl has lost a very important memento."

"My ... my ... my locket," sobbed the pretty blond girl, who looked to be around ten years old. "My dad ... my dad gave it to me, before ... before he went to Iraq. And it was around my neck, and I took it off because I didn't want to lose it ... and then ... and then ... it was gone." She broke down into agitated sobs.

"Can you help us find it?" her mother said, tears pooling in her eyes.

"Hey, I remember seeing a locket. I put it in the bag, tucked inside a shoe."

"Yes, yes, my shoes were there, too. I was just so worried about the locket."

I looked around the room, but didn't see the bag anywhere. I walked over to one of the staff workers closing up the ballroom divider wall, making one room into two, and asked him if he had seen a big black garbage bag.

"Oh yeah, I put that in the Dumpster," he said. "Someone forgot to throw it out last night."

Ack!

"No, no, that was the lost and found. You put it in the Dumpster? What Dumpster? Where?"

"Out back."

"Why would you do that? Why would you throw it in the garbage?" I asked, irritation and anger scoring my voice.

"Uh, because it was a *garbage* bag," he said.

Great. The little girl and her mother were eyeing me anxiously, and Bonnie was glaring at me, so I asked him for directions to the Dumpster and then went out the back entrance of the ballroom, into the arctic-chilled inversion. I saw the Dumpster but I really wished I hadn't, because it stunk. Bad. Best I could hope for was that the bag would be right on top.

It was one of those great big, industrial-sized Dumpsters, and it was taller than I stood, so I couldn't see into it. I looked for a foothold, finally finding a cement block that must have been used to block the door from time to time. Definitely not fire code, but who was I to say anything. I set the block on end and carefully stepped onto it, balancing as

I put first one foot, then the other on the narrow block. It put me just high enough to throw open the lid, and I spied a relatively clean-looking black garbage bag toward the back. I reached toward it, the block tottering, and I stopped to steady myself. When I had my balance back, I reached again, slowly, grabbing the bag and hauling it toward me.

"Will you hurry up?" screamed a voice behind me, setting me off balance again. I pitched headfirst into the garbage. Great. Just great.

Bonnie cackled with joy—I swear she cackled!—and I tried to push myself up out of the mess, my hands sinking into the garbage all around me.

My legs were still sticking out, but I couldn't push myself backward because the garbage was so soft. The block had obviously fallen so I had no choice but to pull my legs into the bin with me. I pulled the garbage off my face and out of my hair, and I tried to find something firm to stand on to get me out of this stinky, smelly mess and into Bonnie's face. Something to the left of me caught my eye, and I turned to see I wasn't alone in the Dumpster. Next to me was the body of Jason Kutcher, former hip-hop choreographer extraordinaire.

Jason would never dance again.

FOURTEEN

I know I screamed long and hard, although I didn't have much memory of it. Bonnie had finally figured out I wasn't messing around, and got some help. While we waited for the police, the staff member who had thrown out the lost-and-found bag clearly began to worry that someone might finger him for something more—like, say, a murder—because he started talking fast and furiously and explaining that he had seen nothing the night before.

Six uniformed officers showed up, Tate following fairly quickly on their heels. After I was questioned, I was led to a hotel room where I was allowed to shower. Bonnie grudgingly gave me some Hollywood StarMakers gear to wear—a T-shirt and sweatpants. My bra and underwear had, thankfully, remained clean. The other dance clothes I had worn would go first to evidence and then in the garbage.

The shower and the fresh clothes did nothing to soothe my emotions, however. Though I hadn't been particularly fond of Jason, the sight of his dead body had left me thoroughly shaken. One of the most vivid things I remembered about the body was the big red imprint on his forehead. A print that looked an awful lot like a tap shoe.

And I couldn't help but remember, also, that the last time I had seen Kutcher, he had been arguing with Enrique Perez, who just happened to be the tap-dance teacher for the convention, something he was not particularly happy about.

All of this I shared with Tate after I got out of the shower and dressed, joining him and the other police officers in the main ballroom.

"You think Perez did this?" he asked me.

"No, I can't see it. He seems too nice, but he was the last one I saw with Kutcher, and they were not saying nice things to each other. Theirs was not a mutual admiration society."

"I guess we are just going to have to call this convention off," Bonnie said. "Bill's gone, now Jason's been killed, and all we have left is, well, you two and Enrique."

She pointed in the direction of me and James, who had shown up about three minutes before, almost late as usual.

True, there was no Bill. And now there was no Jason Kutcher, hot young hip-hop choreographer, who had to be a big pull. And if things kept going the way they were going, Enrique would be pulled in for questioning, so even the tap classes would not have a teacher.

I grabbed the schedule out of my bag and surveyed it.

"Bill would not want this convention to stop because of this," I said firmly.

"Hello, Jenny, dead body," James said, aghast.

"He has put his life and his soul into this, and something like a cancellation would destroy his business. I'm not going to let that happen."

"It's my business, too, and I call the shots. And I don't see how we can pull this off," Bonnie said. "We simply don't have the manpower. Or the talent." She looked at me derisively.

"You wouldn't know talent if it climbed out of your—"

"Jenny," James said warningly.

"Look, we need to question Enrique, and everyone else, Jenny. I just don't see how you can make this work, with all the problems." Tate was trying to be nice, but I was not willing to see Bill's dream die. Plus I really needed that twenty-five hundred dollars he was going to pay me.

"James, call Amber. Tell her we need her. And have her call Sal. We need him, too. He's really good. And he can choreograph a routine at the drop of a hat."

"Sal," James said, his voice dripping with derision.

"Yes, Sal. And Amber. Between us, we can run all the classes. And Enrique's classes weren't scheduled until the afternoon, so the cops can question him and then he'll be free by the time his classes are scheduled."

"You're being optimistic, Jen," Tate said gently. "What if we don't release Enrique?"

"You're charging Enrique?" James said, his voice aghast, alarm on his face. "Why, he wouldn't hurt a fly. He is the nicest, kindest, hottest man I have ever met. And you're charging him with murder?" With each word his voice went up an octave, and Tate started to look alarmed.

"They are not charging him with anything, James. They just need to talk to him. He was the last person who saw Jason alive."

"He is *not* a murderer." I half expected James to rend his shirt and howl at the sky. Drama was his strongpoint.

"No one is calling him a murderer," I pointed out, although I noted Enrique, who had arrived shortly after Tate, did not look happy as he answered questions fired at him by Agent Carson Keller—a man who was looking remarkably awake, and quite handsome, despite the early morning hour.

"You can't pull this off," Bonnie said with a sneer. "Why, Bill said—"

"Hey, you really ought to start off questioning her," I said to Tate. "She probably knew Jason better than anyone, aside from Bill of course. That's where I'd start."

He fought back a smile and walked toward Bonnie, who immediately began protesting her innocence.

"Call Marlys, too," I told James. "I'm going to need her organizational skills if I'm going to pull this off."

CONVENTION classes started about a half hour late, but considering the events of the morning, that had to be some kind of miracle. I would have called Grandma Gilly and asked, but she was still pretty peeved about the whole patron saint of dancers thing. She gave me one of those necklaces and told me the story about the saint, some guy who was murdered for confessing his faith, or something like that. I failed to see the importance, or connection between that and dance. After that, I stopped asking her Catholic questions.

I ended up with the oldest girls, while Sal took the youngest dancers, and James started with the girls in the middle age range, Amber assisting. Marlys ran from room to room making sure everything was flowing.

"Keep an eye on Sal," I whispered to her when she poked her head into the room to tell me all was going fine. "I have no idea how good he is going to be at this teaching thing."

We had a good class, but my mind was weighed down with thoughts of Bill and the murdered Jason Kutcher, so I was glad when the time was up and we had a ten-minute break. It had originally been slated for twenty minutes, but we had time to make up due to our late start.

I quickly scurried down to the room where Sal was teaching, and was surprised to find his class still in session.

"Time's up," I mouthed to him when I caught his eye. "Time to change classes."

He shrugged his shoulders and mouthed something I couldn't understand. And kept dancing. So I walked up closer. "Sal, it's time to quit. The girls need a break before their next class."

Sal stopped, then walked over to the sound system and turned off the music. The girls, who had been following his every move, groaned. One little redheaded girl looked up at me. "We don't want to switch classes. We want to stay with Sal. This is fun. Dance is *never* fun, but this is a blast."

I was awfully glad she wasn't one of my dancers. Dance is never fun? I'd rather dance than eat. Well, most of the time, anyway.

"Sorry girls, but everyone else needs a chance to dance with Sal, too. And you guys are coming to my class next. It'll be so much fun."

"Oh," said the little redheaded girl, and I suddenly felt like Charlie Brown, carrying his trick-or-treat sack filled with rocks.

"Come on, girls. Go get a drink, use the restroom, and then switch to your next class."

They all ran up and hugged Sal, then reluctantly went to gather up dance bags and shoes, and drink some water before the next class started.

"Well, seems like you're a hit," I said.

Sal looked down at his shoes and squirmed like a bashful five-year-old. "Aw, Jenny, I'm just glad you trusted me enough to let me do this."

The next group of girls filed in, and I just patted him on the arm and told him to keep up the good work. I didn't have the heart to tell him that I was desperate, and he was a last resort. But hey, he was doing a great job.

The morning flew by, and before I knew it, lunchtime rolled around. The girls ran off in a million different directions, some sitting with parents who had brought them meals, and others buying food from the Marriott vendors set up to serve them.

I wandered off in search of Tate and Agent Keller, as well as Enrique, but all I could find were a few uniformed cops stationed throughout the hallways.

I went into the small room reserved for conference staff and found James and Amber eating sandwiches, apparently from a nice selection set up in the corner of the room. There were also sodas, milk, juice, bottled water, and an assortment of desserts. I really liked the way Bill did things. Bill. *Where was he? Was he okay?*

I sat down next to them and unwrapped the turkey sandwich I'd selected, listening to them discuss the murder of Jason Kutcher and who would have wanted him dead.

I didn't join in, as my thoughts were still with Bill. James claimed he had never really gotten over me, which I found hard to believe. I was a very get-overable girl, at least as far as I could see. But the fact he was now missing made me look back and remember the way we were— please don't sing along.

I had a lot of fun with Bill, but truthfully, most of our relationship had been one big double date. Everything we did was tied in with the group of people we hung out with. We had a great time hanging out with people, and we were close. We shared heartache and success and disaster and joy, and I really thought that was what he missed. It couldn't really have been about me, but rather that time of our lives.

"Don't you think, Jenny?" James asked me.

"Sorry, I really wasn't paying attention. Don't I think what?"

"I was just saying, don't you think it's a little strange and coincidental that Bill disappeared right after or during the time one of his teachers was murdered?"

"Yes, that's more than a little strange. I'm worried. I hope he's not—"

"Oh no, Jenny, are you saying you think he's been murdered, too?" James's face went white, and Amber covered her mouth with her hand.

"I don't know what to think, but what I do know is that he's missing, and I'm pretty worried."

There was a knock on the conference room door, it opened, and in came Tate along with Agent Keller and two other men in suits I did not recognize. Enrique was not with them.

I jumped to my feet. "Hi, Tate, did you find Bill yet?"

He just shook his head, and I knew something was terribly, terribly wrong from the look on his face.

"Tate?"

"James Marriott, we need you to come with us," Agent Keller said, his voice not quite so singsongy and charming as it had been the previous day.

"Tate, what's going on?"

"We found the murder weapon, Jenny. It was a tap shoe, used with great force, and unfortunately, we also found the owner."

"I don't understand."

"The shoe belonged to James, and we have witnesses that reported seeing him with Jason Kutcher late last night, sharing drinks and a meal. Apparently, after he argued with you and Enrique, he took off and ran into James."

James looked wild-eyed, and nervous, his gaze darting back and forth as though he were watching an invisible tennis game—or looking for an escape route.

"James, were you with Jason last night?" I asked him.

"Don't say anything," Amber interjected. "Anything you say can and will be used against you in a court of law." I was impressed. Apparently, Amber watched more television than I realized.

Tate rolled his eyes.

"Look, you know the drill," Tate said. "We need to talk to James, to clear this up. I'm a reasonable guy. Just ask Jenny. But I have to cover all the bases. If James had nothing to do with it, he just needs to tell us his story, and we'll take it from there."

"He's a reasonable guy," I said, nodding my head.

"So let's just go down to the station and discuss this."

"The station? The police station? As in the police station where the *jail* is?" James turned white and his eyes started to roll around in his head.

"Um, is he okay?" Agent Keller asked.

"He's a little dramatic," I said. "James, snap out of it! It's going to be okay. They just need to find out what you were doing with Jason, what time you left him—you know, the usual stuff."

"The usual stuff?" James said, horror filling his voice. I was very confused by what was going on here. Why was James hooked up with Jason instead of the dreamy Enrique? Jason had appeared to be hitting on me. Were appearances deceiving?

"It's going to be okay," Tate said, very slowly as though speaking to an imbecile. "Let's just go take your statement, and then we'll get you back here."

"Whoa, whoa, take him? Take him!? I didn't think this through, did I? You can't take him. He has a class to teach. I have busted my butt to keep this conference running, and I'll be darned if anything, even a murder, is going to stop it!" The implications of everything that had happened, and what they wanted to do, finally hit me.

"Uh, Jenny, we really need to do this, and we are going to do this. I realize you are a little uptight about this whole thing, but this is a *murder* case." Tate was being very reasonable, but I was feeling very panicked.

"I can teach the class," Amber said.

"But you don't do choreography. I mean, you're a great dancer and all, and you're great at working with the students, but you don't make up dances. It's one of the things I like best about you. You are absolutely no threat to me." *Ulp.* Not sure I should have admitted that, but it was a stressful situation.

Amber just laughed. "She's right. I don't make up the dances. I just follow."

"I can help you," said Enrique, who had appeared in the doorway.

"Hello!" said James, suddenly not the slightest bit hysterical or woozy. "*You* teach tap. And *she* can't design a dance. This is a *jazz* class. What is wrong with you people?"

What was wrong with my life?

"They'll make it work, James," I said, pushing him toward Tate. "Go get this taken care of. Tell them what the heck you were doing with Jason Kutcher—and you best be sharing that story with me later, by the way—and clear yourself, and then get back here. It's the only thing you can do."

"Good advice," Tate said solemnly.

"Now, we have classes to teach," I said.

Marlys came through the door and looked around, eyeing Tate and Agent Keller, the other two cops, and James, Amber, and Enrique, and then she turned to me. "Your life is never boring. Some days, I wish I had even an ounce of the excitement you have. Today is not that day."

Then she turned around and walked out.

"I like her," Tate said, chuckling.

"I bet you do," I said with a big sigh.

I sent Marlys to check on Amber and Enrique about seven million times, while trying to keep my head together teaching the last of my three groups for the first session. Normally, when a traveling competition-convention came to town, they would have events on Saturday and Sunday, but because of our unique religious environment in Utah, all the events were packed into two days: Friday night competition and Saturday convention. So I had the entire evening ahead of me to work again with each group of girls, as did each other teacher.

The night would end with a parent showcase and awards and scholarships.

Bill better get his behind back here soon, or Enrique and I would be choosing awards and scholarships. I hadn't seen hide nor rabbit of Bonnie since early that morning. I suspected that was her normal behavior, and it probably added to Bill's stress. I just didn't understand why he would leave now, with so much on the line. Unless he really did have something to do with Jason's murder. But they'd seemed like good friends. But if he wasn't involved, why had he run? Unless he was hurt or murdered, in a Dumpster somewhere himself!

I looked out to a sea of young faces, all gazing at me expectantly, and I realized I had completely stopped moving as I tried to think the puzzle out.

Marlys came bustling through the door right then, alarm on her face. It took a bit to get her alarmed, so I immediately knew something bad had happened.

"Jenny," she stage-whispered. "We need you out here, now."

"What's going on?"

"Outside, please?"

I had one of the better dancers, who had picked up the routine pretty fast, come up and lead the girls through the steps while I hurriedly followed Marlys outside.

"What's going on?" I asked her as she led me down to the ballroom where Sal was teaching.

She opened the door and I stared aghast at the chaos. Little girls were running around screaming, and some were sobbing in the corner. In the middle of the floor, on the hardwood portion reserved for dancing, lay a woman. An old woman, rather large. Two Marriott staffers stood over her, fanning at her, while she moaned, but her eyes were closed. Sal stood to the side, fanning his own face, eyes wide.

"What the—?"

"It's James's mother," Marlys whispered. "We've called 911, but I thought you should know. She came down to see James work, and when she couldn't find him, came looking for you, but found me. When I told her James was at the police station, she just fell down."

"Well, why did you tell her he was at the police station?"

"What did you want me to say? It's not like I said he was under arrest and they were doing a full body-cavity search!" Marlys's voice wasn't quite as low that time, and I heard Sister Marriott—as she insisted on being called—mutter, "Cavity search . . . ooohhhh."

"Shhh," I told Marlys and then walked over to kneel over James's mother. Since I was hardly her favorite person,

I was a little nervous about how she'd react to me. "Uh, Sister Marriott? Are you okay?"

Nothing, except her eyelashes fluttered.

"Sister Marriott?"

Her left arm twitched and she moaned louder, and then she opened her eyes. "You. You . . . You are the reason. You . . ."

"I am the reason what?" I was beginning to suspect I knew where James had gotten at least some of his theatrical nature.

"You broke James's heart. You are a sinner, and you broke his heart and you . . ." She moaned again, then clutched her left arm.

I wavered between irritation and concern. Irritation weighed in pretty big, but her clutching of the left arm and the sweat beads on her forehead told me that something was probably really wrong. I was no doctor, but I had spent a short amount of time as an emergency dispatcher, and I had read the handbook about signs of a heart attack.

Two paramedics bustled into the room, followed by a couple of cops, and I sighed. This entire convention was just doomed. Somebody really did not want this to go well. Maybe God, but then again God didn't firebomb my car, or leave me threatening messages, or chase me with a snowplow. As far as I knew, God dealt in massive floods, lightning strikes, stuff like that. God was a bigwig. My tormenter was definitely small-time. But very, very irritating.

Of course, whoever was behind the threats had nothing to do with Sister Marriott's current condition. At least directly. The stress of hearing that James was anywhere near the jail had probably aggravated the heart condition I knew she already had, but I was sure they hadn't planned this. Just my luck!

A loud explosion boomed through the building and I jumped up, as did the paramedics, and all the girls began screaming again, running around, hands in the air, squealing like only little girls can do. The cops took off like a shot out of the door in search of the source of the explosion.

"What the hell was that?" one of the paramedics said, and then grimaced as Sister Marriott moaned her dislike of profane language.

"We better get her out of here," the other paramedic replied.

I left Sister Marriott with the paramedics, told Marlys to get to the girls I had been teaching, and followed the cops down the hallway to one of the ballrooms, where big plumes of smoke billowed out of the doorway.

"Holy crap," I said, aghast. This was the room where Amber and Enrique had been teaching. They had about seventy-five little dancers in their class, too. I pushed ahead to force my way through the door, without thinking, obviously. The policeman would not let me through, and then I heard a coughing noise and Enrique came out, Amber by his side, holding his hand. In turn, each of them had a line of girls holding on to hands, and all of them were coughing and crying, but they were alive and safe.

"Good thinking," I told Amber. "Getting them to hold hands and getting them out of there without leaving anyone behind. You didn't leave anyone behind, did you?"

She coughed. "No, we got them all. But it wasn't me. It was Enrique."

He just shrugged, and coughed into his hand, and the policemen began directing everybody out of the building.

"We need to evacuate the entire building. Everyone, please move in an orderly fashion outside," one of the officers shouted above the fray. Please. Have you ever told little kids to move in an orderly fashion? They responded as I thought they would, running and screaming toward the exit. All of them except the ones who were holding hands tightly, trailing behind Enrique and Amber in two lines.

More emergency personnel and police officers showed up, and as we were hurried out I saw the SWAT van pull up, along with a truck that said "Bomb Squad."

It was freezing outside, and the police officers were

pushing everyone to move at least one hundred yards away from the building, while more and more people streamed out of the hotel. Some were dressed in pajamas or had wet hair, and I knew they had been staying in the hotel and had to flee when the officers knocked on their door.

It was so cold a lady with wet hair was turning into a popsicle.

Little girls minus coats and gear were shivering, and an idea hit me. My studio was no more than four hundred yards away, on the other side of the Marriott parking lot. "Hey, my dance studio is right over there," I yelled at the officer who seemed to be in charge of keeping the hordes of people away from the hotel. "These people can wait in there and be relatively warm, at least until the evacuation is over."

I had Enrique, Amber, Marlys, and Bonnie—who I'd spotted milling among the hotel guests—help me round up all the little girls, and we told anyone else who was in earshot to walk over to the studio. I had left my purse in the staff room of the hotel, and so I didn't have my keys, but I knew Marco and Jack would be at their store right now and they could let us in.

As we started a little parade toward my studio, I saw the paramedics wheel Sister Marriott out on a stretcher and load her into an ambulance. I didn't have time to check on her, but I hoped this was a false alarm, that she was not really having a heart attack.

The police officer who seemed to be in charge continued to direct people toward my studio, and I led a big group, mostly little girls, across the parking lot.

Soon we were inside, relatively warm, some little girls sobbing and sitting on the floor, others running around and playing games, dashing in and out of each studio room and the bathroom. I was always amazed at how some children were so resilient and others so easily traumatized. More and more dazed hotel guests came into the studio, wandering around like zombies, wondering what had happened.

Marco and Jack walked around the room and checked on people, and paramedics were also present, checking on the girls who had been in the room where the bomb went off.

Bonnie stood back from it all, distaste on her sharp features, alternately surveying the people in the room and staring at her nails.

"Somebody really doesn't want this convention to be successful," Marlys said, standing by me as we watched the mess.

"I know. But who? Could it be Bill? I mean, he disappeared pretty conveniently, considering that we have now found a dead body. And nobody's seen him since. But he has his whole life invested in this. Why would he want it to fail? That makes no sense to me."

"What about his girlfriend, that Bonnie woman?" She pointed over to where Bonnie stood, now talking to the hotel manager and a police officer. She appeared to be shouting at them, although the room was filled with so much noise I couldn't hear her words.

"This is the first I've seen her since this morning, when she was all about canceling because of all the trouble. My money would be on her. Plus, she's a real pain, so I'd just like to see her get in trouble."

"But she has money invested in this, too, doesn't she?"

"As far as I know she does. But I might be wrong. Bill was a little unclear about it, but of course I never came right out and asked him, either."

Tate Wilson and Agent Keller walked into the studio and headed straight for me.

"It's like you have this black cloud that just follows you around," Tate said to me, irony lacing his words.

"I am not responsible for this. Someone is trying to make sure this convention does not finish up, which means it will be a huge disaster for Bill financially."

"I guess the thought it could be the missing Bill himself has crossed your mind, right?" Tate asked.

"Yes, the thought has crossed my mind, but it makes no

sense. I don't believe it. I think whoever is behind this is also behind his disappearance. I just hope he's not already dead. This is bad. Somebody could have been seriously hurt. Good thing I took over running this, or he would lose all the money and possibly face some lawsuits. Dance parents are psycho. They would all be screaming for refunds if I didn't keep this going."

"Uh, Jenny?"

"Yeah?"

"You *can't* keep this going. Someone just set off a bomb in a garbage can while seventy-five little girls danced close by. What if one of them had gone over to the can to throw something away, right as it exploded?"

"It was a bomb in a garbage can?"

"Yes, a low-level explosive, nothing major, but it could have really hurt someone if they had been close. And now the entire hotel is being evacuated. The bomb squad has to sweep for other bombs, and it will be hours before anyone is allowed back inside."

My mouth dropped open. "But I have to keep this going, Tate. I can't quit now. I can't let this convention not be successful. It's become more than just making it work for Bill. I need it to work for me. It's personal now."

"Honey," he said gently, "there's just no way to make it work."

"We can call my Auntie Vi. She'll get us a Mormon church to practice in, like she did in December, when they shut my studio down. She's great at that. She can help!" I was starting to sound a little frantic, I knew, but I just couldn't let this fail. I'd stepped in to run something really, really, big, and it had become terribly important to me to finish it. To show I was capable, and not just a neurotic, eccentric thirty-something dance teacher.

"Jen, it isn't going to happen," Marlys said. "It's one thing to do this with girls from our studio. We know how to contact all the parents, and it's easier to round them all up. But we can't feasibly move all these girls. And their records and contact information are all back at the hotel. We have to keep them here so when parents hear about the bomb, they can find their kids and don't panic."

"At this point, Jenny, it's not about dance. It's about keeping people safe," Tate said.

And I knew he was right. No one was going to dance anymore today. The person who had threatened me, bombed my car, assaulted me, had won. The Ogden portion of the Hollywood StarMakers Convention and Competition was a bust. It was over.

"I really tried to make it work," I said, a tear leaking out the side of my eye. Damn sneaky tears, always caught up with me when I least expected them.

"You did a good job," Tate said. "But someone very dangerous is out there, trying to sabotage this. And there's nothing you can do about it."

"Are you humoring me? It sounds like you are humoring me, and right now that would probably not be a good choice. I'm in short supply of humor right now, but I sure don't need any of yours!"

Tate just shook his head and pulled me to him, embracing me, then let me go and walked over to talk to a police officer who was asking the girls if they had seen anything or anyone suspicious.

I walked over to the door and looked across the stretch to where the hotel was. Through the thick fog I could hear sirens and could just make out the shapes of people traipsing over toward my studio, blurred figures led by a police officer. Behind him I saw a television crew and an anchorwoman from the local station, and I sighed.

I didn't want this to be over. The really stubborn and stupid side of me was screaming at the top of her lungs, "You can do this! Just finish it! And buy enough Top Ramen for a year!" But the other side of me—the one that didn't show herself enough—knew things had gotten too serious. It was one thing for me to be in danger. I was kinda getting used to that. It was another to jeopardize someone else's children.

And for whatever warped reason, that's where this was headed. Someone else could get hurt. Or die. Possibly a child. Maybe even one of my students. I couldn't let that happen.

I had to wave the red flag. Or was that white?

Didn't matter. It was over.

FIFTEEN

"So, do we talk to you about getting our money back?"

The dance mom standing in front of me was not one of mine, and as personally as I had taken this entire situation, the truth was, I was just a dance teacher, trying to help out an old friend.

"Nope. Talk to her," I said, pointing over to Bonnie, who had made herself right at home in my studio, pulling a chair out of the office and sitting in it.

Parents had started to file in a few minutes before, having been alerted by the news media that the hotel had been evacuated. Most were worried about the health of their children. A few were mostly worried about their money and their child's impending stardom, or lack thereof because of the cancellation of the rest of the convention. There would be no prizes and scholarships given away, and that would not sit well with some of these parents.

Tate and Agent Keller had gone back to the hotel, leaving us with a few patrol officers who were trying to keep the kids under control and the hotel patrons happy.

"Go talk to her," I said to the dance moms queuing up in line behind the first one who had asked me about a refund. "She's a partner in the venture. I'm just a teacher."

"Are they still going to give out scholarships?" asked a tall lady standing behind the first one, holding her seven-year-old daughter's hand. I remembered trying to teach the little girl a few simple steps, and I could tell the mom right now, based on that experience, this child would not ever be getting a scholarship to anything that involved rhythm or balance. But I wouldn't say that.

I pointed in Bonnie's direction.

"My daughter left her street clothes and her lunch bag in there. Do you know if I can just run in real quick and grab it?"

"Well, they're searching for more bombs, so I'm guessing probably not." *Unless you want to sneak past the SWAT team and take a chance on getting arrested for broaching a crime scene. That is, if you don't get blown into a million pieces first.*

Hmm. I was getting cranky. Must be dinnertime.

The woman's face dropped and she turned away, grabbing her daughter's hand and pulling her toward the exit.

A line had formed in front of Bonnie, and she glowered in my direction every chance she got as she reassured parent after parent that StarMakers would refund their money.

"I hope they had insurance for this kind of thing," I said.

"I'm pretty sure they would have to have some," Marlys said. The crowd began to dissipate as parents picked up their kids, but the hotel people were still sitting around, looking shell-shocked, as the all-clear had not been given to reenter the Marriott. About one hundred of the three hundred dancers were still milling around in the studio, too, so it was pretty crowded. Looking out at everyone, I wondered again about how much insurance the convention carried. It had to be enough to cover incidental medical costs. And there were no major injuries, thank goodness, only some cases of smoke inhalation.

"Insurance. Insurance. Someone wanted this to fail, and

I think Bonnie is looking pretty good for that. But would she get something from the insurance?"

"Granted, she isn't very nice, but why would she want it to fail?" Marlys asked, her natural skepticism showing through. "I mean, she has to have an investment in it, too."

"I would guess so, but I don't have details. But I bet Alissa could figure it out."

"Yeah, but she's been so busy, she's never around."

"Well, I'm going to call and leave her a message."

I walked into my office and found about six girls in there playing some sort of game under my desk. I only hoped it wasn't doctor, since they all looked pretty guilty when I discovered them. I shooed them out and shut the door on the noise.

I dialed Alissa's cell phone number, and it went right to her voice mail, which was usual these days. "Yo, Lissa, call me. Um, I'm at the studio right now. So call that number. I don't have my cell. And I won't be staying at my place tonight, so you probably will have to call me now, or you can call Tate's cell phone and . . . Oh, never mind. I'll call you later."

Why was my life always so complicated?

I jumped when the studio phone rang. "Jenny T. Partridge Dance Academy."

"Jenny, it's Alissa. Lots going on down there at the dance convention, huh?"

"Yeah, it just follows me wherever I go."

"Think it's related to the snowplow attack?"

"I don't know how it could not be related. And I had some ideas, but I need your brain to help me research them."

"Okay, but I'm working. I get off at 9 p.m."

"That works. Meet me at my place," I said.

"I'll bring the ice cream," Alissa answered.

Sixteen

THE Red Cross came in and served dinner, drinks, and snacks to the refugees still waiting in my studio. They had all been guests at the hotel, which I was guessing was not at full capacity—either that or some of the evacuees had left to find bars to drink in—because there were only about forty people remaining.

A steady line of girls using the studio phone had resulted in the last of the dancers being picked up about a half hour earlier. Marlys had gone home then, too. Bonnie had disappeared for parts unknown. Probably Salem. I didn't see her go, so I was unsure in what direction she was headed.

Around 7:30 p.m. a very tired Tate showed back up at the studio, shadowed by Agent Carson Keller. They'd been in and out several times as they investigated. The hotel building had been cleared for people to go back in, and most of the remaining guests who had taken shelter in my studio filed out, leaving behind a lot of garbage.

Sal, Enrique, and Amber were all in the other studio

room, playing cards on the floor, music wailing in the background. I swear they would have lit a bonfire and roasted marshmallows if it had been feasible. They'd been joined by a few hotel guests who didn't seem to be in any hurry to return to the Marriott.

"Boy, what a day," I said to Tate after he walked over to me and gave me a quick hug and a sexy smile. Even tired, he still set my heart racing. Agent Keller ambled over, too, giving me his killer grin, and I felt that guilt tickle in my tummy. Oh boy. I started talking quickly to try to cover my discomfiture, but I could see Tate's eyes narrow. He was a detective. He paid attention. He did not miss much. I was in trouble. "First James's mother keels over in the middle of the dance room, and then a bomb goes off and . . . Hey, where is James? I'm surprised he's not here, right in the middle of all the excitement."

Tate gave me a funny look.

"Tate? Why the look? Where is James?" For about half a second I'd been grateful for the diversion, until I realized that James really was missing. And he would never miss good drama. Ever.

"He's still at the station."

"Why would James still be at the station? You acted like it was all a formality. I mean, you and I both know he didn't kill anyone, especially Jason Kutcher. So why would he still be there?"

"Well, actually, Jenny, he's been booked into the jail. Now don't freak out, but there's a lot of evidence that James, is, well, the killer."

Telling someone not to freak out is sort of like saying, "I know you are a total nut job, and need medication, and will freak out the minute you hear this news, but I feel like I need to tell you not to freak out anyway, just because there might be a slim chance you will listen. Even though I know you won't."

"Uh, evidence?" I willed myself to be calm. "What evidence?"

"I can't share that with you right now, but just know that it's pretty firm evidence, and so I really have no choice. I have to hold him. They are going to press charges Monday morning."

My heart skittered a beat, and I considered Sister Marriott, who was probably in a hospital bed right now, clinging to life, moaning because her beloved James was not by her side. James wasn't the only one with a flare for drama.

I took a deep breath. "Okay, listen up, Tate. You and I both know that James is a pain in my patootie, and he drives me absolutely batty, but if there is one thing he is, it's a lover and not a fighter, and he sure is *not* a killer. On top of all that, he had absolutely no reason to kill Jason Kutcher. So they had drinks together. So what? That doesn't make him a suspect."

"Jenny, you've known me a few months, right?"

I just gave him one of those head-tilted, frowny-face, eyes-wide looks.

"There was some fairly substantial evidence, Ms. Partridge," Agent Keller said in his good-old-boy country accent. I suspected if he told me with that same tone that he was now going to pluck my eyeballs right out of my head, I'd just sigh with contentment and smile in agreement. But right now it wasn't working.

"This is dumb. You know James didn't do this," I said, pointing my finger and poking it into Tate's chest. He didn't much like that.

"No, I do not know James didn't do this. I know that people will do all kinds of things when pushed far enough. You should know that, too. And there was enough evidence to charge him."

"So how was he pushed far enough?" I asked. "He barely knew this guy. Last thing I saw he was flirting shamelessly with Enrique, and the next thing I know you're charging him with Jason Kutcher's murder. This makes no sense."

"Well, Enrique's not gay," Amber said. She, Sal, and

Enrique had heard the commotion and come into the main
room to listen in. Everybody loves a party.

"I'm not gay," Enrique said, nodding his head in confir-
mation. "Everyone thinks I am, because I have this whole
pretty-boy thing going on, but I'm straight."

"This is nuts. James said he was going out to have
drinks with you," I said, pointing to Enrique. "He was very
excited. He even winked."

"Well, I do drink. I'm just not gay. I was just being polite, and James lost interest anyway, especially after I asked
him to bring some of his single girl friends along."

"He's not gay," Amber said again, patting his chest in
approval and giving him loving glances coyly from under
her long lashes. Oh boy. I wondered how tropical-vacation
boyfriend was going to feel about this.

"Maybe it was a crime of passion," suggested Amber.
"Maybe James hit on Jason, and Jason was pissed, and
threatened him, and James defended himself, and suddenly, voilà, tap shoe to the head."

"How'd you know about that?" Tate asked, narrowing
his eyes at Amber.

"Jenny," she answered helpfully.

He turned to glare at me.

"Hey, nobody told me I couldn't say a thing about the
body I discovered. A dead body, I might add. I should be
in counseling. It was very traumatic. I had to talk to someone!"

"This is a very unusual case," Agent Keller said. "I feel
right at home here. Things like this happen in the South all
the time, but I always heard it was different out here."

"Never a dull moment when Jenny's around," Tate
grumbled, giving Agent Keller the evil eye. I swear, he was
getting grumpier by the minute.

"So, who's the killer?" asked a rotund bald man wearing a business suit. "Anybody have any ideas?"

"Who are you?" Tate asked curtly.

"Elroy Swanigan. From El Paso, Texas. I'm here in

Ogden on business. I have to admit, I wasn't looking forward to coming to Utah. It's usually fairly quiet and boring, but this has been a real excitin' evenin'."

Tate had reached his limit. I could see that in his eyes. I wasn't the best at gauging limits unless they were my own, so I guessed that if I could tell he was well past his, he must be barely holding on to his composure.

"All right, time for this party to break up. Hotel guests can go back to the hotel. Jenny needs to close up her studio and I need to get her home. She's had a long and busy day." Elroy and two other men, as well as a forty-something woman wearing a bathrobe, moaned their disappointment but finally gathered up their belongings and trudged out the door to head back across the parking lot into the Marriott Hotel.

That left Agent Keller, Sal, Enrique, Amber, and, of course, me and Tate.

Enrique and Amber said good night and walked out together, and Sal just gave me that beleaguered puppy-dog look, but I wasn't buying. "When will your ride be here, Sal?"

"Well, actually, I borrowed Sam's car. So I can drive myself. But I was having a pretty good time. More fun than I've had in months!"

"Understandable, since you were on a Mormon mission," I said.

"Well, I'm going to get going then, unless you have something else you want me to do?" He looked pretty hopeful.

"Nope, we're done here. Time for me to go home."

After Sal left, Agent Keller shook my hand, holding on to it a little too long, and earning a glare from Tate, and then excused himself.

I scurried around the studio, picking up mounds of garbage, food wrappers, abandoned dance clothes, shoes, and more from the floors. I piled all the garbage in my one big garbage bin, and tossed the shoes and clothes in the lost-and-found bin. Tate followed me around, picking up stray items, including a bra that he lifted by the strap, as though it might be carrying some horrific disease.

"How does someone get out of here and not notice their bra is missing?" he asked as he added it to the pile. "This place is a college boy's dream."

I laughed, and switched off the lights in the back studio room, then moved to the office. "I need to go get my purse and coat and stuff from the staff room at the Marriott."

"I'll walk you over," he said.

We locked up the studio and traipsed down the metal stairwell, and walked in companionable silence across the parking lot that led to the back entrance of the Marriott.

Fatigue filled my bones, and my eyes suddenly felt red and raw, my legs and arms weak.

I'd been running on sheer adrenaline for quite a few hours—really since the early morning hours. Now, with the necessity to make due gone, I was hit with reality—hard, like a punch in the face. James was in jail. His mother in the hospital. Bill and two dancers missing. The convention had been a big bust; I'd not been able to save it.

Someone had wanted badly for Hollywood StarMakers to go bust and had gone to great lengths to make sure it happened. And I was going to find out who. This was personal now. I did not like to fail.

We reached the Marriott door and I thanked Tate for walking me over, but he gave me a funny look.

"What?"

"Why don't you just ride home with me? I'll drive you back for Bessie tomorrow."

"Uh, that's okay. I think I need to go visit James's mother in the hospital and see how she's doing, since I feel kind of responsible. Not that she'll be glad to see me, but you know how it is. And then I'm going to go home, get into bed, and sleep until noon."

"Did you forget you're staying at my place?"

"Oh, well, that's not really necessary anymore, because

the person behind all this—who I believe is Bonnie, by the way—got what they wanted. The conference failed. We're both tired, and we both need sleep."

I also had plans to meet Alissa and do some snooping of my own, but I didn't intend to share that little item, knowing full well that Tate would not approve.

"How do you know the danger is gone? Maybe they didn't want to just end the convention. Maybe they wanted to hurt *you*. Maybe it's another psycho dance mom gone off the edge."

"Not likely. They mostly resort to calling me seventeen million times and leaving umpteen messages. Or sabotaging my hair. It's pretty rare that they turn violent."

A half grin quirked up one side of his mouth, but he was too tired to give it his all. I felt bad for him. He looked exhausted, and I knew, as nervous as James made him, that it couldn't have been fun arresting him.

"Well, I'll walk you inside to get your stuff and then escort you to the truck." He held open the door for me and we entered the warm hotel, the door suctioning shut against the cold behind us.

"You don't really think James is responsible for this murder, do you?" I asked him.

"My gut feeling? No. But the evidence . . . well, the evidence points to it. But I'm going to work this case until I either prove conclusively that he did or did not do it. I won't let him go down if he's innocent, Jenny."

"He's innocent, Tate," I said, my voice soft. "I've known James a long time, and he drives me crazier than anyone I know, but he is not a killer. He would never hurt anyone that way. And besides, whatever this is started before James knew anything about it. I mean, with the two dancers disappearing. He couldn't have had anything to do with it."

"I know that part doesn't add up. And if you're right about his innocence, then I'll just have to find the evidence to prove it. But Jen? Sometimes these things really do just happen."

He leaned in and kissed me. I was surprised he wasn't

fighting harder to have me come stay at his house. Further proof he really was exhausted, I thought. I *hoped*.

I stopped at the room that had served as staff quarters for the convention, and pushed open the door. My purse and coat were still there, as were James's things, Sal's coat, and Amber's purse. Now why hadn't Amber taken her purse?

Oh boy. I grabbed it, and James's, coat and bag and Sal's coat, and took them with me, so they wouldn't get stolen.

Tate walked me back outside, and I shivered in the cold and fog. We reached Bessie, and I opened the door and got inside. It took about four tries to get her started, but once she rolled over she roared. Loud.

"Lock your door at home," Tate said. "Both locks. And call me as soon as you are safely inside your house. And I'm waiting here until you drive away. I'm not convinced this is over, and we do still have three missing people."

"Four," I said.

"Four?"

"Bonnie. She skipped out of my studio pretty early on. I think she's the one looking good for this. I believe I mentioned that before."

He chuckled. "I know you don't much like her, but there is not one shred of evidence pointing in her direction."

I hoped to change that this evening, but again, that was something I didn't intend to share with Tate.

"Well, she really tried to get me to cancel the convention this morning," is what I said. "And she was absolutely no help at all in running it, and I would have expected that as Bill's partner, she'd have as much invested in it as he did. I mean does." I was alarmed to realize I had referred to him in past tense. I didn't know where Bill Flanagan had gone off to, but I didn't want to think he'd been murdered. I didn't want to believe he was dead, too.

"What a crazy case," he murmured, leaning into me and kissing me again, gently. I could barely hear him above the roar of the old truck, and the exhaust was starting to fill the cab. It was cold, and I was shivering, but Tate's kiss felt so nice I wanted to stay there forever. Well, maybe forever if it was just a little, tiny bit warmer.

"Get some sleep," I told him. "Then find the evidence to clear James. He didn't do this, Tate."

"I hope you're right," he said.

$\mathcal{S}$EVENTEEN

$\mathcal{M}$Y best guess was that James's mother had been taken to McKay Dee Hospital, just off Harrison Boulevard, so I put Bessie in gear and headed in that direction. I didn't really want to visit her, and undoubtedly, I was not the person she most wanted to see, either. But I felt an obligation since James was—I hoped temporarily—detained in the Weber County Jail.

James and I had done quite a few duos together when we were dancing with Camelot. We seemed to have a natural rhythm and cadence, and our bodies seemed to speak to each other, knowing just which way to move, almost anticipating it before it happened. Of course, that was the *only* speaking our bodies did. Obviously. But I had some pretty good memories of James and I together, as dance partners. No matter what trouble he got me into, I felt an obligation to him, and thus, his mother. *Sigh.*

I parked Bessie in a space pretty far away from the entrance, mostly because it was too hard to maneuver her into a tight spot next to other cars. That meant, of course, that I had to trudge a ways in the cold, thick fog.

I was on edge because of the experiences of the past few days, but the lights of the hospital were fairly bright and I could see my way to the front without too much trouble, although admit I spent a fair amount of time looking behind me. Was it possible the inversion was lifting a little? I was afraid to hope. We hadn't seen the sky in a very, very long time.

I entered the hospital through the main entry lobby and headed straight for the information desk, where a pink-jacketed elderly lady sat manning her station.

"Hi, I'm wondering what room Sister Marriott is in."

"Well, let me see. Hmm. Three Marriotts. What's her first name?"

"First name?" Perhaps I had never considered that "Sister" was not James's mother's first name. After all, being a non-Mormon, it was entirely reasonable that I should be ignorant of the culture, right? Okay, fine, I knew Sister wasn't her first name, but I was never curious enough to ask just what it was, and certainly never close enough to her to care.

"Um, well, see, I'm her home teacher, and I came to see how she was, but I have to admit, I've never called her by her first name. It's a respect thing, you know," I said, chucking the lady in the arm like we were fellow members of the Relief Society Club.

"I'm Catholic," she said drolly.

Darn! What were the odds?

"So, like, does it tell you what they are in for? I mean why they are hospitalized? Because she has a bad heart. Possibly a heart attack."

"Doesn't say. Just know there's three."

Apparently, since I didn't know the secret password, Sister Marriott's real first name, I was going to be kept out of the club yet again. That had happened to me a few times when I was a kid, and I didn't much like the feeling. I wracked my brain for a minute, trying to think of a time—any time at all—when James might have mentioned his mother's first name, but couldn't come up with one.

The Pink Lady just sat there and stared at me, waiting for me to give her the right name. Was this hospital policy? Were they supposed to make it this hard? Did this woman know my Grandma Gilly? Maybe they played bingo together. Maybe if Grandma Gilly had complained enough about me it would be like this woman knew me.

That wasn't possible, but she was giving me an evil eye just like Grandma Gilly did. It was making me very nervous.

"Oh, I just really don't remember. But she'll feel terrible if I don't just peek in on her. Can't you help me out here?"

The Pink Lady's lips thinned, and then she looked at her list and back up at me. "Two of 'em are guys. Yours must be room 402."

"Bless you," I said, sure that had to be the right thing to say. More evil eye. Maybe not. I scooted off in the direction of the elevator.

I was relieved when it opened up and I could disappear inside, hitting the button for the fourth floor. I swear, I could still feel the evil eye following me. How did these Catholic grandmas learn that stuff?

My Mormon grandma, Nana Marian, was gentle and kind, and sort of oblivious to the real world around her—but the key words here were "gentle" and "kind"! So what if she didn't know what day of the week it was half the time. At least she was nice. She fed me and brought me a copy of the Book of Mormon every month. You'd think I'd be the most learned person about Mormonism around. But you'd be wrong. I said she gave me a copy of it. I didn't say I ever opened one.

I got off on the fourth floor and followed the arrows in the direction of room 402. The closer to the room I got, the slower I walked. What was I supposed to say? The woman wasn't all that fond of me on a good day. On a day like this, she would probably be downright hostile. I know, I know, after dealing with psycho dance moms I should be able to deal with anything, but I found James's mother seriously scary.

And what if she was really ill? What if she were, *ulp*, near death? What then? What if she was comatose? *Yikes!* Hmm. Well, that one might work in my favor.

There was a bustle of activity at the nurse's station, and I was almost half expecting someone to yell, "Stop, fraud!" so I moved quickly into room 402, before anyone could detain me.

The room was dark and I couldn't see anything in the gloom in front of me. A small light on the wall did little to dispel the darkness, and I could hear a beeping sound and see some fluorescent green monitors across the room.

I also heard a whirr and hiss that kept repeating in a soothing rhythmic manner. I realized how tired I was as I inched forward.

"Sister Marriott," I called softly. "Are you awake?"

No answer, just the reassuring whirr and hiss.

"Sister Marriott," I called a little louder. "It's Jenny. I just wanted to check on you and make sure you are okay. I felt kind of responsible, since you were . . . well, I mean I was worried."

Still no answer.

"Sister Marriott?" I wasn't even using a soft voice anymore. But there was no response. I edged closer to the bed and squinted, trying to see by the light of the many monitors.

I could see the outline of a frail figure in the bed. Frail? Sister Marriott was not frail. She was kinda big, actually. It occurred to me right about then I was probably in the wrong room, so I started to back away from the bed, as quietly as I could, when someone jumped up out of a chair that I hadn't seen and started shrieking.

"Nooo, nooo, you can't have him. Nooo," and then the person started whapping at me with leathery weak hands. Now, normally, I didn't like getting slapped, even when it's by someone as ineffectual and weak as the person whapping me. But I was pretty alarmed and I think my heart kinda stopped there for a minute, so maybe the whapping was doing some good by getting it started again.

Suddenly the lights flipped on and a nurse was standing there, staring aghast at me and the small woman who was still whapping me.

"Mrs. Marriott," the nurse said, running forward and pulling her away. "What are you doing?"

"The angel of death is here to get him," the old lady moaned, pointing at me.

"I don't think that's the angel of death, Mrs. Marriott," the nurse said. "Who are you?" she asked me.

"I was looking for, uh, Sister Marriott. The lady downstairs obviously gave me the wrong room."

On the bed was a frail old man, obviously in his eighties, kept alive by a respirator. He was unaware of the commotion in the room. The woman who had been whapping me was at least as old as he was, tiny, and hunched over, but she had a very determined look on her face. I was awful glad I wasn't really the angel of death. I wouldn't want to get whapped to death. As frail as she was, it would take a while.

The nurse settled Mrs. Marriott back in her chair and put the blanket over her, then hustled me out of the room. "Sorry about that. She keeps watch every night. She's just determined she can keep the angel of death away from her husband. I've tried to tell her when it happens it just happens, but she's old. She doesn't believe me."

"I don't think I've ever been mistaken for the angel of death."

"You ought to try working on this wing. Happens to me about three times a week."

"I do not envy your job."

"Who did you say you were looking for?"

"Uh, Sister Marriott?" I still didn't know her first name. I didn't even know why I was trying.

"Oh, LaVerda? She's in my ward. They brought her in earlier today. But she went home hours ago. They ran some tests, and it wasn't her heart. She's as healthy as an ox. It was just a little heartburn, the doctor said."

"She doesn't have a bad heart?"

"No, she'll probably outlive us all."

When I thought of all the things I had forgiven or given into because of Sister Marriott's "bad heart," I started to boil. I was so going to kill James. When he got out of jail that is.

When I got back downstairs and the elevator door opened, I walked straight to the information desk, where the same Pink Lady sat, a smug look on her face.

"You are *not* nice," I told her. "You should be wearing black. That pink is a deceptive color. Pink is the color of niceness. You are not nice."

"You weren't being honest."

"How do you know whether I was being honest or not?"

"Because Mormon women don't have *home* teachers, they have *visiting* teachers."

"I thought you were Catholic."

"I converted after I met my husband. I grew up Mormon." Her mouth was a prim slash of disapproval.

"You must know my Grandma Gilly," I muttered as I headed out the front door.

"Gilly? Gilly O'Toole? We play bingo every . . ."

I knew it. I didn't wait to hear the rest. This woman probably knew my whole life story. Although my mom and dad seemed to like me okay, I'd turned out to be a huge disappointment where Grandma Gilly was concerned. I suspected she'd wanted a more Virgin Mary–like granddaughter, and she got stuck with me.

Now that *my* heart was working well, it was time to go to my apartment and meet Alissa. I wanted to see what we could dig up on insurance, Bonnie French, and maybe even Bill Flanagan, although I still wanted to believe he was innocent.

Since he wasn't here to defend himself. Where was he?

EIGHTEEN

"So, what's the plan?" Alissa asked me. We sat at the small desk where my home computer sat, mostly collecting dust. I did not much like the computer and suspected it felt the same about me, but my parents swore it was necessary for life in today's world, and so bought it for me and paid for my AOL access.

Once in a while it came in handy. This was one of those times.

Earlier, at my studio, the thought of insurance had set my rusty wheels spinning, mostly because I watched a lot of television, and often heard the words "insurance" and "scam" pretty close to each other. That stuff was always happening on *Law and Order*. And it made sense. What could be gained from shutting down the convention? It could only be one of two things: the destruction of Bill and his company, or the collection of some money. In my thinking, Bonnie was good for both.

Alissa turned on the computer and waited for it to boot up. I went into the kitchen and dished us out some ice cream—pralines and cream, yum!—and let her do her magic. She was very computer literate. Among other things. It wasn't fair. Tall, gorgeous, smart, computer savvy, and she could also shoot a gun. All I could do was dance.

I carried the ice cream back into the other room, then jumped as my doorbell chime sounded. I snuck a glance at my watch and saw it was nearly 10 p.m. Who would be at my door at this hour? James, maybe. He was always showing up at the worst times, but I knew where he was, and there wasn't much chance he'd been released from the Weber County Jail late on a Saturday evening.

Alissa pulled her gun out of her purse, and I jumped about ten feet—much farther than I had when the doorbell rang. "Put that thing away," I said.

"Hey, things have been crazy around you lately. Best to be prepared."

I shook my head, then walked to the door and looked through the peephole. I was surprised to see Agent Carson Keller standing there.

"It's the FBI agent assigned to the missing persons case—or is it cases?"

"Why would he be here this late?"

"Um, no idea. Should I open the door, or are you just going to shoot him through it?"

Alissa quickly walked to the desk and put the gun back inside her bag. I just shook my head again, then unlocked the door and opened it.

"Agent Keller. Hello. What are you doing here so late?"

"I had a few questions for you. I'm sorry to come over so late. I just got done with some paperwork, and some things occurred to me, and . . ." He looked up and saw Alissa, and his eyes widened in surprise. "Oh, hello."

"Agent Keller, this is my good friend Alissa Miller."

"Hello," she answered, giving him a simple smile, which, of course, meant it lit up the whole room. Alissa was like that.

"I'm sorry to interrupt the two of you, but I just was

wondering about something. Jenny, did Bill give you any indication he was panicked, or might have had a reason to run? I know the two of you are old friends. Is this in his nature? Is he the kind of guy that takes off when the going gets tough?"

"No. Never. He's always been very reliable. Uh, well, as reliable as a dancer can be, anyway. And he's spent years building up this business. He wouldn't just walk away."

"Well, all the indicashuns we're gettin' point to a real drinking problem." He must be tired, because his Southern accent was very pronounced right now, much more so than I had ever heard it. "His girlfriend told us she'd even recommended rehab."

"She's who I would look at," I said to him. "I told Tate the same thing. That Bonnie is trouble, with a capital 'L.' And she's gone, too."

"Capital 'L'?"

"Uh, loser." Sometimes my mouth got ahead of my brain. You might have noticed.

"And what do you mean, gone? I just talked to her about an hour ago. I don't think she's gone."

"Well, she left my studio after the hotel was evacuated," I said. "And she's hardly the outdoorsy type, so she had to go somewhere. Maybe she has Bill and the two dancers held captive somewhere. Is she from around here?"

Agent Keller chuckled. "Boy, you don't like her much, do you? The woman has no criminal record, and there's no indication she is involved in this at all. But to answer your question, yes, she was raised in Utah. I believe she's been living in California for more than ten years now, though. Why do you think she had something to do with it?"

"Because she is *not* very nice," I said, then realized how stupid that sounded. Sort of like I was one of my young dancers. *Great. Very mature, Jenny.* "And, well, she didn't get along with anyone, as far as I could see. She wasn't much help to Bill. She tried to cancel the convention, too. Why would she do that?"

"Maybe because she didn't want to do the work involved?" Alissa said. "I mean, it sounds, if anything, like she just didn't want the hassle of it."

"I think there's more to it than that. I'd just look at her very, very closely, if I were you."

"And you're sure there's nothing about Bill Flanagan that you can think of, anything at all, that would explain his disappearance?" Keller asked.

"No. This was his life. He wouldn't willingly walk away. When you get this involved in dance, you don't just leave it behind. I know I can't, and I know he couldn't."

"Even if he killed somebody?"

"Well, since you guys already have someone under arrest for that murder—someone who would not be able to kill a fly, by the way—I would think no, he wouldn't run. And Bill's not capable of murder, either. This is all so stupid. Why do these things keep happening around me?"

"Keep happening around you?" If Agent Keller had had antennae, I knew they would be twitching right about now.

"Last Christmas one of my dance moms got a little whacky and sorta killed another one, and then there was the whole witness protection thing, and . . . well, you know."

"No, I don't, but I would love to hear about it. But maybe another time." Agent Keller raised his eyebrows, in a look I couldn't interpret, and then said, "Well, I guess I'll get out of here. I just wanted to see if you thought there was anything else about Bill I should know."

"Your cell phone does not work?" Alissa asked drolly.

"I like to do my legwork in person. You get more out of it if you can see the person's face," he said, giving her a serious but thoughtful stare. "Part of my job is reading people. Sounds like you do that yourself. Are you with the force?"

"I'm at the academy right now," she admitted, now not looking quite so sure of herself. I knew she was still a little insecure about her transition from 911 dispatcher—a position that didn't really get the highest respect from officers, even though the people who worked it were responsible for every officer's safety—to cop.

I also knew, because she'd shared it with me, that she was worried she would forever be known as that "dispatcher" who got too big for her britches.

"Cool," was all Agent Keller said. "Good for you. I know a lot of people who have worked their way up from dispatch, and they end up being the best cops, because they know every end of the system."

"Thanks," she said, beaming a little bit.

"Well, I'll be going now," he said. "Sorry to bother you so late. Good night, Jenny. Good night, Alissa."

He headed out the door, and I shut it behind him, shaking my head.

"Why are you shaking your head?" Alissa asked.

"I just don't know why he came over. I mean, didn't that strike you as a little strange? Coming over here, this late?"

"Yep. Totally out of character. I wonder if he was wired?"

"Why would he be wired? You think he's been drinking too much coffee? Oh wait, you mean, wired, as in wearing a wire?"

"Yep."

"What's going on?"

"Look, Jenny, something is not right here. He knew who I was."

"Of course he knew who you were. I introduced you."

"No, he looked surprised to see me, number one. Two, he said he admired my desire to work my way up from dispatcher. Remember? Except I never told him that. And we've never met. Unless you told him that."

I thought back. "No, can't say that I've had that many conversations with him at all. And they were mostly about missing people, and Bill. So, no, I didn't tell him."

"So, he comes here pretty late, and you don't know him all that well, and frankly, that's not kosher behavior for an FBI agent. I mean, they learn to cover their butts, and they don't open themselves up for false accusations. Which, in all reality, could happen, if he showed up at the wrong female's house, and she cried rape or molestation."

"I would never do that!" I said, aghast.

"You would if it were a legitimate complaint, wouldn't you?" she said.

"Where are you going with this? I'm so confused."

"I'm not going anywhere. I'm just trying to figure out why FBI Agent Carson Keller just showed up at your door, late at night, asked us a few silly questions he could have asked over the phone, and then left. Several things come to mind. One, they suspect you are involved in something, and he was wearing a wire. Two, he's hot for you and thought this was an appropriate way to express it. Or three . . . Hmm, not sure what three is."

"He is *not* hot for me. That would mean Tate, Bill, and Agent Keller all at once, and that kind of stuff only happens to you. Not me."

"Bill?" she asked.

"Long story. James claims he's carrying a torch for me, or something stupid like that."

Alissa just raised her eyebrows.

"He's *not*," I said firmly.

"Who are you trying to convince, me or you?" she asked.

"Let's just search out Bonnie, and insurance scams, okay?" I knew I would never win in this conversation with Alissa, and so I wasn't going to try.

Bill was *not* carrying a torch for me. And Agent Keller? I was not going there.

W E searched for about two hours and found all kinds of information on insurance, insurance for dance companies, cancellation insurance, and more, but nothing that jumped right out and screamed, "Here's the scam, Jenny." Why couldn't life be easier?

"We haven't learned much," I said dejectedly, leaning back in the hard kitchen chair I'd pulled up next to Alissa's more comfy desk chair—another item garnered by my dad at one of those school district sales. Since she was the computer guru and I had a hard time finding the On switch, it only made sense she got the comfortable chair and the driver's seat.

"Well, we are searching blind here. I looked Bonnie French up on Google but didn't find anything interesting."

I'd put a lot of hope in the computer and Alissa, because the last time I'd found myself in a bind, we'd discovered some very important information on this very computer. Not today.

It was after midnight and my eyes were red, raw, and tired. "I guess this is going nowhere."

"At least for now. Although it could still be an insurance scam, depending on who is on the policy and what they were insured for. For example, did the cancellation insurance just cover the refunds of tuition, or did it cover payroll, salary, operating expenses, and all the rest? And was there a clause for the damage from an incident, like a bombing, in it? If that existed, then the obvious suspects would be Bill and Bonnie. But we have no way of knowing. We would have to find out that information before we could really do anything else. Did Tate tell you anything about it? Is he looking into it?"

"No, he doesn't tell me anything. About anything."

"That sounds like Tate."

Four words. That's all it took, and I was back worrying about just how well Alissa knew Tate and what their relationship had been in the past. I'd always been too chicken, or too stubborn, or maybe too in denial to actually ask.

Maybe I didn't really want to know. No, it was time to take this cow by the horns and get some answers.

"Just how well do you know Tate?" I asked Alissa.

"I wondered if you were ever going to ask me about that."

"I wondered if you were ever going to offer it up."

"I didn't see the point," she said. "But I knew sooner or later it would drive you crazy. You'd open Pandora's box, just because you couldn't stand not knowing what was inside."

"Who the heck is Pandora, and what does she have to do with this?" I asked, totally confused.

"It's an old myth. But the moral of the story is, are you sure you want to open the box, because once you do, you can't put the things back in it."

"I'm pretty good at packing things away," I retorted. "Tell me."

Alissa shook her head and then started talking. "We dated. Right after I started at the sheriff's office and he came on as a deputy. We were pretty close for about a year, right up until the time he discovered that I not only liked his gun, but I intended to carry one myself. He pulled some chauvinist crap about how no woman of his would ever be in the line of fire, and I made it easy on both of us. No relationship, no problem."

"And that's it?"

"Obviously, I summarized."

"Do you regret it?" I knew my voice had gone timid and soft, but I needed to know. Would Alissa ever come back looking to mend those broken gates with Tate?

"Sometimes," she answered honestly. "That's probably why I'm not so nice to him. Because he's basically a very decent, honest, hot guy. But with Tate Wilson, there is no two-gun relationships. It wasn't meant to be."

He wouldn't have to worry about that gun thing with me, that was for sure. Although lately various dance accessories had been used as deadly weapons, too.

"Are we okay?" Alissa asked me. "You understand it's over and done with, and we've both moved on? I would never hurt you, Jenny."

I understood. But I also knew the ghost of Alissa Miller in any relationship would be a hard one to shake.

A sharp, sudden pounding on my door made us both jump. Then the doorbell rang several times, insistently.

"Sheesh, who the heck is that?" I muttered as I walked over to the door, Alissa trailing me.

I looked out the peephole and jumped back, gasping.

"Who is it?" Alissa asked, alarm in her voice.

"It's the she-devil. Bonnie French."

The witch had come to pay me visit. How had she found my apartment?

NINETEEN

I slowly opened the door and made sure my coolest, calmest dance-teacher look was pasted on my face. Bonnie didn't even give me a chance to whip off some witty comment about her unwanted presence.

She pushed past both me and Alissa, and began pacing the length of my living room.

"Where is he?" she ranted. She headed down the hallway and threw open the bedroom door, then the bathroom, checking out each room, and finding them empty. She returned to us and stood in front of me, hands on her hips, glaring.

Her hair was a bit in disarray, but her clothes were immaculate. So was her makeup. Only the hair went with her wild manner.

"Where is who?" I asked.

"You are aware you were not invited in and that constitutes trespassing, right?" Alissa said to her.

"Who are you?" Bonnie replied. "Her attorney? The way she lives her life, she sure needs one."

My arm went up reflexively. Just two minutes around the woman and I was ready to deck her. She brought out some violent tendencies in me I didn't know I had. Alissa caught the arm, and I yanked it away and lowered it. I knew I shouldn't hit Bonnie French, but she really, really deserved it.

"Where is he?" she said again. "Where are you hiding him? I knew coming here was a mistake. I knew we should never have added Ogden to our list of cities to visit."

"If you mean Bill, he is not here," I said. "I haven't seen him or heard from him."

"Oh please. In trouble, he'd turn to you. I know he would. It was always, 'Jenny did this,' and 'Oh, Jenny did that.' All I ever heard was Jenny, Jenny, Jenny. I'm not dumb. When he disappeared, I put two and two together. You're hiding him. I know it."

"First of all, why would it be necessary for him to hide at all? Is he afraid of you?" That I could see.

"He's hiding because he's a stupid coward. Whenever anything goes wrong, he runs. And this whole thing has been wrong from the day we landed in Utah."

"Look, Bonnie, I don't know why you think I've seen him, but I'm telling you now, I haven't. I have no idea where he is."

"You're lying." She was still staring at me, wild-eyed, but I swore I could see a teardrop in the corner of her eye. Maybe Bonnie the Beast was human.

"I'm not lying. I don't know where he is, and Bill and I are nothing but friends."

"You really don't know?" Her face crumpled a bit, as though she'd been so sure she would find Bill with me. Or that I would give her a thread to go on.

"I don't know where he is."

She full-out cried then, tears pouring down her face, Alissa and I standing there staring at her. I felt like I should comfort her, but that would involve touching her, and I really had no desire to do that. I steeled myself, and reached out and patted her shoulder, hoping she wouldn't bite me.

"Uh, it'll be okay, Bonnie. He'll show up. The police are looking for him. It'll be fine."

"It won't be fine. It won't. He's with someone else. I know him. At least if it had been you, I would know it wouldn't last. No man would leave someone like me for someone like you."

I jerked my hand away. She had bitten me, with big, sharp words. Comfort time was over.

"Please leave," I said crossly, pointing to the door.

She wiped at her tears as she went to the door, then she turned and hissed at me, "If I find out you are lying, I will hunt you down and I will hurt you."

"That sounds like a threat," Alissa said calmly.

Sounds like a threat?

Bonnie slammed the door behind her, and I turned to Alissa and just shook my head. "I really hate her."

"I can see why."

Why was she so threatened by me? I was worried about Bill, too, but why did he hold this candle for me? Was it because we had spent so many hours in the dance studio together, rubbing each other's sore muscles or commiserating about a part we didn't get?

"I really wanted that role," I cried as he held me tight in his arms. We were in his small studio apartment in Salt Lake City. And the role of Carmella in the Spanish sequence had gone to someone else. Someone tall and dark and leggy. I knew I was not that type of dancer, but I had tried to overcome my height, my hair, my coloring with my passion for it. It hadn't been enough.

"You deserved it, Jenny. But Olden was always going to give it to Ginnie. He created it for her, with her in mind. You knew that."

"But I thought I could convince him."

"You sure convinced me," he said softly, pulling my chin up toward him. "You were the best. You were on fire. You did better than she did. But it was made for her, so you would never have won. That doesn't mean you didn't score the

*real victory. You took a role meant for a tall, dark-haired
señorita and made it yours. You should be proud."*

*I cried a little more and then settled into his arms, and
we talked about our dreams and aspirations.*

*"Someday, I'll have my own studio, and you can teach
for me. We'll be partners, both in life and work. A big studio, with hardwood floors and hundreds of students, and
people clamoring at our door to get in."*

It had sounded so good. But when our love faded away,
so had the plan. Bill was not a one-woman man. He cheated,
I cried, we moved on.

AND now he was with Bonnie, who could care less
about dance, and his dreams. I still cared. I wanted him to
succeed, and I'm sure he knew that. And I was really worried about him.

"I wonder where he is? I hope he's okay."

"I hope so, too, Jenny," Alissa said gently.

TWENTY

I woke up Sunday morning with a raging headache, located right between my eyes. I blamed Bonnie the Beast, combined with a late night and a restless sleep full of nightmares in which Bonnie alternately tried to steal my studio and all my students, and then went after Tate.

I didn't like my bed much right now. I preferred Tate's, with its nice expensive sheets and down comforter, fluffy pillows, mattress from heaven, and most of all, with him in it.

And he hadn't called me last night. Okay, so I was supposed to call *him*, but I thought he would call, check on me and make sure I was okay. But he hadn't. I wished that didn't bother me.

I got up and padded to the bathroom, startling myself as usual as I looked in the mirror. My hair did not do restless evenings well, and thanks to my recent haircut, courtesy of psycho mom Carmen, it was even worse than usual, with short, shaggy pieces standing up all over my head.

I showered and calmed my hair as best I could, and then dressed in a nice pair of jeans and a cute (and warm) sweater that Marlys had given me for Christmas. I lightly applied some makeup, and then I walked into my kitchen, opening the fridge to find that, of course, I had nothing in it. What was new? And the money from Bill wasn't going to come now, either. Unless there really was insurance that covered that kind of thing. I knew that Bonnie had told the dancers' parents they would be getting refunds, at least for the convention, so I figured there had to be something. But even if there were, that could take months. Why did things always work out for me this way?

I went back into the bathroom and brushed my teeth, then grabbed my jacket and my purse, making sure my phone was inside, and headed out into the dismal morning, complete with fog and arctic temperatures. It had been fourteen days without seeing the sun. That was two weeks! Surely this inversion would lift soon.

I shivered as I started Bessie up and waited for her to quit hiccupping so we could drive off.

Alissa had arranged for me to get in to see James. It was not a visit I was looking forward to, but it was a necessary one.

The Weber County Jail was not a place I spent a lot of time, nor did I want to. I suspected that it was one of the last places on earth, probably right there next to Kmart, that James wanted to be.

So I was pretty surprised when they brought him up to the glass partition and he sat down, looking freshly scrubbed and clean, and in very good spirits.

"Are you okay?"

"Oh yes, I'm doing okay. Not great, but okay."

"You look pretty good."

"Puh-leeze. I had to use regular soap on my face, and it was harsh. And shampoo? Oh my, let's not go there. And this?" He tugged at his orange clothes. "Not attractive. No one could look good in this. Well, almost no one."

He had a strange look in his eye, and I squinted at him. "What is going on with you, James? I figured you'd be hysterical, sobbing, begging me to get you out of here."

"Well, normally, I would not be enjoying this at all. But I have met the most lovely man, and he is a biker. He rides a Harley, Jenny. And he is gor-geous. Just your type, but I saw him first. Long, dark black hair, dark blue eyes. And the stories he tells. I've always been intrigued by bad boys, and he is as bad as they come."

I sighed. "James, this is not summer camp! You're in jail." And should I really have to remind him of that?

"I know, but it's just not as bad as I thought. Although I am anxious to get out of here. Do you know when I can expect to be released?"

"No earlier than tomorrow, I'm afraid. You have to go before a judge, or something. Unless we find evidence that absolves you."

James looked at me intently. "It wasn't me, Jenny."

"I'm well aware of that, James."

"I was with Jason, and we had a drink, but he was perfectly straight and perfectly boring, and I left, and forgot my dance bag."

"Why did you forget your bag?"

His lips tightened up, and I knew that what he was about to tell me—or not tell me, as the case may be—was not going to be something I wanted to hear.

He stayed silent.

"James, why did you forget your bag? Where did you go?"

He sighed heavily and then looked around, as though someone might be listening in. "I met Cullin there, okay? He dropped in with a few friends, and one thing led to another and—"

"James!" I said, not sure what was worse: the fact he had hooked up with the dastardly Cullin, a man who was living a lie, married with two children and courting James on the side; or the fact that he had hidden this from the police, most likely to protect Cullin. "You have to tell the police. You have an alibi. Cullin can get you out of here."

"It would ruin his life, Jenny. If his wife found out, she'd divorce him, and his kids would be devastated."

"Well, it's certainly better that yours is ruined then, since you only have your mother to worry about!" I was pretty glad I didn't have to tell him that his mother was in the hospital, due to the fact he'd been arrested.

He gasped, and put his hand to his mouth. "Does she know?"

"Yes, she knows, since she came down to see you at work and someone let it slip you'd been arrested."

"Oh no, her heart. This could kill her!" His face blanched.

"She'll be okay," I said gruffly. "I talked to a nurse at the hospital, and she said your mother is perfectly healthy. Nothing wrong with her heart at all."

All James heard was the word "hospital."

"She's in the . . ." He could barely speak, his breath coming rapidly, and I had no way to get a paper bag to him, even if I had one. Which I didn't.

"Breathe, James. She is home, fine. There is *nothing wrong with her heart*."

His breathing slowed. "She's fine? Her heart's fine?"

"Yes, she's fine."

"Oh, this is just a huge mess. A huge mess. I should have just told the truth, Cullin be damned."

"I agree," I said. "Okay, I've got to go, but I wanted to make sure you were alive and well. Go back to your biker, but be careful. I doubt he's gay, and since this is the Weber County Jail, and you're being processed, I doubt he's a long-timer, either, desperate for, uh, companionship. You don't want to get beat up before we get you out of here." I didn't tell him I intended to get him out today. Cullin was going to have to own up to something, for once in his life.

"Thanks for coming, Jenny. You're a true friend." He got a little teary, and I decided to scat before the scene got mushy.

"Look, I'm going to get you out of here, but on one condition."

"What's that?"

"You tell your mother the truth. She doesn't have a bad heart. She might even already know that you're gay, which is why she is keeping up the charade of bad health. She wants to keep you in line. Maybe she thinks she can change you. Whatever it is, the time has come to be honest."

"I can't tell her, Jenny."

"Well, at the least, you can tell her that you and I will never be an item, or married. Ever." I thought about Cullin. "Actually, I have another condition."

"What's that?"

"No more Cullin."

"Jennifer—"

"I'm not kidding. If I get you out of here you have to promise. You will stay away from him for good. And get your mother off my back, too."

"Well, I really intended to do that all along, Jenny. It's just not that easy—"

"James!"

"Okay, I promise."

"Now, I gotta go, James."

"Jenny?"

"Yes?"

"Thanks. I owe you."

"Yes, you do."

$\mathcal{A}$FTER I left the jail I pulled my cell phone out of my purse and dialed Tate's number. He answered with a sleepy hello.

"You're still in bed? It's 10 a.m." Although I couldn't blame him. I wanted to be in his bed right now, too. Preferably with him in it.

"Out all night on a case. And you didn't call me. What's up?"

"Doesn't sound like you were too worried. We need to talk about James. Would you like to meet me for coffee?"

"No," he said, his voice a throaty growl.

"Oh."

"What I would like is for you to come over here, now, and climb into my bed with me. I'll make you warm in places you've never imagined. I'd give up sleep for that."

I knew I was blushing, and was glad the street was deserted, since it was a Sunday morning. During an inversion. Fog everywhere. Probably no one could've seen my face anyway. Good thing.

I hesitated for a minute. Oh, who was I kidding. Mystery Man or not, this was going to happen. It was inevitable. I didn't know what tomorrow would bring, but I was diving in.

"Jenny?" he said.

"I'll be there in twenty minutes."

TWENTY-ONE

THERE were a lot of things about Detective Tate Wilson that I really, really liked. I liked the way his black hair fell over his forehead, just slightly, but enough to make him continually push it away. I liked how if I looked close I could see some silver starting to show through. I liked the way his blue eyes lit up when he studied me, and I liked the way the scar over his eye made him look slightly dangerous.

Maybe, like James, I really liked bad boys, and police officer or not, Tate was a bad boy—tamed. It was there, in the scar and in the eyes. And there was the whole Mystery Man thing he had going. Tate was anything but an open book.

I let myself into his condo with the key I still had. I reminded myself, as qualms of fear shook me, that he had not asked for this key back. And that meant he was not afraid I would show up, suddenly and unexpectedly, and find him with someone else. I think.

I walked toward the bedroom and then heard running

water coming from the bathroom. He walked out and I gasped, as all he wore were a pair of boxers and a big smile. His hair was recently combed, but he sported a dark shadow of beard, and his lids were low, his eyes dark and full of intent.

"Why don't you stay awhile, Jenny," he said, and his voice sent shivers up my spine. "We got interrupted the other night. This time, I don't intend for that to happen."

He walked over to me and reached out, pulling off my coat. He grabbed my sweater by the bottom and then pulled it up over my head, dropping it on the floor next to my coat. That left me wearing only a small camisole over my bra, my jeans, and under that, a thong. I'd taken to wearing thongs to avoid panty lines in my dance clothes, but it seemed it would serve a different purpose today.

He stopped, and looked at me intently.

"What?" I whispered. Not for effect, but because that was the most sound I could manage.

"You're shaking," he said softly. "Are you okay with this?"

Was I okay with this? He moved forward and kissed me, gently at first, then harder. Spirals of excitement swirled in my stomach. Oh yeah, I was okay with this.

He reached for the button on my jeans, expertly popped it open, and then pulled the zipper down as he leaned in to kiss me. Slowly, he moved down, kissing first my neck, then the vee between my breasts, and in a straight line down to my belly button.

How did he do that? Keeping a straight line, I mean. At least I thought it was a straight line. My thought processes were starting to get a little fuzzy.

He picked me up, sweeping me off my feet for the very first time in my life, and walked me to the bed, gently setting me on it. He helped me shimmy out of my jeans, a wolfish, feral smile on his face as he eyed my skimpy underwear choice.

"This I like . . ."

"You like?"

"Yes, let's take it off . . ."

"But I thought you liked it . . ."

"It's in my way."

"It's not big enough to be in your way . . ."

"It's in my way. I want to see all of you."

He got his wish.

And I got more than a few of mine . . .

TWENTY-TWO

I could almost see the headlines of the Grandma Gilly Gazette. Jenny T. Partridge is a bad woman! It would do no good to argue with her. She'd been convinced I was bad news since the day I dressed up her Virgin Mary statue in my Barbie doll's bootie shorts and halter. It was a tight fit for the clothes, but I made it happen. Afterward, my behind was sore for a week.

I didn't care right now, though. I was an adult. She couldn't spank me. As long as I didn't get close enough, that is, and I stayed far, far away from Grandma Gilly.

"What are you thinking about?" a lazy-lidded Tate asked me as he propped himself up on one arm, staring at me.

We were still in his bed. I think it had been three hours, but boy had it passed fast.

"Grandma Gilly and her Virgin Mary statue."

"Uh, why would you be thinking about that?"

"Never mind. Tell me something about you. Something that I don't know, which pretty much opens up an entire spectrum. You've seen me in all kinds of weird and vulnerable positions, and you've even met my mother and my Auntie Vi, and my dad and cousins. I don't know anything about you."

"Your cousins scare me." He'd had a run-in with my cousins Kim and Terri, thirty-something single Mormon girls looking for love, when they'd staged an intervention of a sort for me, because they suspected me of poisoning the missionaries. Long story. He'd also pulled a gun on my Auntie Vi, and I knew I'd love him forever just for that. *Ulp. Love.*

"You're changing the subject," I said.

"No, really I'm not."

"Yes, you are."

"Fine, what do you want to know?"

"You grew up an only child, right?"

"Right."

"You have a half sister."

"Right."

"And her name is?"

He hesitated for a minute, then answered. "Malece."

"And she lives with her mother?"

"Right now, she is currently living with my grandmother—when she comes home."

"In Brigham City?"

"Yes, in Brigham City."

This conversation was not going well. It was like pulling teeth. "And she doesn't come home a lot?"

"She just turned eighteen. She thinks she's an adult."

"Well, technically, she is."

"She's not very mature."

"And what is she like?"

"Sullen, dark, angry."

"Do you have some pliers?" I asked him.

"Huh?"

"Well, it might be a little easier to get more than four-word answers out of you if I had a pair of pliers to pry them out. Or maybe some truth serum. You're a cop; don't you have some of that laying around?"

Tate chuckled. "It's just something I don't like talking about, Jenny. It's personal."

"Yeah, like your mom and dad, and your friends, and basically every part of your life. All personal. While I lie here, naked in your bed, realizing that your lack of getting personal means that what just happened means it was only about sex, because God forbid we should get personal." I was surprised when a tear rolled down my cheek, followed by another and then another, and I wiped at them furiously and turned away, flopping down on the pillow.

Tate reached out and pulled me into him, but I refused to turn to face him. Okay, it was just sex. I could handle that. I was a big girl.

Why did I want it to be so much more? I'd been alone for a lot of years now. Alone was less complicated. I could handle this. *Stop crying!*

"Please don't cry," he whispered into my hair. "This is hard for me. I'm just not the kind of person that shares things. I've always been this way. Quiet and private. My mom's the same way, which has led to her denying her husband ever had an affair, or has another daughter. She's grown cold from the pressure of trying to keep it all in. My parents no longer talk, although they live in the same house. I don't want that. Even though I don't talk about me, I want you to know me. It's just something I have to work on. Okay?"

"Okay," I muttered, a little mollified by his explanation. I sniffled for a minute, then said, "So what does your dad do?"

He burst out laughing. "You crack me up, Jenny T. Partridge."

"What?"

"Nothing. My dad is a real estate developer and a rancher. My mother is a professional Mormon debutante, at least as far as Mormons have debutantes. But she's the queen bee of Brigham City. A little different from how she acts at home."

"Okay, I feel better."

"Because you know what my father does?"

"Because I know something. Because I'm not as worried you are going to just . . . Never mind."

"Jenny, I am not going to just."

"Just what?"

He cracked up again. "Let's make some food. I'm starving."

WE sat at his kitchen table eating a very good omelet off one shared plate. He'd made toast, too. I slathered my piece with blackberry jam and he smiled as he watched me eat.

"You were hungry," he commented.

"I'm always hungry," I said. "I think it comes from worrying where my next meal is going to come from. After I pay my studio rent and my apartment rent, and the phone and utilities, I have nothing. Literally nothing. If it weren't for the charity of my parents and friends, I'd starve to death."

"So why do you do it?"

"Teach dance?"

"Yeah."

"Because it's the only thing I'm good at."

"I don't believe that."

"It is. I tried the sheriff's office, as a 911 dispatcher, and I hated that, and I was also very, very bad at it. I worked for a day in a dentist's office, but I messed up all the appointments, and they asked me not to come back. I can't type. I can answer the phone, but once I pick it up, if it ain't about dance, I can't help you. In short, this is all I can do."

"I still don't believe you. I think you do it because you love it."

"Yeah, I do love it. I love it a lot. Except when the psycho moms are on a rampage. Then I wish I were back working for the dentist."

He chuckled, and leaned in and kissed me. He smelled like egg and toast, and warm, yummy man. I shivered with delight.

"You cold?"

"No, for the first time in weeks I'm really, really warm."

"I'd say you're hot."

I blushed, and took another bite of the omelet. Then I thought of Bill, and the other missing dancers, and a strong jolt of guilt gushed through my body. How could I be here, eating, enjoying carnal activities with Tate, when Bill was missing? What kind of person was I? As usual, I did not want to know the answer to that. But the guilt wouldn't go away.

"What happened? You just went so somber."

"I was just thinking about Bill, and Twila and Eldon, and wondering where the heck they are. What if they are hurt? What if they are . . ." I stopped and gulped.

"Jenny, you have to leave this to the professionals, okay? This isn't your job, and you are way out of your league here. We have a lot of people looking for them, and so does the FBI."

"I know, but Bill and I, we go way back. I mean . . ."

He frowned a little bit and then leaned forward. "Do you still have feelings for him?"

"God no," I said, astonished he'd think that. "I mean, we had a lot of fun, but it was always just . . . a lot of fun, I guess. But we stayed friends. We both stayed in the dance world, and it's a small one, you know? Everybody knows everybody. He's my friend, and I'm worried."

"I understand. But you can't go looking for him. Things get bad when you go looking for trouble. It finds you without any help, so promise me you won't get involved."

"I promise." I meant it, too. That didn't mean, as Tate noted, trouble wouldn't find me. It usually did. I took another bite of omelet, trying not to stress out about what I could not control.

"So, how did your visit with James go?" he asked me.

I put up a finger while I chewed and swallowed, and then answered. "It was fine. He was actually happy in there, you know, because he is in holding with some cute biker dude. I swear, he is such a trip . . . Hey, wait a minute. How did you know I got in to visit James?"

He raised his eyebrows. "I know everything."

"You do not. Alissa called you, didn't she?"

"You don't believe I know everything?"

"Tate!" I punched his shoulder.

"Okay, yes, Alissa called me. She told me she got you cleared to visit and that she was worried you might do something drastic to try and prove his innocence. She also let me know, in no uncertain terms, that James was not capable of this crime, and if I chose to hurt you, I could kiss my cojones good-bye."

It was my turn to chuckle. "Sounds like Alissa."

"Yup."

"Speaking of James, I got the truth out of him. He's covering for that creep Cullin. He hooked up with him the night of Jason Kutcher's murder, and that's why he won't say anything. He's trying to protect Cullin and his carefully built house of lies, so his wife and kids won't find out he's really gay. James said he left his bag behind, and I believe that, because when he sees Cullin, all rational thoughts fly out of his head."

"Well, Jenny, that's not really proof. I mean, I would need to talk to Cullin and get his signed statement."

"Then let's go. I think James has suffered enough. Although he did not really look like he was suffering too much, to be honest. He almost seemed a little gleeful."

"Scary."

"Yeah. But things could turn bad fast, and it's not a good environment for anyone. He's my friend. I owe it to him."

"Do we really have to do this now? I had more plans for you, my bed, and maybe even . . ."

I blushed and stood up. "If we could just take care of

this, I promise we'll come back and not leave your bed for the rest of the day."

He groaned and stood up. "Fine. Let's go talk to Cullin."

WE caught Cullin just as he was returning home from church with his wife and two kids. He apparently was already in the house, his wife and kids trailing behind. I had to admit, they were darned cute, those kids. Both little blondes, they left the car, and his daughter, who looked to be around six, skipped inside, talking to her mother a mile a minute. The boy, maybe eight, ambled behind, stopping to pick up a rock or a bug. Maybe not a bug. It was freezing outside, and the fog was still thick. So it was probably a rock. Whatever it was, he found it fascinating.

I guessed in some ways I could understand why Cullin was lying. These kids were cute. They would still be his kids whether he was gay or straight, but our society was not so accepting of gay people. Who knew what damage a divorce would do? Who knew how accepting the kids would be? I decided to tread carefully here. Maybe Cullin wasn't the big snake I thought. Maybe.

"Hi," said his son, who had spotted us exiting Tate's car. "Who are you?"

"We need to talk to your dad, son. Can you go ask him to come outside?" Tate sounded friendly but authoritative, so the little boy quickly ran inside.

A nervous and anxious Cullin poked his head out the front door, then blanched as he saw me standing on his walkway. I knew he wanted to just slam the door and will me away, or maybe chase me off even, but he eyed Tate and must have changed his mind. Tate looked like a cop, and Cullin had to have known what he was.

He might even have known James was currently in jail, on suspicion of a crime that Cullin could exonerate him from. Yep, he was a snake.

"Cullin, we need to talk to you. Please come out."

"I think I want a lawyer."

"Well, sure, that's okay. Let's just go down to the station then, and we'll get you a lawyer and read you your Miranda rights and all of that."

"Station?" He gulped, his Adam's apple bobbing in his throat. Cullin was tall and slim, but with broad shoulders. He dressed impeccably, his hair was always coiffed perfectly, and he had dark green eyes and dimples on both sides of his lush lips. In short, he really was pretty. I guess I could understand why James had a hard time saying no, despite the fact the man couldn't hold a job for more than a week at a time.

"Yes, station. If you're going to want your lawyer, then we need to do this right. Just following the ropes, you know."

"Cullin?" His wife stood behind him, curiosity and a small amount of fear in her clear blue eyes, and I felt a stabbing pain in my gut. I didn't really want to be responsible for this woman's disillusionment and upset when she discovered that her husband was not what he said he was.

"It's okay, Brenda. I just need to talk to these people for a minute. Go get the kids started on dinner."

"But Cullin—"

"Brenda, go." His voice was firm, and I saw the fear in her face again, and some anger, and I wondered, did she have some inkling? Did she know?

He shut the door firmly behind him and then walked down the walkway like he was headed to his own death sentence. He wore a nice blue suit, a designer label, and I knew that his wife came from money and she worked for her family's construction firm. She was the breadwinner, and her family wasn't all that fond of Cullin, kind of like me. I knew all this because my Auntie Vi had her finger on the heartbeat of all of Ogden, and what Auntie Vi knew, everyone else knew, too.

Nonetheless, they tolerated Cullin because their daughter loved him.

"So, here's the deal, Cullin. You can make this easy, or you can make this hard," Tate said. "We've got some pretty good proof you were with James Marriott on the night that

Jason Kutcher was murdered, and as you may have heard, that murder has been pinned on him. I would think that as a matter of honor you would come forward, just so he wouldn't be put through unnecessary trauma of being charged with a murder he didn't commit."

"I don't know what you're talking about," Cullin said stiffly, his eyes going to his house, then back again to Tate. Whenever his eyes settled on me, they hardened. We didn't much care for each other.

"Oh, knock it off, Cullin. For once in your life, do the right thing and tell the truth."

"I . . . James is being charged with murder?" His voice got a little faint and the color drained from his face, as Tate's words sunk in. I must have been wrong about him knowing, because he looked pretty upset at the thought.

"He could very well be, Monday morning, if you don't step up to the plate. We have evidence that places him at the scene, but we have also heard that he was with you. His life is in your hands. Are you really going to let him go to prison for a crime he didn't commit?" I had to admit, Tate's argument was very persuasive.

"I . . . You don't understand." He cast another nervous glance back at his house.

"Maybe I don't, but this can be painless. Were you with him on Friday night, and from what time until what time?"

"If my wife or her family finds out . . ."

"They won't find out unless it goes to court, which will definitely happen if you don't back up what we are hearing. Because he will be charged. At that point, he'll probably have to get a lawyer, and his lawyer will subpoena you, and then—"

"All right, all right. Can you promise me this won't go any further?"

"No, I can't. But if you were with him, and will swear to that, it will go a long way to helping him get released from jail."

"Swear to it where?"

"In a statement. You can come in Monday to the station.

For now, though, I just need to know the truth. Were you with James?"

"Yes, I was with him," he said, looking totally dejected and still throwing nervous glances back at his house.

"Times?"

"We hooked up about six and went to a couple of bars. I think we finished up around midnight, and then . . ."

"And then?" Tate said pointedly.

"And then ended up at his house." Cullin's lips pursed together and he glanced back at his house yet again. "I stayed over. Called my wife and told her a friend and I were practicing for a gig and it was going to run late, so I would just crash on his couch."

"A gig?" I said disparagingly, and Tate gave me a pointed glance.

"Yes, a gig. I'm in a band, and we're pretty good. We have a guy interested in us recording a demo, and then I'm going to finally show—" He stopped, as if realizing he was giving out too much information. "Anyway, yes, I was with him, and I'll sign a paper, but only if it won't ever be made public."

"Can't guarantee that," Tate said, "but I can tell you that the odds are in your favor, as long as someone can back up your story."

"You don't believe me?"

"Let's just say I want a second source."

"Bartender at Pete's Pack House. That's where we were until about ten, and he's a friend of mine. After that we went to Butterfly and Fawn, and then Diego's."

"Gay bars," I faux-whispered to Tate, and he gave me another glare.

"Cullin?" It was his wife, standing at the door, anxiously wringing her hands. "Dinner's getting cold. Aren't you going to come in? The kids don't want to pray without you."

"Be right there," he said. She disappeared back inside the house.

"Can I go now?"

"Make sure you come in and find me Monday morning." Tate handed him a card. "Thanks for doing the right thing."

"Yeah, yeah, I just hope this doesn't destroy my life."

"What about James, huh? What about the fact that—"

"Let's go, Jenny," Tate said, interrupting what was about to become my tirade.

"Fine."

Cullin disappeared back inside his house, and I knew that even though he was a master liar, his wife would be wondering. His life was on the edge now, and although I thought he deserved it, I wasn't sure his wife or kids did.

We headed back to Tate's car and he held the door open for me. After we were back on the road, I said, "Well, can we get him out?"

"Not today, Jenny. I have to follow proper procedure. Normally, it's the job of the defense to get him released. It's our job to find the bad guys, not prove them innocent."

"But he's not a bad guy. He's not a killer. I've known him a long time, and I know he's not capable of this. Did you really think he might have done it?"

"If there's one thing I've learned doing this job, it's that you can't always know what people are capable of," Tate said, his expression deadly serious. "You may think you know them, but sometimes there's something lurking underneath that you can't anticipate. In the right circumstances, some people are capable of anything and everything."

"Not James. I can't believe you think he'd really do something like this."

"The evidence all pointed to him."

"That must have been some evidence."

"It was pretty damning. We definitely had enough to charge him. With Cullin's testimony, if I can get some backup, I might be able to get him out. But that's going to require work on my part that I don't usually do. And it also means that if Cullin's story about their whereabouts doesn't add up, I won't be having him released, so you should prepare yourself for that."

"He didn't do it, Tate."

"I hope you're right."

TWENTY-THREE

THE rest of my Sunday passed in a bit of a blur, spent as it was with Tate. I had periods of uncomfortable reverie, as I thought about James, Bill, and the other missing dancers, but Tate quickly figured out my "guilty" look and reminded me that I would not and could not get involved. I wasn't really happy about his ultimatum, even though I knew he was right.

And I was grateful for the diversion, because I'd somehow convinced myself that I would have James released and back home by now. Don't know where I got that idea. Probably television. Determination didn't count for a lot when it came to the justice system.

I had to place my faith in Tate, that he'd take care of things tomorrow. And pray a little bit that Cullin was telling the truth, and others would back up his story and James's alibi.

While I was in bed with Tate, my cell phone rang incessantly in my purse, but I ignored it. I had more pressing things to worry about.

I woke up Monday morning around 10 a.m., all alone. That was good. Alone was good, at least right now, because I was so sore I figured I would have a hard time walking. And of course I had to teach dance today.

I turned to snuggle into Tate's pillow, pulling it into me to smell his unique scent. It was earthy and tangy, and slightly spicy, too. Kind of like him. I sighed a bit as I remembered how many days it was until tuition was due, and how I was not going to be getting that big payment I'd been expecting. I refused to let that ruin my day. I was in a great mood.

I forced myself to get out of the bed, shrugging into the T-shirt Tate had left on the floor after our latest encounter, and as I made my way toward the bathroom I heard my cell phone buzz. It was in my purse, on the kitchen table where I had dropped it after we returned to Tate's place yesterday. I remembered the incessant ringing and figured I probably had thousands of messages, and the voice mailbox was full again. My home phone was probably the same way. Some things never changed.

I quickly scanned the calls to see if anyone important had called—like, say, Bill, who was missing. I saw that most of them were from Tamara Williams—you know, April's mom—along with a few from assorted other dance moms, most of whom were not psycho, although I'd noticed a funny trend. A totally normal-seeming mom could suddenly go off the deep end and join the psychos when her daughter got a little bit good.

It was almost enough for me to want my students not to improve. Almost. After all, they were out there dancing with my name attached to it. For that reason alone, I would have to deal with the psychos.

I didn't see any calls I thought I needed to return, including the three from my mother. *Ack! My mother! Sunday dinner! Tate!* I was in deep trouble. A phone call wasn't going to be enough to fix this one. I was going to have to go over there and beg for forgiveness. But what could I possibly say? "Sorry, Mom, I was busy in bed with Tate."

Oh no, that was not going to go over well. And how did Tate forget he had promised my mom he would come for dinner? He was a cop. I was pretty sure he remembered everything, or was supposed to. *Must've been the thong.*

My phone rang as I stared at it dismally, and I jumped and dropped it.

I quickly picked it up and saw my mother's number, again. I supposed it could be my dad, calling to ask me "What in tarnation is going on?" He asked me that a lot. But no, my senses told me it was my mom.

The call went into voice mail. Phew. Then it rang again. And went into voice mail. And rang again. And all this time I was holding it in my hand, staring at it as though it were possessed.

It wasn't going to stop. I had to answer.

"Hello?" I said, my voice a little shaky. What was I, twelve? It sure felt that way.

"Jennifer Tamara Partridge, what in tarnation is going on?"

"Uh, hi, Dad. Nothing's going on. Just getting ready to go teach some solo lessons. The dance moms are anxious to get their daughters ready for the regular solo competition season. What's up with you?" All three names. I was in deep doo-doo.

"Your mother has been calling you nonstop since you failed to show up for dinner yesterday. She's now convinced you are dead in a Dumpster somewhere, much like that young fellow they found in the Dumpster at the Marriott on Saturday. She shouldn't watch the news. It gives her ideas."

Yikes!

"No, no, Dad, no Dumpster for me. Tell Mom I'm fine and really, really sorry. I got busy teaching solo lessons and just forgot about dinner."

I was so going to hell for lying to my parents.

"I went by your house about six times, and Bessie wasn't there any of them. I was supposed to be watching football, but since your mother was having a meltdown, I kept going by your house. You weren't there. Your mom put on quite a spread, you know. She was thinking your friend was going to come."

"Yeah, well, I had a really busy day, Dad. Really busy. Trying to earn some extra money because it's a tight month. Now, with no car, I really have to put in some extra hours."

"Well, your mother will be relieved you're okay."

"Tell her I'm really sorry. I'll come by this week and explain personally. I really just forgot, because I was really, really, busy."

"That would be good. Make sure you don't tell her *you* discovered the dead body in the Dumpster at the Marriott, or that James is in jail suspected of killing the boy. That kind of information wouldn't set well with her. You know."

My dad did not play fair. Where did he get that information? Damn Auntie Vi! I knew she was behind this, somehow. She always was.

"And Jenny?" Phew. He must be calming down. I wasn't Jennifer Tamara anymore.

"Yes, Dad?"

"Maybe you should get some pepper spray. Trouble seems to follow you around."

"Thanks, Dad, I'll think about it."

"Okay, I've gotta go now and let your mom know you're okay. She's probably already got your funeral planned. Please stop by soon so she can see you in the flesh."

"I will."

I hung up my cell phone and sighed, deeply. The things I forgot. The phone rang again and I jumped. I looked at the caller ID. Tamara Williams. If I didn't take it, she was going to use up all my minutes leaving me stupid messages.

"Hello?"

"Hello, Jenny? This is Tamara Williams, April's mom."

"Hello, Tamara."

"I'm down here at the studio, because April was supposed to have a solo lesson at ten, and I'm wondering if you are coming."

Crap. Yet another thing I'd forgotten. It was all Tate's fault, and yet it had been worth any unpleasantness I'd be forced to suffer in the next few days. I think. Maybe I should take that back. "I'll be there in fifteen minutes. Just wait for me, okay?"

I pulled up to my studio twenty minutes later, parking next to Tamara's car. She and I shared a name—although I was awful glad it was my middle name and no one used it except my dad when he was mad—but that was about all. She was driving a Lexus. Bessie didn't really measure up, no matter what my dad said.

"Hi, Tamara," I said, stepping out of the truck. "Sorry I'm late."

"Well, I almost left, but April really needs this solo lesson," Tamara replied as we headed toward the metal stairs leading to the studio, April lagging behind, dragging a big dance bag. "If you gave her even one-tenth the time you give the other girls, she could have competed at the Star-Makers competition and probably would have won."

Maybe on the sixth Tuesday of the month. During a meteor shower. With a bag over her head. I must be hungry, because I was cranky. I decided to ignore her comment and started up the stairs to my studio.

They followed me in, Tamara complaining the whole time, and after I set April up doing stretches, I went into my office and saw the flashing light on the answering machine. Probably half the messages were from Tamara, and I thought about ignoring them, but I was a little irked, so decided to listen and mostly delete.

"Jenny, this is Tamara . . ." Delete.

Delete.

Delete.

"Jenny, it's Bill. I need your help. I don't know where I am. I passed out in my hotel room and I woke up in this strange place. I'm locked in. I need your help. I don't know where I am."

There was a click as he disconnected, and I felt a chill roll down my spine. I played the message again, and I could tell he was disoriented and a little groggy. Had he been drugged? Was someone really holding him hostage? And if so, why? And if someone was holding him hostage, how did he get to a phone? Stupid kidnappers?

Didn't matter. It was time to call Tate.

Tamara was pretty peeved that I worked with April for only thirty minutes, while I waited for Tate to show, but she was just going to have to deal with it. I told her we'd meet up again on Thursday morning, since April was currently off track, as she attended a year-round school in Davis County, not far from Ogden.

Tate showed up with Agent Carson Keller in tow, and I felt that funny little squirm in my stomach again. Was it betrayal to think someone else was really, really hot? Especially since Tate and I had finally consummated our relationship. It couldn't be. I was just looking. Looking was harmless. And he had showed up at my house, late at night. Was it possible he was doing some looking, too?

After I played the message for them, they rewound and replayed it a few times, listening closely, and then confiscated my answering machine.

"Sorry, Jenny," Agent Keller said, with that breathtaking smile. "But it's necessary for the investigation. I'm actually kinda glad you have this old answering machine, because it's so much harder to deal with the phone companies and voice mail."

"You might be doing me a favor taking it," I said, thinking of all the messages from Tamara Williams. Maybe I should give him my cell phone, too.

"Why would he call here?" Tate asked.

"I think this is the number he has. When he called to ask me to work the convention, he called here, too. I'm not close enough to him that he'd have my cell or home number. Not anymore anyway."

Tate gave me a slightly dark look, which actually brightened my spirits. Was that jealousy I saw?

"Be careful," Tate warned me before he left with Agent Keller. They didn't seem real chummy, or happy to be working with each other, but necessity is the father of . . . what is that saying?

I realized I was alone in my studio, with nothing to do until my first class of Tots showed up, which wasn't for a few hours, so I decided to head to my mother's house and face the music—and hopefully get something to eat. Unless she was too angry. Maybe she'd feed me bread and water.

The front door opened and Sal and Enrique came through the door.

"Hey, Jenny," Sal said. "I thought I'd come run some routines before the classes start."

Enrique looked a little downhearted, and I guessed that Amber had gone on her tropical vacation as planned. It was hard to say no to the Bahamas, I guess, even for someone as gorgeous as Enrique Perez.

"Hi, Jenny," he said. "The cops won't let us leave, and since Bill had our plane tickets, I can't really go anyway. Bonnie is being a beast, as usual, and when I saw Sal headed up to the studio, I thought I'd come hang out over here, since I have nothing else to do."

"Where is Bonnie hanging out?" I asked, still convinced she was behind all of this.

"In her room or the bar of the hotel mostly."

"Well, I was just going to head to my mother's house. I need to talk to her."

"Oh," Enrique said, looking so sad I had to invite him along.

"You can come if you want." After all, my mom could hardly get really angry with me if I had other people there to act as a buffer. And she loved to feed people.

"Can I come, too?" Sal asked eagerly. "Oh, and I brought my bag for the week, since I'm staying with Tate. Maybe we could drop that off on the way."

"Uh, okay, but . . . maybe it would be better if you stayed at my place." *Maybe then I could stay with Tate in his comfortable bed*, I thought to myself.

"Well, whatever works," Sal said amiably.

The two men followed me as I locked up the studio, and then we all got into Bessie and waited for her to warm up. It was a tight fit in the front cab of the truck, especially with Sal sitting in the middle, although he looked perfectly happy and content. I guess after that mission thing, every day was a picnic to him. The inversion was still covering the valley, and it had been fourteen days since I had seen the sun, and I was getting really tired of it. I was ready to just drive myself up the canyon so I could at least get a glimpse of blue sky and temperatures that were hardly balmy, but at least not well below freezing.

My phone rang in my purse, and I carefully checked to make sure it wasn't psycho Tamara Williams. I saw Alissa's number, so I answered it. "Hello?"

"Hey, Jenny, it's Liss. Listen, I found this really cool search engine tool, called ZabaSearch. Can you write this down?"

"I'm driving. Hey, Enrique, can you get a pen and paper out of my purse, and write this down?"

Enrique shuffled through my purse, accidentally came out of it with a tampon and blushed mightily. He stuck it back inside, trying not to touch it even though it was wrapped up tight. He gingerly sorted through the rest of my purse, a look of apprehension on his face. He was probably worried about what other secrets of womanhood might pop up to terrify him. It took a really strong man to go through a woman's purse.

He finally found a scrap of paper, probably a receipt, and a pen.

"Will this work?"

"Yes. Okay, so it's what, Alissa?"

"It's www.zabasearch.com."

I repeated it and Enrique spelled it back to me to make sure he had it right.

"So what exactly is this supposed to do for me?"

"Look, I'm in class, and then I have to work, so I can't do anything with it right now, but I thought you might want to get a head start until I can come help you. One of the guys here at the academy told me it's this really invasive search engine that can find names, property listings, and all kinds of info on just about anyone."

"Really invasive. Lovely. And somehow you think I can operate a computer well enough to figure out how to work an engine?"

"It's a search engine, Jenny. Just like Google."

I knew what Google was, especially since we had spent some time using it, but her patient tone irritated me, so I decided to play her a little. "Google is what little girls do to little boys, right?"

"Jenny . . ." It worked. Patience was gone and irritation took hold.

"I know what Google is, Alissa. I just don't think I know my way around a computer well enough to get this search engine up and—"

"I can help," Sal said.

"Me, too," Enrique added.

"Sounds like you are having a party there, Jenn," Alissa said, humor filling her voice.

"It's just Sal and Enrique, and we were headed over to my mom's. Guess we'll head to my apartment instead and check out this search engine."

ENRIQUE seemed to know quite a bit about computers, which I found surprising for a tap teacher. Maybe I just found it surprising because computers befuddled me, and I was a dance teacher. Not tap, but still dance.

Sal had no interest whatsoever in anything computer related and settled himself on my couch, which despite its man-eating proclivities just couldn't seem to swallow Sal. He was too big. He found the remote and set about getting caught up on all the daytime television he has missed while serving his mission. From all the "bleep" sounds coming from the television, it had to be the *Jerry Springer Show* or something like that.

Sal was entranced.

Enrique had the ZabaSearch site up in a flash, and we began to do searches on the names "Bill Flanagan" and "Bonnie French." Well, technically, I just watched over his shoulder. He was doing all the work, but hey, I was making suggestions. We had to narrow it down to Utah and California listings, because there were too many listings of each name. We got addresses for both Bill and Bonnie, living together in Burbank, California. We found no Utah listings for either a Bill Flanagan or a Bonnie French, although there were a few B. Frenches and a few B. Flanagans.

"This one looks kind of promising. It's in Park City," I said, pointing to a listing. B. French. "No, never mind. The date of birth is 1956. Bonnie is not that old."

"So, neither of them owns any property here," Enrique said. "At least not under their own names." He didn't look very surprised. I guess it was a long shot, but in my experience, oftentimes long shots were the only shots I got.

"Okay, well, let's think this through," I said, tapping a finger on my chin. "Three people are missing, and there's been no sign of them. Even the FBI can't track them down, and they have all the bells and horns anyone could want or need. So we aren't looking for something obvious."

"No, definitely not something obvious," Enrique muttered. I gave him a funny look.

"Sarcasm does not become you," I said, trying to sound just like my mother. Or maybe Alissa. Could've even been Marlys. Hard to tell.

"Two other people, besides Bill, are missing. Although Bill is the only one we've heard from."

"What do you mean you've heard from Bill?" Enrique asked, turning away from the computer screen to look at me. I didn't know how top secret that message from Bill was supposed to be, so I just shrugged. "A message on my answering machine. That's all. Could've been old."

"What answering machine?"

"At work. It was probably old, okay?" He was being pretty persistent.

"What did it say?"

"It was kinda garbled," I ad-libbed. "Something about needing help. Probably for the convention. The more I think about it, the more I think it was definitely old."

I didn't know why Enrique was questioning me so closely, but I was a little nervous about it. I hadn't exactly been given the go-ahead to tell the world Bill had called and left a message claiming he was being held against his will. In the wrong hands, this would undoubtedly be dangerous information. Geez, listen to me. I sounded like a spy movie. Still, I didn't feel comfortable divulging it, so I just changed the subject. "Hey, try Twila Clark and Eldon Ramsay," I suggested. "They are missing, too."

Enrique gave me a hard look, then finally accepted I wasn't going to answer his questions—at least not with the response he was apparently looking for. He typed Twila's name in first, with no matches that fit what we were looking for. He tried "Eldon" and came up with quite a few Eldon Ramsays scattered across the Wasatch Valley, but none that seemed to fit. Of course, the fact we had no idea what we were looking for didn't help.

"This is getting us nowhere," I said with exasperation, and my stomach growled unhappily, reminding me I had been on my way to my mother's house to make peace, and hopefully break bread, when I had gotten sidetracked by this computer search.

I hated computers. I was hungry. I was broke. It was

dismal and freaking cold outside. One of my oldest friends was missing, and apparently in extreme danger. In short, life sucked. I sensed my cranky genes humming into gear. I think I inherited those from Grandma Gilly. She'd probably been the one who'd suggested my silly middle name, too. Jennifer and Tamara did not go together. Back in the days of the Camelot Dance Troupe, Bill used to call me J.T. just to irritate me. I got him back, though. I called him LaMar on every occasion . . .

"Hey, try this. Try LaMar Flanagan, or LaMar William Flanagan."

"LaMar?" Enrique said, a hint of humor in his voice. "Who names a kid LaMar, especially when your last name is Flanagan?"

"Mormon Irish people, I guess," I said, trying to keep the cranky genes in check. "It's common around here. LaMar, LaVar, RaeVel, LaDell—I think it's a combination of the parents' names, or something. All I know is Bill hated it, and the first time I saw his driver's license, I knew I had some good fodder for bribery."

"Hey, look at this," Enrique said, leaning in closer to the computer screen. "This is the record of a home in Eden. Registered to LaMar Flanagan. No middle initial or any other info, though. Where's Eden?"

"Up Ogden Canyon, past Huntsville," I said. "In the canyon. Above the inversion. Where there will be blue sky and warmer temperatures. Let's go for a drive."

"Don't you think you should call the cops with this information?" Enrique said. "Call your detective friend first and ask his opinion? Oh, and can you call me a cab? I think I better get back to the hotel in case anyone is looking for me."

It was a pretty abrupt shift, and I knew Enrique had something up his pant leg.

"Who would be looking for you?" I asked, although alarm bells were starting to go off in my head.

"Oh, you know, some of the staff, maybe Bonnie. The police might have more questions."

Chills ran down my spine. He hated Bonnie. And the police weren't really hanging out at the Marriott Hotel. I knew exactly where Enrique Perez was going. He was headed up to Eden, Utah, to check out this house. The only thing I didn't know was why.

TWENTY-FOUR

"THIS is very exciting," Sal said as we bounced along in Bessie, headed in the same direction as Enrique. I knew it was a mistake to do this, but I'd left four messages for Tate, none of which he'd returned. Of course, I had told him only that I was going to drive up to Eden and check out a hunch.

I also tried to contact FBI Agent Keller, with absolutely no success there, either. I'd even called Alissa, but she must have been in class. I wanted to scream at all the answering machines and secretaries, but what could I say? "It's an emergency—I found a house owned by LaMar Flanagan! LaMar! Bill's real name. Really. Heh."

The argument wasn't even working with me, and God knows I'd talked myself into some pretty bad decisions in the past.

LaMar, the one that owned the house that is, was probably eighty-two, retired, with no hair and false teeth. There was no real proof this meant anything. I might not even have given it a second thought had I not seen the light in

Enrique Perez's eye, or noted his hasty exit from my apartment.

He was looking for Bill. But why? Was he a murderer? Had he been the one who killed Jason Kutcher after all, framing James? And if he was a murderer, what the heck was I doing following him? Furthermore, why did I care? I knew it was about Bill. I needed to know he was safe.

I called Marlys and asked her to set up a substitute to teach the Tots class, since Sal was with me and James was most likely still in jail. She said she would call one of the Senior girls, who were old enough to be reliable and had been trained by me.

"Don't bother calling Tate and tattling," I said. "I already left him a message."

"This is dumb, Jenny."

"No, we're just looking around. I just need to know Bill is okay, that's all." She didn't say anything else. She didn't have to.

"This is not exciting," I told Sal. "We are staying very, very far back. We are just watching . . . just making sure nothing bad happens."

"What is it you think might happen?"

"I don't know." And I didn't. But Enrique's behavior had all of my nerve endings on fire. I might not have been able to get ahold of Tate, but I made sure I had my phone, just in case things went north fast.

As we headed up Ogden Canyon the fog dissipated. I could see blue sky, and I knew that even though this was most likely a wild-hog chase, I felt better than I had in weeks. Even though I had no money. And it was a long time until tuition was due. And one of my oldest friends was missing. *Sheesh! Enjoy the sun, Jenny.*

We rounded the bend past Pineview Reservoir, which was iced over, all the trees around it laced in white snow. The sun reflected off them, and the icy lake sparkled; everything looked new and shiny. We headed past Huntsville, a companionable silence in the cab of the truck. The radio in old Bessie did not work, but we didn't talk. Sal looked peaceful, leaning up against the side of the door, head tilted against the window, eyes half closed, enjoying the slight warmth of the sun as it penetrated through the cab.

It was quite a change from his life just a few days before, when he had been proselytizing for the Mormon Church—and apparently, not very well, by his own account. He'd been trying to fit himself into a world where he didn't belong. I'd tried that road myself, although not for long. Not the mission thing, of course . . .

We took the turnoff for Eden, and I realized I was humming, and relaxed. I hadn't felt this way in quite a while. It was a wonder what a little sunshine could do.

Sal snored lightly, lulled into sleep by the sun, the movement of the truck, and maybe just sheer relief that his life had changed so much.

When we reached downtown Eden—was this a downtown? A gas station–fast food mart, a small grocery store, and some city buildings—I pulled out the map I'd printed out from one of those Internet services. I was mighty proud of myself for managing that after Enrique had left. I'd seen Alissa do it before, though, and I really did understand Google. Really. Kind of. I'd typed in "map" and hit Enter, and it led me to a service that asked for an address. It took me right to a map.

I'd printed it out (another major accomplishment), and Sal and I were on our way. I didn't mention my concerns about Enrique Perez to Sal. I was pretty much in denial about them myself.

I followed a two-lane country road that led higher and higher into the back hills of Eden, until I came to a remote area that had a state park on the west side of the road and a long driveway on the east. Ahead I could see the road's end and a lot of mountainous terrain. I stopped the truck and considered my options. If I headed up the driveway, and someone was there, I would be alerting them to my presence. And yet I had pretty much convinced myself that this was just a waste of time, so what was I afraid of?

I decided that even if this was a long shot, I was going to use caution. The fact that I was up here, with no one but Sleeping Sal for company, told me I had already cemented myself into the too-stupid-to-live category you always saw in movies. You know, the pretty but not-so-smart girl who walks into a dark alley to investigate a noise, when everyone knows that there is a killer waiting there. Well, maybe not the pretty part. Attractive, maybe. The "too stupid to live" I had down pat.

I turned to the west, pulling down the long, inclined drive, into the wooded, shady park. Everything was covered in snow, but unlike in the valley, here the sun was shining brightly, and the sky was blue. In this park, however, with all the trees, there were plenty of dark spots. I chose a parking place next to a copse of trees. It wasn't hidden, but since the park was totally empty, I doubted anyone would see my truck.

I nudged Sal.

"Huh, wha? No, I don' wanna read the Scriptures again. No, no, no more prayer. Just let me sleep until six," he moaned. He must have been having a relapse dream from his mission, but he sure was a heavy sleeper.

"Sal, wake up. We're here." I poked at his shoulder, and he continued to sleep.

"Sal!" This time I yelled and he shot up like a bolt.

"Are we there?"

"Yes, we are there."

He peered around sleepily, rubbing at his eyes like a little kid. "This does not look like a house."

"It's not. It's a park across the street from the house. Well, not really across the street. It looks like that on the map, but I swear the driveway looked like it went up about two miles. You up for a hike?"

"Sure," he said, yawning and stretching, hitting the roof of the truck with his arms, he was so big.

We bundled up again, zipping coats and jackets, and I pulled a pair of warm gloves out of my purse. The sun might be shining up here, but I knew it could be deceptive. Though it was well above zero, it would still be cold, especially in the shade, and we were going to be sticking to the trees.

We hurried up to the entrance to the state park and then crossed the road to the driveway of the house we were headed for—the house where I hoped to find Bill Flanagan and the missing dancers.

We traveled quickly—Sal moved gracefully and fast, despite his size, a testament to his ability to dance—moving on the side of the driveway, about twenty feet in, keeping in the trees and covered.

Our boots crunched into the snow, which was not newly fallen and had a hard crust on it. The sound made me wince, as it echoed throughout the vast silence. I shivered; we were in the trees and the sun was not penetrating them very well. All I could hear was our footsteps. There was no traffic, no birds, nothing but crisp silence. I shivered again, and this time it wasn't the cold. I was spooked. It took us about ten minutes to reach the house, which was surrounded by a large fence.

"Wow," Sal said, staring at the palatial mansion in front of us. "That's big. Way big."

That was an understatement. The home in front of us was at least three stories, all burgundy-colored brick, with dark window accents and huge paned windows. It could probably fit four or five families comfortably, although I doubted that had been the intent—unless it had been built by one of the many polygamists we had living in Utah.

"So, what do we do now?"

"I have no idea."

"I don't see anyone."

The house did look very empty, but it was so large, who could tell?

"Maybe I'll go around by the garage and see if there are any signs of cars or vehicles," I said.

"You? You aren't leaving me here. I'm a little freaked out by all this nature and silence."

That made two of us. We kept to the perimeter of the yard, moving counterclockwise toward the side of the house where I suspected the garage was located. It was not visible from our vantage point, but I knew the driveway led to something, and that something was undoubtedly a forty-five-car garage.

When we were directly horizontal from the garage, we looked across but could see nothing but three large garage doors, all closed.

"What now?" Sal asked.

"I'm going to go around back and just see if I can spot any signs of life. Anything."

"That sounds like a bad idea. That sounds like something Detective Wilson would *not* approve of."

"Well, I don't see Detective Wilson here. Do you?"

With that, I continued my perimeter walk to the back half of the house. There was no sign of life in the house. One little peek in the window, and I would know that I'd been right. Crimes were not solved this easily.

I dashed across the yard, Sal right behind me, even though he had voiced earlier disapproval. We crouched down at the back of the house, and hunched over, staying low while we headed for a large back window.

"Okay, I'm just going to peak inside, and if there's no one there, we'll leave."

"Okay, you peak inside."

"You know, you are a little taller, you might be able to see more than I can."

"Good try. Not buying it. This was your idea."

"Fine. I'll look." I slowly rose and put my hands on the windowsill, then pulled myself to my full height, peering through the window.

The toothless face staring back at me screamed.

I joined in. Then Sal was screaming, too. It was a screamfest.

Then whoever was inside hit the ground, with a thunk so hard I could even hear it through the closed window.

I heard another, higher-pitched scream and I turned to run just as two big, huge, really, really big dogs came dashing, snarling, and barking toward us, let out from a side door.

Sal screamed again, high pitched and terror filled. I could understand.

We were about to be torn limb from limb.

TWENTY-FIVE

THINGS happened pretty fast after that. Apparently we had scared the homeowner, Marlon T. Spriggs, half to death—literally. His wife had heard his scream, came running, let the dogs out, and called 911. At least that's what she told us.

She had ordered us inside at gunpoint—a very large rifle-looking thingie, to be exact. Mr. Spriggs was recovering on the sofa, having taken his nitroglycerin pills. He was still very white, and with all the heart concerns, had not bothered to put in his false teeth. Mrs. Spriggs managed to tell us all of this while marching us inside. She looked older than dirt, but boy she was holding that gun steady.

Turned out that Mr. and Mrs. Spriggs were the "Spriggs" in Spriggs Rifles and Automatic Weapons. Utahns were big on personal freedoms such as carrying deadly weapons to kill large or small animals; protecting home and property; and of course the right to take your weapon to church, school, or anyplace else, just in case someone tried to steal your temple recommend or raid your food storage supply.

The Spriggses had done well here, in their home state, and had retired to their fortress in Eden, and guarded it with guns manufactured in their own factory.

Also turned out that map program I was so proud of having found and used on my computer was notoriously flawed, giving us the wrong directions. The house we were looking for was about a mile and a half back, and up a very deserted dirt road.

"I don't think you want to go there," the now kindly Mrs. Spriggs said. She'd put the rifle down after she discovered I was just a harmless dance teacher from Ogden, looking for a friend. I left the rest of the stuff out. "That house has been abandoned for years. We were excited when some California guy bought it, and we thought the new owner was going to repair it, but nothing's happened."

Sal was still doing deep breathing, trying to recover from our close call with the Spriggses' dogs. Luckily, Mrs. Spriggs had called them off at the last minute.

"So, no one is staying there?" I asked her about the house that Bill apparently owned. "No one's been seen?"

"Not a soul. At church Sunday, Phyllis told me that she and ArDell are just about fed up with the place and want it torn down, but the city says there's nothing they can do."

"Hmmmph. Well, I guess that's that," I said.

"Your friend told you he'd be staying there?"

"Well, maybe he just said he might be there. But I guess he was wrong."

Mrs. Spriggs invited us to stay to dinner. I guessed that was only common courtesy, especially after she'd almost killed us, but I figured we were even, since her husband still hadn't recovered from the shock.

"Alzheimer's," she whispered to me as she escorted us out. "Most days he doesn't remember his own name, let alone mine. I had to lock up the guns because he kept shooting up the trees and the yard, and sometimes the dining room furniture. The only one still out is this one, and I keep it hidden in a place he'd never look—the broom closet. Man's never done a day of housework in his life. Of course, *that* he remembers."

We bade Mrs. Spriggs good-bye and sprinted down the drive. It was heading into late afternoon, and the sun was starting to go down, and the temperature along with it.

"Well, that was fun," Sal said. "Life is always fun around you, Jenny."

"Yeah, you say that now you're breathing normally."

"Well, you gotta admit, those dogs were scary. And the gun? My word."

We headed across the street and down the drive leading into the park, jogging to where I had parked Bessie. Where had I parked Bessie? I distinctly remembered pulling her under the copse of trees in the far corner, as far away from prying eyes as I could get her.

"Where's Bessie?" I asked Sal, as if he hadn't just endured dogs, guns, and old people with me for the past half hour.

"Gone," was his answer.

"Wow, very insightful," I said sarcastically.

"I was with you," he pointed out.

"I, however, was not," Tate said, coming out of some trees behind us. He definitely gave me another start—like my heart needed any more motivation to pump wildly today.

He held my dad's spare key in his hand. I recognized it from the rabbit's foot key chain dangling down. *My father, the traitor!* I thought. At the other end of the parking lot I saw Tate's car.

"Jenny, what are you doing? I got your message. And I had to ask myself, 'Does this woman have a death wish?' "

"It was just a hunch. Nothing concrete." He didn't say anything. Just stared at me like Grandma Gilly always did, especially when she was really PO-ed. "Hey, I called! I tried to get ahold of you. I just—"

"You just wanted to step into a huge mess, and maybe

almost die again?" There was definitely tension, and something else, in his voice.

"No, I just wanted to—"

"Jenny, this is a police case. Do you get it? You are not a cop. You are not a PI. You're a dance teacher, in Ogden, Utah. You teach little kids to shake their butts. You are in way over your head here. You could have been killed, and you could have gotten Sal killed with you."

This was probably not the best time to mention my new friendship with Mrs. "Shotgun" Spriggs.

"I'm okay," Sal said. "It was a trip. It's always fun with Jenny."

Tate didn't answer Sal. And neither did I. Because his words began to sink in, piercing through my skin and roiling around inside me, bouncing and caroming off my heart and lungs, like I was a giant pinball machine. A dance teacher? Teaching kids to shake their butts? *Shake their butts?* I taught jetés! I taught chene turns! I taught relevé, and piqués, and . . . Shake their butts?

"Whoa, your face is red, Jenny," Sal said, alarm crossing his face. "I think your head might explode."

"I think you might be right," I said in short, sharp, clipped words.

Tate was still glaring at me, so I guessed his head was ready to explode, too.

"Where's my truck?"

"I had it towed. Turns out it might not be street legal."

"It is *too* street legal. And that's my dad's truck. No one messes with my dad's truck. Why would you mess with my dad's truck?" I guessed he could see I was getting pretty worked up.

"Okay, fine, I just moved it. I was looking for you, and I didn't want you getting away before I found you."

"What if I needed to get away? What if, say, three rabid dogs and a gun-toting granny were chasing me, huh? What then? I could have died!" It was only a slight exaggeration.

"Gun-toting granny?"

"Oh, yeah, she was pretty—" I elbowed Sal to make him stop talking.

"There really was a gun-toting granny?"

Sal nodded his head before I could stop him.

"And the dogs?"

"They weren't rabid," I said before my large Samoan friend could get me into deeper hot water with Tate. "They all had collars and dog tags. Dogs with dog tags don't have rabies."

"Yes, but they do have teeth." Tate looked amused again, although I could still see the tension and something else— concern?—on his face.

"Where's your car, anyway? And how did you find us?"

"I'm a cop," he said.

"That is a very vague answer."

He just raised his eyebrows.

"Great, Mystery Man again. Where's the truck, Tate? I want to get going," I said.

"Or you want to go find the house you were looking for in the first place?"

"Okay. Just spill it. How did you know? I only told you to call me, it was important. I did not tell you where I was going."

"I have my ways."

"Oh, now we are Secret Agent Man?"

"Yes, and if I told you how I found out, I would have to kill you."

Even Sal groaned at that one.

"Fine, just tell me where the truck is." It was Marlys who had told him. I knew it. I was so going to fire her . . . after the competition season was finished, of course, because I couldn't pull that off myself.

He motioned us to his car, and I sullenly followed and got in, with Sal right behind me. We didn't speak as Tate drove us out of the park and a couple hundred yards down the road to where Bessie sat parked.

"I'll be over to deal with you later," Tate whispered in my ear as I got out.

Somehow, that sounded more like a promise than a warning.

Twenty-Six

"Boy, I am starved," Sal said as we headed back toward Huntsville and the road leading down Ogden Canyon into the city. "Can we stop at that store so we can get some chips or something?"

He pointed to one of the three businesses in Eden, a Maverick Station that offered gas, food, and—judging by the tables and seats inside—good local conversation.

I pulled Bessie over and parked in one of the spots in front of the store, a few old farmers walking by, refillable coffee mugs in hand. They eyed Bessie as though she were Marilyn Monroe. They eyed me like I was a two-headed monster, especially after Sal got out.

He looked like Bigfoot, although accessorized nicely for winter, with a puffy white down jacket, a burgundy scarf and matching gloves, and black fur-lined snow boots. He also had on a pair of UFO pants—large, puffy, hip-hop-style pants with lots of pockets. I hadn't paid much attention to his attire before, because that was the world in which I lived. Hard to believe that just a week before he had been living in suits and ties. I had on my Hot Chillys, black leggings that were made for cold weather, covered with a long sweater. On top of that, I had on my down jacket, and on my hands my warm winter gloves. On my feet were a pair of faux Ugg boots. I couldn't afford the real ones, of course, but Payless made a nice imitation.

In short, we looked like artsy dance people. And in Eden, Utah, we stood out like Sharon and Ozzy Osbourne on Temple Square.

"Uh, let's make this quick."

Sal picked out some Doritos and I grabbed some nuts, and we paid and quickly headed back out to the car. The teenage cashier whispered to her coworker as we exited through the glass door, and I felt as if I was on display, all the old farmers staring at us, mouths agape, through the front windows of the store.

I was pretty relieved to be back on the road, until I noticed a Humvee following us. I did not like Humvees. I *really* did not like silver Humvees. Sal saw my anxious glances into the rearview mirror, and he turned and looked back, then blanched. He had been with me during the infamous bus chase, when someone in a Humvee had been shooting at us.

"Um, Jenny?"

"I see them. It's probably a coincidence."

He didn't look like he believed me. I wasn't sure I believed it myself. The police had never really figured out who was driving the Humvee and shooting at me, so the attacker was probably still on the loose. Although I wouldn't think he or she would be hanging out in Eden.

I came to a four-way stop and decided not to use the turn signal, idling there for a minute while deciding which way to go. The Humvee coasted closer, and I gunned Bessie and turned sharply right, tires squealing. I'd like to say we jetted away, but this was Bessie. A school bus could not outrun a Humvee, and neither would this old truck. When I saw the Humvee make the same turn and then accelerate, I knew we were in trouble.

At least I thought that until I saw a blue Ford Taurus cruise up behind the Humvee, and I knew it was Tate. My whole body relaxed, and I turned into a big noodle, which is not a good thing when you are driving a very old truck without power steering. I didn't quite make the left curve I needed to make, pulling wildly at the wheel, and Bessie headed off into a field, stopping only when she crashed into a large telephone pole.

My chest hit the steering wheel and I gasped, trying to breathe. Sal had braced himself with his big arms, and as far as I could tell, had sustained no injuries. Neither of us had been belted in, as the seat belts in the old vehicle had been nonfunctional for quite a while.

My door flew open and I heard Tate's voice, although with all the dots swimming before my eyes I couldn't really see him or focus. I was just trying to breathe.

I heard him say, "Call 911," just before I passed out.

T WENTY - SEVEN

$\mathcal{A}$N ambulance was not my ideal mode of travel. Not that I had ever been in one before, and considering what I was driving—and had just wrecked—it was pretty nice, but still.

I also didn't care much for the hospital, which I knew I could not afford. Turns out men can be pretty bossy when they are worried. And Tate was definitely worried. He even said he was going to pay my medical bills, although I didn't intend to let that happen. I'd figure it out. Somehow.

My chest was black and blue, and I was sore as hell, but there was no major damage done, just bruised lungs and ribs. The doctor told me I had been very lucky, and then I got a twenty-minute lecture on using seat belts. I was too sore, tired, and upset to tell him that Bessie didn't have functioning seat belts.

I would live to teach and dance again, and that brought a huge sigh of relief to my soul. And man did it hurt to sigh.

I had made Tate promise not to call my parents, but as I've mentioned before, my Auntie Vi knew everyone in Ogden, and some nurse at the ER must have ratted me out, because my parents rushed into my room about two minutes after the doctor had finished his lecture.

My mother was crying, and my father looked really, really stern—it was his worried face. "I'm okay, Mom. Please don't cry. I'm just bruised."

She hugged me tightly and I winced. This situation was not good. I knew Auntie Vi and my spinster Mormon cousins couldn't be far behind, so I motioned to Tate. I sorta peeled my mother off me, and said, "I've been released. So I can go home now."

She wiped at her eyes and peered at me anxiously. "I'm taking you home with me. Enough of this. You could have been killed! You could have died."

"That's okay, Mom. I'll be fine at my apartment."

"Jennifer, your mother is taking you home." That was my dad. And he meant business. Nothing like a little car accident to turn you back into a twelve-year-old. A twelve-year-old who wrecked her dad's prized hunk of junk no less.

"I think that sounds like a great idea," Tate said. "Don't let her out of your sight. I'll give you my cell phone number, in case she gives you any trouble."

"Hey," I protested. "I'm not a prisoner of war. Or a child."

"You know what? Tonight you are," Tate said. He was getting really bossy. I wasn't sure it was endearing anymore.

MY mother tucked me into my old bed, in my old bedroom, and went to make me food. I was sore and tired, and more than a little freaked out about the silver Hummer that I was blaming for this whole mess, although the truth was, lots of people drove Hummers these days. It could have been a coincidence. The vehicle had not run me off the road, and no shots were fired from within. So why was I so freaked out?

I supposed the dead dancer in the Dumpster, three other missing dancers, a firebomb to the Pepto Mobile, a bomb at the dance convention . . . All those things might be adding to my angst.

Tate had told me that he didn't get the plate of the Hummer, because I crashed right as he got close enough. He admitted to being a little unnerved by the sight but said there were no indications it was anything but a coincidence.

I wanted it to be just that. A coincidence. It had to be. Nothing else made sense. But why didn't the driver of the Hummer stay to make sure everything was all right? Wasn't that what normal, concerned citizens did?

I heard the phone ring and my mother's voice answering it. She had taken my purse and hidden it away right after we got home. She'd probably thrown my cell phone out in the road. She took her mothering very seriously, and it had been a while since I'd allowed her to do any of it.

She'd been my biggest supporter growing up, taking me back and forth to ballet, jazz, tap, and solo lessons, with never a complaint, even though she herself had never had a desire to dance. She'd recognized that fire in me—the all-consuming need to dance, and be the best, and she'd supported it both emotionally, physically, and of course, financially. Looking around my room, I could see all the trophies and tiaras I'd won at competitions as a young girl. They were still proudly displayed. Probably dust free. A physical reminder that my parents did love me.

I got a little teary eyed. Of course, my mother chose that time to poke her head through the door and saw I was awake. "Are you okay? Why are you crying? Are you in pain?"

"A little bit." I wiped at the tears. "Mostly just overwhelmed, I think."

"The doctor said to give you these for pain," she said, handing me two tablets and a glass of water she'd pulled from behind her back, sort of like a magician pulling off a really great trick. Gotta love moms.

I obediently took them, because I *was* in a lot of pain. It hurt to just think about breathing, let alone do it.

"Marlys called, and she said that Sal covered your classes, so you shouldn't worry."

"Okay," I said listlessly.

"Jenny, are you okay?"

"Every day is hard, you know? I mean, it's always something. I guess that's life. But these past few days have been really, really hard. And I'm not sure I'm up to this life anymore. I want to crawl into my bed and just stay there. It's safer, and easier."

"You're just hungry," Mom said, patting my hand with hers. "I'll go fry up some chicken and make mashed potatoes and gravy. You'll be feeling better in no time."

I have to admit, my spirits perked up quite a bit at the thought of my mother's fried chicken and potatoes and gravy. She knew the way to my brain was through my stomach. I felt better already.

At this rate, I'd be better—and much fatter—in no time. I don't know if it was the pain medication, or the events of the day, but I dozed off, then awoke to find it was completely dark.

My first thought was, "Damn, I missed fried chicken."

My second thought was, "Who is standing by my bed?"

My third thought was, "Wow, that's a big gun."

TWENTY-EIGHT

BONNIE French was not my friend. She had no business in my room. She certainly had no business in my mother's house. So why the heck was she here, pointing a gun at my head?

Was this a hallucination, brought on by the pain meds? A vivid dream?

"Bonnie?" I asked, my voice tentative.

"Get up, Jenny. It's time to go."

"Why are you here?"

"I need you to lead me to Bill's hiding place."

"I don't know where that is."

"Yes, you do. I know you found it. I followed you."

"Do you drive a Hummer? Have you been stalking me since December?"

"What are you talking about?"

"Why are you here?"

She sighed impatiently. "I told you. Now get up!"

She jabbed the gun at my chest and poked me, and I gasped in pain. "Whoa, chill Betty. That hurts."

"Uh, my name is Bonnie, and *get your ass up*."

I tried to comply, mostly because I didn't want her poking my chest with that gun again, but the world was spinning alarmingly. I was having a hard time grasping what this situation was all about, especially in my drugged state, but I knew one thing. My father had the ears of a cat. He could hear a mouse fart on Neptune—should there be mice on Neptune, of course. There'd been no sneaking out or sneaking around when I was a kid, mostly because my father always heard any noise that didn't belong in our house. He couldn't hear me ask him to drive me to the mall, but raise up a window to try to get outside of the house after curfew, and the man was like radar. Or sonar. Whatever that technology was.

I crawled out of my bed, slowly, mostly because I was sore but also because I was stalling, and waited for my father to appear in the doorway. I never welcomed that as a teenager. Right now, it would be the most beautiful sight on earth.

Bonnie prodded me again and pointed me toward the door. I was dressed in a pair of my mother's flannel pajama pants and a large T-shirt of my father's that said, "Teachers do it with class." I did not want to know where that came from. And speaking of my father, where the heck was he?

"Where are we going? I need shoes. And my coat."

"I told you, we're going to find Bill's hideaway."

"And I told you, moron, that I did not find any hideaway."

She whapped me on the back of the head with the gun and I cried out, which made her poke the gun in my back and threaten to shoot me.

"Sorry. Pain medicine must have made me loopy."

"Pain medicine made you loopy? You were born loopy."

I considered turning and wrestling her for the gun, then smacking her hard, but I was having a hard time just walking, so I thought I'd just wait for Mr. Eagle Ears to come in and save me. Where was he?

"Oh, and don't make any more noise. Your mother is so nice, she made us coffee and fed me fried chicken and mashed potatoes while we were waiting for you to wake up. She had no idea I slipped something in her coffee. She's out like a light."

Bonnie the Beast ate *my* mashed potatoes? And drugged my mom? I wasn't sure which one was worse. Probably the mom thing, but still . . . It was my mom, for Pete's sake . . . And my mashed potatoes, too! My stomach rumbled at the thought.

"And don't get any ideas," Bonnie whispered behind me as she pushed the gun into my back. "I'll shoot your mother before I shoot you. I have a lot to lose here, and frankly, your mother is pretty nice, so she doesn't deserve it. But I'd do it just to torture you."

I'd been right all along, apparently. When I told everyone to look in Bonnie's direction, I'd been correct in my assumption that she was behind the . . . The what? The disappearing dancers? And why was she asking me about Bill and his hideaway?

I opened my mouth to ask her, and then thought of my mother, and decided to wait until I got outside. My father had a room in the basement, where he stayed up late at night watching television and doing crossword puzzles. He was a bit of an insomniac, which explained why he woke so easily when I was growing up. But the older my mother got, the less tolerant she was of his night-owl habits, and so they had compromised with him watching television in a room far from her bedroom.

The renovation of our basement had taken him six months, and when it was done, he had his own private mecca. He was quite proud of it. I suspected he had retired down there after he'd eaten, and wouldn't be up for a few hours. So much for Mr. Eagle Ears. The good thing was, eventually, he would come up. And he would find my mother drugged and me missing. I hoped.

Bonnie herded me out into the cold night, and I shivered.

I only had on socks and the T-shirt and pajama pants, hardly enough for subfreezing weather. Although it didn't feel quite as cold as it had been earlier. I could see a vehicle parked on the side of the road, in front of my mom's house, and in the faint light of the street lamp it was pretty apparent it was not a silver Humvee. It was a white minivan, in fact, almost the polar opposite. The moon was about half full, and the night was not completely black, but dark enough to give my current situation ominous undertones.

Wait a minute . . . The moon? The car on the street? I could see! There was no fog. The inversion was gone!

Just in time for the end of my life.

"The inversion's finally gone," I said to Bonnie.

"Who cares?" she asked, pushing me toward the mini-van.

Actually, I did. I'd been waiting for more than two weeks to see the sun, and when it came up tomorrow, I was going to be alive to feel it on my face.

Even if I had to kill Bonnie French.

I wasn't thrilled with making another trip up to Eden. Especially at gunpoint. Tied up. Bonnie had bound my wrists together, probably to keep me from smacking her. Good move on her part, because I *really* felt like smacking her.

She drove with her left hand on the steering wheel, the right pointing at me. I figured her arm would get tired long before we got to Eden, and I could make my move then, knock the gun away, and maybe throw her out of the moving vehicle. That might make me feel better.

It was a flawed plan, mostly because Bonnie had a better one. And accomplices to boot.

She pulled over in the parking lot of Rainbow Gardens, located in the mouth of Ogden Canyon, and two big, burly men climbed into the minivan. She ordered one of them to put me in between them and keep an eye on me.

Great.

"Just what the heck is going on here, anyway?" I asked Bonnie. She didn't answer, and one of the big guys nudged me, probably telling me to be quiet. I recognized both men, after a few minutes of watching them. They were the roadies, the men driving the truck that went from town to town with the Hollywood StarMakers sound equipment, trophies, and other stuff that couldn't fit on a plane.

"Look, Bonnie, if you followed me, you know the police were there, too, and I know Tate. He undoubtedly found the right address—which I did not. Do not ever trust Mapmakers, by the way. Anyway, it was a wild-hog chase. And Bill left a message that he was being held against his will, so he would hardly be holed up in his own house, right?"

She just snorted. Not a terribly attractive sound, either.

She headed up around Pineview and then took a left shortly after we passed the exit to the monastery.

And that's when my pain medication wore off. Or my brain started working. She'd said she wanted me to take her to Bill's hideaway, but she wasn't asking me for directions. Not only that, but she was headed in a different direction, turning at least ten minutes before we reached the outskirts of Eden. She wound her way through the streets of Huntsville, a small community located on the banks of Pineview Reservoir.

"You didn't really need me, ever, did you?" I said to her.

"Nope, not really," she answered cheerily. She turned again and then pulled up to a large condominium complex, putting a code into a keypad and waiting for the gates to open. She drove down a long road to a building on the very end of the street, and hit a garage-door opener.

The door went up, and we drove inside, and I felt the blood drain from my face as the door lowered again.

The two big guys grabbed me by the arms and escorted me out of the van. Bonnie traveled ahead of us, and we went inside through the door that connected the garage to the house.

Inside, I was surprised to see Bill Flanagan and another woman tied to the kitchen chairs, mouths gagged, terror on their faces.

TWENTY-NINE

THERE were four kitchen chairs. Two had been taken. A third was reserved for me, and soon I was tied to it, glaring at Bonnie and the two men.

"What the heck is going on here, anyway?" I asked her. The pain medication really had worn off now, and my chest and insides were throbbing. I wanted to scream with the agony of having my hands bound behind my back, but I fought back the pain and clenched my teeth.

"Why don't you explain it to her, Billy," she said, walking forward and yanking the gag viciously from his mouth.

Bill spluttered and licked his lips, and then just looked at me. Sorrow filled his eyes, and I thought I saw a hint of tears. The woman next to him sobbed softly. I guessed she was Twila Clark.

"Tell her," Bonnie said again, her voice harsh. She pulled her gun from the pocket of her fur-lined jacket and pushed it against his forehead. "Tell her what you are really all about, William Flanagan. The woman I could never quite measure up to is here, so tell her. Tell her what you really are."

The woman she could never measure up to?

He just shook his head. Bonnie shook her head in exasperation, then turned to me. "I got tired of hearing about Jenny T. Partridge, and how talented and quirky and funny she was. Really tired of it. I thought it was me. The whole time, I thought it was me, but the truth is, Bill was just living in the past. He couldn't be faithful to any woman. Just ask Twila there."

The other woman just continued to sob. She had long blond hair, big blue eyes, and fair skin. She was thin, with a dancer's build. And somehow she was tied up—heh, get it? Tied up?—in all of this. I guessed there was still some pain medication in my system, because it was a miracle I could find anything at all amusing about this situation.

"Anyway, we set up this whole thing, to get some money, so that Bill and I could retire and build a dance studio for him to run in California. He was tired of the road, and I was just trying to make him happy, so it seemed like a good plan. But Bill . . . Bill didn't want a numbers person. Oh no. He wanted a dancer. Someone to replace you. So he stupidly decided to cheat on *me*. No one cheats on me."

Her eyes sparkled with venom and hatred for me.

"I don't understand what any of this has to do with me." Well, I kind of did, but I was going to play stupid until I figured the rest of it out, or got out of this situation.

"Don't be stupid, Jenny, if that's at all possible for you. After I found out about his cheating, I convinced Bill that there was big money in an insurance scam. And of course, the perfect time to pull it off was when we were in Ogden, so that I could rid myself of not just two problems, but three."

"But it isn't about an insurance scam, is it?" I said.

"No, of course not. That kind of thing is too hard to pull off. Too many paper trails and money investigations. But Bill was easy to convince, because he's money stupid, and he had no idea I was on to his affair with Twila. He'd even planned to bring her on board and have her teach at the studio, where the two of them could carry on their sordid little affair right under my nose."

Twila cried some more. She was starting to get on my last nerve. And Bill? He couldn't even look me in the eye. He was a criminal, too. He'd gone along with it, after all. It seemed that some of what James had told me was true. Bill held me up as some sort of ideal, but it sure wasn't enough to keep him on the straight and narrow. I was no guardian angel to him. I was just a memory of a time in his life when things were less complicated and more carefree. He'd idealized that.

Bill finally looked up at me, and I saw the shame there, but also something more. Despair. He knew he'd lost. He'd given up.

I turned to look at Bonnie. "Look, if this wasn't about insurance, then what is it about?"

"Drugs," said Enrique Perez, his gun aimed squarely at Bonnie French's head.

THIRTY

GOD, I had so terribly misjudged this situation. Enrique Perez stood, calm and studied, the gun in his hand pointed at Bonnie, but covering the two big men at the same time.

"Get on the floor, now," he ordered the two men. They didn't move. One of them pulled a gun out of his pocket, and in a heartbeat Enrique fired, shooting the man in the hand. He dropped to the ground now, screaming in pain, holding the hand to his stomach, blood pouring out of the wound. A metallic smell filled the room, and I felt my stomach churning. My chest ached from my earlier accident, and I could get no relief, so tightly was I bound.

"Throw your gun over here, Jackson," he ordered the other man, who apparently wanted to keep his hand in working order. Jackson immediately complied, and dropped to the ground.

Bonnie stood with her gun pointed at Enrique. "You lying sneak," she said, anger filling her voice. "You rotten, no-good weasel. You cheated me and conned me, and now you're trying to take it over, aren't you? You rotten no good—"

"Can it, Bonnie," Enrique said.

The man who had been shot moaned softly, but the other man was completely silent, prone on the floor, arms outstretched.

"Maybe you guys should put away the guns. I mean, as far as I can see, nothing good ever came from guns," I suggested. They both ignored me. I figured they would, but it was worth a try.

"She's right, you know," Bonnie said finally. "Nothing good ever comes of guns. So why don't you just put it down, Enrique? Put the gun down, or I shoot her." With those words, she moved swiftly to the back of my chair and yanked my head back roughly, pushing her gun against my head.

"Calm down, Bonnie. Just calm down. We can talk this through," Enrique said, but he didn't put the gun down. "I don't care about her, but you really don't want to shoot her now, do you?"

I was so confused as to what was going on. I'd been worried about Enrique's involvement with this situation, and I guessed I'd been right. Apparently, he had been working with Bonnie, but had now turned on her.

"Put it down, Rico. It isn't going to work. You lied. You were supposed to be with me, but now I have to wonder, were you working with her? Is that what is going on? Is that why you're concerned about me shooting her, because I can tell it bothers you to think I would put a bullet through her brain."

She jabbed the gun at my forehead and I winced.

"Just one little shot, and what little bit of fluff is in between this ditso's ears will go flying all over the room."

"Who you calling a ditso?" I said, and she roughly shoved the gun against my forehead. I decided to shut up for the time being. I'd get her back. Somehow.

"Put the gun down," Bonnie said again. I didn't know Enrique very well, but I didn't think he was going to listen to her. I was kind of confused as to who the bad guys were here. Bill looked as baffled as I was.

"Okay, I'm putting it down. Just be calm. Don't do anything rash. Let Jenny go, and I'll put the gun down. See, I'm putting it down."

He bent down and gently placed the gun on the floor, and stood back up, arms up, palms splayed outward. "Now what?" he asked her.

"Kick it over here. And then kick Jackson's gun over here, too."

"I'm not going to kick my gun," he said, outrage written all over his face.

"Kick the damn gun," Bill and Twila thundered in unison.

He glared at them, and I stared at both with surprise. Maybe Bill hadn't given up yet. Maybe we might get out of this alive.

Enrique kicked the gun toward Bonnie, and she ordered the man called Jackson to stand back up and help her. He rose and quickly traveled over to her, taking his gun back. She ignored the other guy, who had a serious wound in his hand and who looked close to losing consciousness.

"Bonnie, what the heck is going on here?" I asked. "Why are you doing this? Bill's always been a bit of a ladies' man. You can't really take that personally."

"Hey," Bill said indignantly. "I resent that." So much for the shame he'd been feeling before. He'd always been pretty arrogant.

I glared at him, and he shut up. I was trying to side with Bonnie, to connect with the she-devil in some way, like I'd seen people do on television, and he was not helping.

"Jenny Partridge, you are so, so simple. Can't you see? This is not about Bill. I couldn't care less about Bill and his bimbo, Twila. Their silly scheme to rip off the insurance company? Doomed. We were all in it together, Bill, Twila, and I, and they never knew. They never knew that I had bigger plans. That I knew it would never work. I knew that from the get-go. It was just the perfect cover for me."

"Cover for what?"

"Bonnie's been using the Hollywood StarMakers tour to transport drugs from state to state, without raising any

suspicion at all," Enrique said. "The two goons were helping her with the hiding and delivery. No one would suspect
a children's dance competition and convention of being a
major drug supplier. It was the perfect cover. Especially
when the lid blew off the insurance scam. No one would be
looking any deeper. Except I already was. Only she didn't
know it. And after she killed Kutcher, she needed someone
else. So she turned to the street kid from Los Angeles."

"I should have known," she said, sudden enlightenment
in her voice. "God, I really misjudged you. I knew you
weren't very good at what you did, but I didn't think
you were a cop. I could tap-dance better than you. And I
can't tap. But a cop? Following me? Never occurred to me.
My bad."

Enrique was a cop?

"Hey, I'm not that bad," Enrique protested.

"Well, actually, you weren't all that good," Bill interjected. "With your resume, I was really expecting you to be
better. I was thinking of letting you go."

"Oh please," I muttered. "What is going on here?"

"Are you daft? Haven't you been listening? He's a cop,"
Bonnie said. "At least I think he is. Undercover, apparently,
trying to destroy me and my plan. And I almost fell for it.
Wow, I guess I should thank you, Jenny. If I didn't have
you as a hostage, if I hadn't come to your house to get you,
just because I hate you so much, I might not have found
this out until it was too late and the whole thing blew up in
my face."

"Uh, glad to help," I said crossly. "You're a cop?" I
asked Enrique.

He just shrugged his shoulders but didn't own up to anything.

"This isn't what I planned, but I can still make it work.
Jackson, untie Twila. She's going to be the killer. The rest
of them will die in the fire. Smoke inhalation if they're
lucky. Burned alive if they're not. It will look like murder-
suicide. And they'll be looking for Twila. But she'll be
nowhere to be found."

Twila blanched and turned ghostly white. Jackson untied her quickly and lifted her up. She collapsed weakly, and he just hefted her over his shoulder and carried her out into the garage. There was no noise. Fear and anxiety filled my stomach. Did he just kill her out there? Was she still alive? Would I live to see the sun tomorrow? I'd been so determined, but now it seemed so hopeless.

The "burned alive" comment was making my stomach seriously hurt, and sparks of fear were coursing up and down my back.

Bonnie just shook her head. "This isn't the movies, Jenny. Things don't always get wrapped up nicely at the end. And believe me, this is the end. At least for the four of you." I was guessing she meant Enrique, Bill, Twila, and myself. And possibly the other goon, because he was now lying unconscious on the floor, although she hadn't counted him.

She ordered Enrique to sit in the chair vacated by Twila, and Jackson tied him up tightly.

Bonnie took a small bottle of lighter fluid out of her pocket, and started squirting the luxurious carpet in front of us, dousing it liberally as she walked backward.

"This isn't going to work, Bonnie," Enrique said softly. "We've been tracking you for four months. We were just getting ready to move in and arrest you. If you do this, they'll know it was you. You'll be on every most-wanted list in the nation, including the FBI's. You can't get away."

She stopped and turned to him, a feral, vicious look in her eyes, her mouth a slash. "Well, they won't find me. And the insurance scam is all there, all documented, too. I made sure of that. I was feeding the cops information the whole time. I'm guessing you were working undercover, right, Rico? Maybe DEA? An agency that trusts no other agency? No one is going to believe it or you. I'm not worried about my chances of getting away." Enrique winced, and I figured what she was saying was probably true. If he was deep undercover, he wasn't going to share that with other agencies. I'd watched a lot of cop shows on television. I knew.

She continued to douse the floor with lighter fluid, until the can was empty. She threw it to the ground. Of course, she'd been wearing gloves the entire time, so there would be no fingerprints. No way to trace the accelerant back to her.

And time had run out. I wouldn't be seeing the sun tomorrow.

I'd never watch a line of ragtag little dancers hopping around trying to hold leg extensions. I'd never sigh with despair at the failure of an older dancer to spot a turn. I'd never see my studio, my team, my friends again. And I wanted to. I didn't care how bad they danced, I wanted to be there to see it. I wanted to do my best to get them better. I wouldn't get that chance.

"I'd say it's been fun, Jenny, but I'd be lying. You are a pain in the ass to be around. I suspect more than a few people will be glad to see you go. I'm probably doing the world a service."

Bonnie pulled out a pack of matches and slowly struck one, her eyes wide, her smile big as she watched the fear on our faces.

Jackson left the room and went into the garage, and Bonnie backed up to follow. "Good-bye, Bill. You're a loser. You always were. Now, you'll be a dead loser. But at least you'll have your precious Jenny."

You know how in movies, time suddenly slows down, and it takes forever for something bad to happen, even when you know it isn't real? I watched her strike the match and throw it through the air, and it took an eternity for the flame to fall and ignite the carpet. After that, though, things went really, really fast.

THIRTY-ONE

ENRIQUE hopped violently in his chair until his was behind mine. I couldn't see him, but I knew he must be trying something. The flames were flicking up pretty high, but I stared at them perplexed. They didn't seem to be traveling.

Bill screeched like a little girl. Right now, I had no warm feelings for Bill at all.

"Would you shut up," I said to him.

"Jenny, in my right pocket, I have a knife. It's a sharp blade. I'm right behind you."

I wiggled my fingers and touched the denim of his pants. The movement made a fresh burst of pain roil through my chest and I gasped.

"Are you okay?"

"No time to explain. Tell me when I'm close."

I used my fingers to make a pathway around his pants, trying to find the pocket. I finally found it and struggled to get one hand inside, not an easy feat with my chest so sore, my hands bound at the wrists. I felt the cold, hard metal and pulled the knife from his pocket.

But now what?

"There's a little button on it. Can you feel it? Be careful not to drop it."

Using my left hand, I felt for the button, and finally found and pushed it, hearing a sharp click. And feeling a sharp stab of pain, too. Great. I'd found the knife and opened it up the wrong way, slicing open my hand in the process. And of course, that made me drop the knife.

"Damn, you cut yourself good. Are you okay?"

"Oh hell, what are we going to do now?" I said, despair filling me. I'd just bungled up our only chance at getting away. I was going to end up Barbecued Jenny.

But a strange thing was happening. The flames were dying down, not traveling as I would have expected. In fact, some of them were petering out completely.

"This whole room should have been on fire by now," I said. "What is going on?"

"I found that accelerant in Bonnie's bag a few days ago, when I was looking for . . . Well, never mind what I was looking for. I took it and poured most of it out, and filled it back up with water. So there's not much accelerant at all there."

"Wow," I said. "But it's still burning."

"Yes, I said most of it. Not all. It had to still smell like starter fluid, at least a bit."

While we weren't entirely safe, we also weren't in danger of going up in smoke anytime soon.

"Okay, time for Plan B," Enrique said. "Help is on the way. I promise. I called for backup just before I came in. But we need to get out of here if we can. It might take them a few minutes to get here."

A sudden flare-up in the flames made my eyes widen, and I tried to hop my chair backward, toward a large-paned window that overlooked Pineview Reservoir. I got it mostly sideways so I could keep an eye on the flames, and then worked at slowly moving the chair away from the fire.

Each jerk and leap made my chest burn and pain shoot through me. I couldn't help but gasp each time.

I knew from the sound that Enrique was hopping his chair toward the window, too. Bill also followed suit.

I reached the windowpane, and Bill was about two feet behind me. I could hear thumping sounds from Enrique's direction and knew he was following my lead. The flames had spread to cover the entire dining room in front of us, and they were quickly encroaching on our territory. The watered-down accelerant had prevented us from being immediately consumed by fire, but now no accelerant was needed. The house was going to burn, and we had to get out of it. Quickly.

I heard a moan from the floor and remembered that Bonnie and Jackson had abandoned Goon Two, leaving him unconscious on the floor. He sat up and screamed at the fire, groggily getting to his feet and lurching backward.

"Get away from the flames," I screamed at him, then began to cough and choke. Smoke was filling the room, and that might kill us before anything else.

I heard a smashing sound and an "oomph," and looked to see that Bill had passed me by and thumped the window hard with the back of his chair, smashing it. Cold air coursed through, and the flames leapt higher as Bill tried to heft himself, chair and all, out the window.

Enrique was right behind me, and Goon Two lurched to the window and dived through it, crying out with pain as he hit the ground. Bill kept tilting his chair toward the window, but he wasn't able to tip himself far enough backward to go out the window.

"Jenny, we have to get out of here now. This is getting bad fast. At this point, our only hope is to get out that window. Do you think you can do it?" Enrique asked me.

I felt hopeless. I didn't think I could. My chest hurt so bad I could barely move. And the more I coughed, the more smoke filled my lungs, and the weaker I became.

Bonnie had won. And I wouldn't be seeing the sunshine tomorrow.

I blinked hard to clear the tears from my eyes but then realized they weren't tears. Water was coming from above. Lots of water.

It was raining inside the condo.

THIRTY-TWO

THE funny thing about rich people is that they have lots of money to spend. Most of us invest in fire extinguishers, because that's all we can afford. But rich people living in ritzy condos, even ones they rent out to other people, have sprinkler systems put in their houses, in case of fire. Sort of like the one now.

I hadn't noticed the sprinklers gracing the ceiling of the condo before because I hadn't bothered to look up, and frankly, they were pretty well hidden. Kudos to the architect or whoever had installed them. A sudden dousing of cold water worked pretty well to wash away my melancholy. I couldn't believe I had been *this* close to giving up.

I figured the next time Bonnie rented a condo she planned on setting on fire, burning four people who could finger her for many, many crimes, she should probably check to make sure the place wasn't equipped with fire sprinklers.

The bad part about sitting under the sprinklers—sprinklers that kept me from being flambéed—was that I was drenched and completely frozen within minutes. The cold air coming in through the window did not help. I was sure my lips were blue. Enrique shook, too. Bill was still trying to tip his chair out through the window and over into the yard, despite the fact he was soaking wet. Maybe he was trying to escape, because he would probably be facing charges for the scam on the insurance company. I doubted he was trying to go after Twila and free her. He wasn't much of a hero.

When the fire department arrived and broke through the doors, they found us shivering and cold.

TWENTY-FIVE minutes later, I was wrapped up in a blanket, sitting in the back of an ambulance, wearing clothes the Huntsville police chief's wife had brought to the scene, and drinking some hot cocoa.

The paramedics were tending to Goon Two's shotgun wound, and the cops were standing close by, talking to Enrique. Bill sat in the back of an ambulance, a cop by his side, talking a mile an hour, probably trying to convince someone he was entirely innocent. I knew that wasn't true.

When three more cars pulled up, I knew it was Tate and probably Agent Carson Keller. Tate came swiftly toward me and engulfed me in the biggest bear hug I had ever experienced. And man did it hurt.

I couldn't help but moan.

"Oh God, I'm sorry. I forgot about your accident injuries, I was just so relieved to see you alive."

"I'm alive because Enrique followed me," I told him. "He'd been watching Bonnie all along. He's a cop."

"I know."

"You know?"

"Agent Keller came clean about an hour ago, but not without some prodding. I'd suspected he was working with someone inside, to get information on the insurance scam, but I didn't know a thing about the drugs. And I guess I really didn't suspect it was Perez, either, because he seemed to fit into the dance world so well." His voice was dark and heavy, and I could hear the anger underscoring each world. "Some detective, huh?"

"Hey, *I* didn't even know, and I know dancers." I was trying to make him feel better but didn't think it was working. "You know, he wasn't bad at tap."

"Apparently, he danced a lot as a kid."

"So do you know how Jason Kutcher was involved?"

"Keller said Jason was working with Bonnie. Perez—er, actually, his name is Agent Rudy Jaramillo—uncovered that. The FBI was watching Kutcher, too. They still aren't sure exactly who killed him, but it's definitely tied to Bonnie. Maybe he was going to bail or rat her out. But after he died, it made it easier for Jaramillo to get his foot in the door with Bonnie."

"Did you really think it was James, then, who killed Kutcher?"

"No, I didn't think it was James, but I didn't know who it was, and there was a lot going on, so I had no choice but to take the action I did."

"And this is the case you were working all along, the one that took you so many hours?"

"Yes and no. Like I said, I knew that they were investigating the insurance avenues, so I was doing a lot of cover work on that, but I didn't know about the drugs until tonight. Insurance scams can be dangerous. So I was nervous. But drugs—people kill for drugs. After Kutcher died, I got really nervous. I started digging, and thought I was being vigilant. I thought I could keep you safe. I'm so sorry, Jenny. I should have watched you even closer." I could hear the remorse and anger in his voice, but also the frustration. I knew it wasn't his fault, but the fact he knew something was up with the dance competition-convention, and that he hadn't told me about it, really bothered me.

"So you knew all along that things were not kosher with this dance competition?"

"Okay, Jennifer, slow down." His voice was gentle and warm, and I fought against the desire to snuggle up against him and just cry. I was still so cold I didn't think I'd ever get warm.

"Who are you calling Jennifer, anyway?" I asked him, tears choking my voice.

"You, little one. Jennifer Tamara Partridge. Look, James knew he wasn't really a suspect. He went along with us and the plan because he thought Agent Keller was really hot, and also you know him, he loves being in the middle of everything. He enjoyed playing the role to the hilt. It was like this big secret no one knew but him—and us of course. He didn't even let you know that he wasn't really in trouble, when you went to see him in jail. But I didn't know that Bonnie was such a cold-blooded killer. And that's what really has me kicking myself."

James, the little fink, had been in on it! I had worried over him needlessly.

"Since I knew Agent Keller was close, and I figured there was another cop inside, although I had no proof— along with the fact I kept you pretty well in my sights—I figured I had you covered. I'm sorry I misjudged it, Jenny."

"Next thing you'll be telling me Sal's a cop, too, and that he was just pretending to be a missionary and a dancer."

"Uh, no. Sal is not a cop. He's definitely a runaway missionary, and a wannabe dancer." Amusement filled his voice. "After I got put on the case, looking for the missing dancers and trying to track down evidence of the insurance fraud, I made sure. I always had someone watching your back. Until you got hurt, and I stashed you at your mom's. I thought for sure you would be safe there, and so I got a little less diligent. I'll never forgive myself for that." Exhaustion, fear, disgust, and a myriad of other emotions tinged his voice.

"I'm okay," I said softly, leaning in against him. "Except . . ." I sat up. "Tell me you got Bonnie and Jackson?

You arrested them, right? They have Twila, too. And Bonnie is wicked crazy. You should have listened to me all along. Why would no one listen to me about her, huh? Twila's in danger. A lot of danger."

"Jenny," he said, pulling me tight again, and making me wince. "They did get Bonnie and Jackson. But Twila wasn't with them. They're going to search for her body in Pineview in the morning."

"Oh God."

"I'm sorry. She was in on the insurance scam, but she really didn't deserve to die."

I sighed, and breathed in deeply, pain filling my lungs. "There's one thing I just don't get. You're a good cop, and it seems like Agent Keller is a good cop. And I didn't know Enrique, er, Agent Jaramillo was a cop, but with all of you guys on this case, how did Bonnie drive to my house and kidnap me? I mean, weren't you watching her? Wasn't Enrique with her?"

"She tried to slip away from him. She used the same drug she used on your mother, but Jaramillo was watching her closely, and he didn't drink the coffee. He knew she was up to something, so he snuck into the back of the van, and there was no way he could contact us without giving himself away. He called us just before he entered the house, but it took us a bit of time to get here. We called the locals but asked them just to guard the perimeter, and not to move in, because we had a man inside."

"Is my mom okay?"

"Yes, she's okay. Your dad found her, and found you missing, and called 911. I already knew things were headed south when we heard from Jaramillo, but that just cemented it."

"This has not been the best week of my life. But guess what?"

"What?" he asked gently.

"When Bonnie kidnapped me and was taking me out to the van, I noticed that I could *see*. I could see clear to the mountains. The inversion's gone. And tomorrow? Tomorrow, the sun is going to shine again."

He pulled me into him and kissed me gently. I felt warmth spread through my whole body. Yep, there was definitely going to be sun tomorrow.

THIRTY-THREE

I had not lost or destroyed a phone since December. That had to be some kind of record. Maybe Guinness Book worthy. I'd have to think about calling those guys. But for now, I had to get back to my regular schedule. Which had never been very regular to begin with.

Eldon Ramsay, the other missing dancer, actually did jump off the plank, going to work for Aiden Bright. Bright admitted he had lied because he was delaying the announcement until right before his next convention date. He had, apparently, not realized that lying to the FBI could get him in hot, very deep doggie doo-doo. Tate assured me he would feel the heat.

After Eldon disappeared, Bonnie convinced Twila to "disappear," and then Bill, and staged the bomb at the Marriott with the help of her two goons—and possibly the help of Enrique, but the cops weren't talking about that. I knew from watching television that there was a certain amount of "going along" that went with working undercover. I knew he would do everything possible to keep people safe, but I had to wonder if he had known it would happen.

The plan, Bill told police, was for he and Twila to stagger into the store in Huntsville a few days after the convention was over, and tell a story of kidnapping. Bonnie had rented the expensive condo, apparently under an assumed name, and Bill and Twila were staying there, messing around behind Bonnie's back, never understanding what she had intended for them.

They never really thought the plan through. They just wanted to collect on the insurance and leave the road behind, building a studio in Burbank and teaching dance there, together, happily ever after—or until someone else caught Bill's eye.

Bill wasn't very smart. Cops were smarter. I sincerely doubted the plan would have worked, but somehow Bonnie had convinced him it would. Of course, I don't know how smart I was, either. The house registered to LaMar Flanagan in Eden? The one that had led us in somewhat the right direction? Turned out it was a different LaMar Flanagan. Sheer coincidence. Life is very weird, and very random. At least my life.

Anyway, it turned out that Jason Kutcher had been the one who got Bonnie involved in transporting the drugs, through his shady connections. He had been sent in to make sure she was able to deliver a particularly large shipment— the one that never made it, thanks to Agent Jaramillo, myself (in a way), and of course Tate and Agent Carson Keller. But it never would have made it anyway.

Bonnie had underestimated the people for whom she was working. Tate said they were very powerful, very nasty, and that she was pretty lucky she was sitting in solitary confinement awaiting trial. Their reach was long, and she would never be safe again, after attempting to double-cross them.

She'd admitted to stealing James's tap shoes after she followed him and Jason to the bar. She'd had a pretty good indication she might have to resort to murder in order to keep herself and her plans safe. She confessed that she'd killed Jason after he threatened to expose her. Bonnie would never see the sun again, unless it was from behind bars or in a prison yard—if she lived that long. The people she had intended to double-cross were not nice.

Jackson, her goon, admitted to threatening me on the phone and to chasing me with the snowplow. He also admitted to helping Bonnie dump Twila's body, which hadn't been recovered. All those charges were sure to keep him in jail for the rest of his life.

Although Bonnie and her goons deserved what they got, I felt a pang at the fact their lives were in danger. Just a small one. Or maybe it was hunger.

Tate said Bill seemed genuinely remorseful over Twila's death. I wasn't ready to forgive him yet for any of this, so I wouldn't be visiting him myself to find out. I also wasn't ready to address the fact that Bonnie seemed to hate me so much because Bill was always talking about me. Even if he was still carrying a torch for me, he was too shallow and self-centered to remember how to light that torch. And he didn't seem to have a very good moral core, either. That was something I hadn't really put my finger on, of course, until Alissa pointed it out to me.

Now she and I were at breakfast, dining at Moore's Family Restaurant with Agents Keller and Jaramillo, Tate, and James. I had eggs Benedict. Yum.

Agents Keller and Jaramillo would be heading back to California in the afternoon. They both had apologized profusely—about a million times—for the fact I had almost been burned alive. I accepted their apologies but told them both they owed me more than one breakfast.

"Anytime I'm in town, I'll buy you breakfast, lunch, and dinner," Agent Keller said, his Southern accent filling me with images of fireflies and back-porch swings. Even though I'd never seen a firefly in my life, except in movies and on television. He'd admitted to me, as they checked me out in the hospital, that he'd shown up at my house that night because he was worried about Bonnie and her drug-running pals. And the fact that Tate wasn't aware of the drug angle. He claimed he'd wanted to make sure I was safe. Then before he left my hospital bed, he quickly handed me his card, with his personal phone number written on the back, and gave me a dazzling smile. "Call me anytime, Jenny. Anytime."

He said the same thing now. It made me a little warm inside, but I wasn't going there. Oh no, I was not.

"That's an offer she won't be taking," Tate said harshly, giving Keller his famed "shooting bullets" look. I never liked that look aimed in my direction.

Agent Jaramillo and Alissa were chatting about guns and ammo, and I could swear I heard flirtation in her voice. Couldn't blame her for that. James, who sat across from me, said very little, his hands on his chin. He'd only picked at his food, and now was staring glumly off into space.

"What's going on, James?" I asked him. "What's wrong?"

"It's Mother. Turns out she doesn't have a heart condition after all. And now she's decided you are far too dangerous for me to be around, so she's setting me up with all the single girls in her ward. And the next ward. And the ward after that. Apparently, your cousins are on that list."

"Uh-oh. Time to be honest?"

"I don't know. If she didn't have a heart condition before, hearing her only son is gay will probably be sure to bring one on."

I chuckled just as my phone rang in my purse. I snatched it out and groaned as I looked at the caller ID. It was Tamara. Tamara Williams. You know, April's mom?

Back to the psycho-dance-mom grind. Competition season started next month. We would be making the rounds of Friday and Saturday competitions for at least two months. Solos needed to be taught and refined, team dances cleaned and perfected, and the claws would be coming out as the mothers fought tooth and nail for their daughters to be in every dance, on the front row, and to get the most extra hours and lessons in.

It wouldn't be pretty. But I preferred it to dealing with insurance scams and drug dealers. My phone rang again. Tamara Williams. At least I think I preferred it.